GW01459059

Dedicated to

Laila, Kieran & Rocco

Vincent G Learoyd

Chapter one

Laila and Mr Tree

The Otherworld exists. But to discover it we must use our imagination.   *Yan Overton*.

In the halcyon woods of Epping, beneath the spreading canopies of deciduous trees, nestling hidden amongst the glades of dappled shade there lies a pond.

A tiny oasis of rippled light that shines like a jewel amongst the variegated shadows for all to admire and delight in contemplative calm. And where, for countless generations young children would frequent on mild spring afternoons in pursuit of tadpoles and great adventures.

Whilst nearby in silent observation upon a steep gravel bank overlooking the pond there stands the grandest and most majestic of all trees, the magnificent Warren Oak.

It looms tall robust and regal like some custodian of the forest. Indifferent to the changing seasons, yet gnarled and lambasted by the relentless storms of time in centuries past. It's myriad of out stretched roots resembling the wrinkled bony fingers of some gigantic primeval hand grasping desperately into the earth around for support, whilst all about the eroded soil gradually crumbles away to reveal its scars. Huge deep basal cavities and tunnels that gouge throughout its core like caves or small rooms, and to all intent and purpose could quite easily be mistaken for the long lost dwellings of Fairy folk or other such beings. A source of great fun for those who with a wild imagination would venture into the forest to clamber amongst its roots and hollows. Now such a setting as this would appear commonplace to the wayfarer, who tramps the tracks and bridleways of southern Britain. Venerable oaks and ponds in woods throughout this pastoral land are an abundant wealth, but a series of strange occurrences were about to unfold in this lowly nook, miraculous events that would one day alter the course of time forever.

It all began one cold crisp morning on the day of the vernal equinox, when the early frosted buds of spring pervade the sprawling boughs of rousing giants, and the bright azure sky was vast yet unblemished by a single cloud, broken only briefly by the transient flocks of Canada geese heading for Connaught waters.

A quintessential English dawn like any other for a young girl by the name of Laila, who would frequently visit the forest near her home.

Like so many of the jaunty children that visited the old pond, she would frolic beneath the spreading limbs of the great oak, losing herself in the land of imagination and claiming to all on her return that the tree, who she aptly named Mr Tree was a gathering place for Fairies.

"He is the king of the woods" she would proclaim, referring to him as if he were an old friend could often be seen holding fanciful conversations with him while spending time there alone by the pond. He was as real a person to her as any person she care to have known, and with a great fondness would visit him religiously every weekend.

Laila was rather atypical of most eleven year old children her age. Solitary and aloof yet content in the fantasy world of her thoughts and full of adventure, often returning home from back wood jaunts looking as if she had come second place in a mud-wrestling bout with some wild animal, her pockets baring the remnants of obsessive forages. Wonderful treasures such as scraggy crooked pigeon feathers, pebbles, assorted leaves, and sometimes the occasional dried up earthworm. She was also deceptively prim and reserved in appearance. Her clothes were always neatly pressed and the colours were made to complement. Her long auburn hair was brushed tightly back into two plaited ponytails creating a centre parting, and with an angelic look to complete the ensemble, you could almost be forgiven for thinking that she was a proper little madam and that butter wouldn't melt, but this would be short lived. For she liked nothing more than climbing trees and tearing everything she wore. Even the rumbustious urchins who gathered in a troop by the pond respected her eccentricity, if somewhat apprehensively.

She awoke bright and early that morning and made her way to the pond wearing a dark knee length denim dress with white cotton tights that would undoubtedly resemble a used dishcloth before the day was through. In her hand she held a small clear plastic bag containing a few slices of bread to feed to the ducks.
It was a magnificent day to saunter amongst the streaming catkins and drifts of delicate ivory

snowdrops that vied for position beneath the boughs of the prodigious beeches aligning the pathways into the forest.

Robins and skylarks sang with a passion on high, while in surrounding fields the march hares gambolled in the misty morning dew. Laila beamed in joyous content as she leisurely wandered along the weathered track towards the old pond.

"Good morning Laila!" said a smartly dressed young woman out walking her dog on the common.

"Hello!" replied Laila kneeling down to greet a small grey muzzled Staffordshire bull terrier.

"How are you today Stripe?" she giggled as the little mutt wagged his tail frantically, Jack knifing his torso with elation at seeing her whilst desperately trying to climb up and lick her face. Laila stood up briskly to avoid his slobbering advances, appeasing his rapture with the customary pat on the head.

Laila knew most, if not all the dog walkers that visited the forest being such a regular there.

"Where are you off to today?" asked the woman endeavouring to restrain her hysterical pooch.

"I'm just going to feed the ducks at Warren pond" Laila replied.

"Have you told your parents where you are?" asked the woman looking a little concerned.

"Oh yes! I told my Mum that I was going to feed the ducks" replied Laila displaying to the woman the slices of bread in her bag.

"Oh and look!" she swiftly digressed.

"My dad bought me this necklace for my birthday". Laila pointed to a beautiful purple amethyst crystal hanging from a fine silver chain around her neck.

"How wonderful! You're a very lucky girl" the woman remarked.

"When is your birthday?" she asked, leaning forward to admire the necklace.

"It's not until next month but my Dad said I could have it now" replied Laila boastfully.

"Well good for you!" she smiled, rubbing Laila's head in affectionate approval.

"Now I had best be off Laila, as I have to get Stripe back". "You take care now" she said trying to coax her dog away from Laila with a biscuit. He on the other hand appeared somewhat reluctant to leave so soon. One can only assume that he hadn't quite fulfilled his squirrel chasing quota that morning, hence his reasons for deciding to lay rigidly defiant on his back

"Come along on Stripe!" she laughed whilst gently tugging at the leash. Yet still he remained obstinate, content in playing dead for as long as annoyingly possible, much to Laila's amusement. But eventually after a little persuasion he succumbs to the morsel and leaps to his feet excitedly, wagging and bounding as he went upon his way.

When Laila finally arrived by the sloping bank that overlooked the pond she paused for a moment to take in the view. Slender beige tufts of reed mace sprang forth from the murky depths like miniature islands at the heart of a great ocean. A light breeze blew gentle ripples across the water surface towards the clusters of Juncus that rustled and danced to the rhythm of the wind. She held her arms aloft to savour the cool zephyr beneath imaginary wings before scampering down the steep incline to the water's edge.

Standing alongside the silted bank close to the margin she opened her bag of bread and began tossing it to the hungry ducks that sped expeditiously like an armada towards her.

The pond was orbicular and quite insignificant in size, containing only a small flush of ducks. Usually a hand full of mallards at best yet, Laila never ceased to relish the opportunity of popping over to feed them. She always took a special delight in feeding the solitary duck that was slowest to intercept the bread.

Conscientiously she would aim a small slice towards each of them, ensuring they had an equal share. And once the bread was consumed she would hold the bag upside down and shake it thoroughly so as to reveal to the ducks that it was empty, all but for a few meagre crumbs left for the starlings to scavenge.

After feeding the ducks Laila began to ascend the sloping gravel bank up towards the Warren oak. The area encompassed within the wide crown spread of the tree was barren and compacted. The ochre pale earth undulated and littered with flint pebbles and the occasional tuft of meadow grass clinging on to life as well as to the sloping bank. As Laila drew nearer to the tree she decided to test her balancing skills by walking slowly and rather precariously along one of the long buttress roots that emanated from the bole of the tree. With arms out stretched she imagined herself to be a tight rope walker at the big top, high up on the wire where the awestruck audience below held their breath, amazed by her dauntless dexterity. With grace and ease she traversed the narrow root towards the stem, although her last few steps were somewhat hastened

as her balance began to falter, causing her to fall
clumsily against the tree in a huge embrace.
"Hello Mr Tree!" she whispered before softly
kissing his coarse tawny bark.
They were old friends after all, and Laila being
animistic by nature made it seem the most natural
thing in the world to do.
"How are you Mr Tree? Sorry I didn't get a chance
to see you yesterday but I was helping my Mum"
she said whilst scaling high into the crown of the
tree. There was a large fork in one of the branches
that made a natural seat and Laila would often sit
there and look across the pond at the horse riders
that passed by in procession along the bridle track.
They would sometimes wave courteously to her in
passing, as she was as much a permanent fixture,
and as common a sight in the old tree as the acorns
in September.
She sat for a short while blissfully, observing the
ducks at play on the pond from her high vantage
point before eventually becoming antsy and
clambering back down again.
Slowly she proceeded to walk a short distance from
the tree before, stopping by the footpath and turning
around.
"I forgot to show you my necklace Mr Tree! My
dad bought it for me as an early birthday present"

she said looking up affectionately at her noble crooked friend.

Putting her hands behind her neck she unfastened the clasp of her necklace and held it up high at arm's length. The beautiful purple stone swung to and fro from the silver chain, catching the sunlight on its many facets.

"Do you like it?" she asked as if expecting a reaction from the hoary giant. Yet all remained silent except for the obvious reply she would have imagined in her head, which no doubt would have been one of great admiration from Mr Tree.

But unbeknown to her someone else was watching the glistening jewel with a greater interest. A curious magpie on a nearby tree hopped excitedly from one branch to another, tilting its head frantically from side to side in an attempt to gain a better view, mesmerised by the refracting light that shone upon its small black beady eyes. It cavorted amongst the sprigs with an uncontainable desire while all the time Laila stood there blissfully unaware of its presence. It was at that very moment when she was just about to put the necklace back on that the magpie seized its chance to steal the pendant.

Falling like a stone from the tree with great menace and speed it flew straight at Laila from just over her shoulder almost nabbing the chain in its bill as it swooped. Fortunately Laila had moved out of the way just in time, startled by the sudden appearance of the birds shadow on the ground, the element of surprise lost. But the magpie was by no means finished. It began to soar up and up to a great height before dipping its wing and returning like a creature possessed. Laila was terrified by the sudden outlandish behaviour and swiftly ran for cover amongst the stems of a goat willow, ducking down low in an attempt to conceal herself, but the tenacious bird simply flew in and amongst the branches, squawking and flapping relentlessly until eventually forcing Laila out from the safe haven of the tree and back out into the open again.

As she raced in terror along the path the magpie clung onto her hair with its feet, pecking violently at her head.

She flailed her arms in a desperate attempt to free it but to no avail. Feathers and hair blew everywhere yet it held on doggedly, stabbing and scratching with an almost incessant rage until eventually distraught and enervated she collapsed helplessly to the ground.

The demented corvine then took to the sky once more but only to circle briefly before a spell of persistent dive-bombing.

Laila cowered on the ground, hoping that the bird
would eventually give up on her, oblivious to the
fact that it wasn't actually her that it was interested
in but the jewel she held in her hand.

Then suddenly all was quiet and there was a lull in
the attacks. Very cautiously Laila looked up only to
see the magpie staring straight back at her on the
ground. Letting out an ear splitting shrill it struck at
her eyes almost blinding her. Instinctively she held
up her hand to protect her face while inadvertently
dropping the necklace. It was then that the
opportunistic bird snapped up the amethyst in its
mandibles and made off in haste.

With the necklace now in its possession the magpie
flew up high cawing triumphantly before landing in
the crown of a nearby beech tree. Laila meanwhile
remained curled up on the ground, unaware the bird
had stolen her necklace, lying motionless in anxious
anticipation of another bombardment.

Time passed and all was still except the whisper of
the wind in the trees. Warily she raised her head
from beneath her arm, timidly scanning the skyline
for the mischievous bird but there was no sign of it
anywhere, yet even so she waited a moment longer
before attempting to move.

Then when it seemed that all was well she tentatively clambered to her feet and brushed herself down while keeping a constant vigil for the magpie.

"Crazy bird!" she mumbled as she slowly made her way back towards Mr Tree.

Just then she realised, all was not as well as she had assumed. Something was missing!

"My necklace, where's my necklace?" she cried while frantically searching her pockets and every conceivable place on her person but to no avail.

"I must have dropped it when that magpie attacked me! It can't be far!" she thought. So feverishly she set about retracing her steps, scouring every inch of the ground scrupulously in search of her beautiful gift only to find the remnants of the bird's downy feathers blowing across the dusty ground.

Every nook and cranny she explored proved fruitless.

And then in the sullenness she heard the familiar sound of the magpie up high the crown of a beech tree. It gave out a loud cu cu cu sound as if to mock her and demand her attention, but by now Laila was no longer concerned or afraid. She was far too focused on her search for the missing jewel to pay it much regard.

Twenty minutes had passed and Laila was gradually becoming more and more distraught at not locating her necklace, and the unrelenting cackles from the magpie were only adding to her torment.

In her fury she began to emulate the bird tauntingly. "Cu cu cu!" she went while flapping her arms as if in some meagre attempt to exasperate it. The bird rocked its head, seemingly intrigued by her strange behaviour before picking up the necklace from its perch and lifting it high and proud in its beak for all the world to admire.

Laila stood aghast at the sight of her precious necklace in the possession of the insane creature. "Give it back you thief!" she yelled racing towards the tree and waving her arms furiously, but the callous bird appeared totally insouciant to her outburst.

So in her rage Laila began to pick up some pebbles from the ground and proceeded to hurl them violently at the magpie forcing it to take to the wing.

Off it flew, up and over the Warren oak and across the pond before resting in the crown of sycamore tree on the opposite bank. Laila dashed around the perimeter of the pond in hot pursuit, stumbling all the way, never taking her eyes off the bird for a moment. In her haste she almost trod on the foot of some poor old gentleman sitting quietly on a bench by the pond.

But as she drew closer to the sycamore the bird simply stretched out its wings and flew off again, soaring high above the tree tops and deeper into the forest .Yet still Laila gave chase, running as fast as her legs could carry her cursing the magpie as she went before inadvertently stumbling over a large protruding tree root and falling flat on her face. With grazed knees and a twisted ankle she could only watch in despair as the magpie gradually became nothing more than a tiny speck in the distant sky.

In her frustration she sobbed and punched the ground in anger.

And then all of a sudden from out of the trees a shadow loomed, and a woman's voice began to speak softly, grabbing her attention and causing Laila to briefly cease her pitiful whines to listen.

"Now, now young lady there's no need to be so sad" she whispered.

Her mellifluous tone was gentle and soothing to the ear.

Laila wearily lifted her sodden face from the ground and looked up to find a tall slender woman smiling back at her. She wore a long black velvet dress with a dark purple hooded cloak draped over her shoulders, which was fastened in the middle by a large silver brooch, inlaid with intricate knot work. Her raven hair was layered and flowing and her eyes were as deep and as dark as a winter's night. Laila had never seen the likes of her before. She appeared as if she had emerged from some bygone age in her archaic apparel. The delicate features of her porcelain smooth skin were not dissimilar that of an Egyptian queen. She was as beautiful as she was mysterious. Yet in Laila's vexation her presence was unwelcomed, as was her empathy.

"Leave me alone!"She sniffed in chagrin while wiping the muddy tears from her cheeks.

"I only came to see if you were ok," said the woman kneeling down beside her.

"Yes, well I am fine thanks! I've just been attacked by a crazy magpie and had my necklace stolen apart from that just great" she snapped sarcastically.

"I know I saw everything, that bird is a really nasty piece of work" the woman replied. Laila frowned and stared suspiciously up at her.

"Who are you?" she asked abruptly.

"My name is Donna," replied the woman with a friendly smile. Laila clambered to her feet and rubbed her dusty hands together.

"Yes, well I can't stand around here all day talking to strangers" she sniffed curtly, whilst trying to retain her dignity.

"I have to get home and explain to my Dad that I have just lost my necklace" she said.

And with that the disheartened Laila solemnly hung her head and ambled back along the stony track towards her home.

"No doubt that delirious magpie has taken your necklace back to his nest with all the other loot he has filched" hollered Donna after her.

"You know! The nest he has in that old Hornbeam pollard up on Broom hill" she wittingly exclaimed.

The sudden revelation caused Laila to pause abruptly in her tracks.

"A magpie's nest in an old hornbeam pollard up on Broom hill?" she muttered to herself. This could only infer one thing. Donna may know the possible whereabouts of her necklace! It took a brief moment to register, by which time the mysterious lady had almost disappeared as quickly as she had arrived.

"Wait! Called Laila running to catch her up.

Donna had only wandered a short distance from the footpath into the underbrush to collect deadfalls when Laila came racing up.

"Did I hear you say that you knew where the magpie lived?" she asked panting from her sprint.
"Of course I know! But I can't stand around here talking to strangers all day." She sneered, and carried on collecting wood.
 "No wait! I'm so sorry for my rudeness back there, there was no need for it, I was just upset that's all. Please forgive me; you see it's just that I really need to get my necklace back, it was a birthday gift from my Dad".
Donna looked at Laila's piteous expression and smiled,
"Ok I'll forgive you!" she said,
"Does that mean you will tell me where I can find the magpies nest?" she asked
"Sure I'll tell you! But under one condition!"
"Anything!" said Laila.
"Under the condition that you help give me a hand collecting firewood" she said handing Laila a large wicker basket.
"Ok sure!" smiled Laila and set about foraging amongst the fresh bracken fronds for deadwood.

As they went about their way collecting wood Donna began to talk in more depth about the Magpie who had stole her necklace.
"He is called Prowler" she said.

"Due to his petty pilfering and the large chip in his prow which he obtained whilst in a fracas with a Carrion Crow. They were fighting over a shiny pebble" she chuckled.

"Why would birds fight over a pebble?" asked Laila bemused.

"Because Corvines are attracted to bright shiny objects, it's just in their nature, which would explain why Prowler was so interested in your necklace".

"But how is it that you know so much about this bird?" asked Laila, intrigued with Donnas intimate knowledge of the magpie.

"I spend so much time in the company of trees, that I have come to know all the creatures that inhabit the woods" she said. This novel remark passed without acknowledgment as Laila endorsed a similar language when referring to the trees of the forest.

"But I am always here in the woods and I've never seen you before!" said Laila.

"Really?" replied Donna with a smile.

"Yet I have seen you on numerous occasions sitting in the branches of the Warren oak".

Laila just glared at her in bewilderment.

"So how come you know where this Prowlers nest is? She asked returning to the subject of the magpie.

"I came across his nest by chance one day whilst out collecting fungi up at Broom hill. I saw him flying into his nest carrying some silver foil, probably from an old sweet wrapper, and then on several other occasions after that".

"So do you think that's where my necklace might be?" asked Laila.

"As sure as there are fish in the pond!" replied Donna confidently

"Could you take me to it?" asked Laila eagerly.

A disquiet look suddenly fell upon Donna's face as if reticent to respond to the request, and she continued on nonchalantly collecting wood as though nothing was said.

"Well? Will you take me?" inquired Laila once more.

A brief silence ensued before Donna finally spoke. Laila could sense a curious shift in her disposition as though there were a sense of foreboding at the prospect of going to Broom hill.

"As I said earlier, I am more than happy to tell you where you can find the magpies nest but I'm afraid I cannot go there, well not today anyhow" replied Donna seemingly agitated.

"Why can't you to go there?" asked Laila bemused.

"Because I, I have guests coming to see me this afternoon and I have to get the fire going before they arrive" she uttered in a fluster before storming off through the trees with her basket of wood. Laila rushed over and grabbed Donnas arm firmly.

"Please!" she begged. "My Dad will be so upset with me if I tell him I've lost my necklace already, as he has only just bought it for me".

Donna pulled her arm sharply from Laila's grip and turned petulantly away.

"Not today I said! Now leave me alone" she snapped, and with that swiftly parted company. Laila put her face into her hands.

"How will I ever be able to tell my Dad?" she cried and fell tearfully to her knees.

Donna had only gone but a few yards before her conscience forced her to give pause and look back at the lugubrious figure alone in the woods.

"Oh come, come now stop, there's no need for that my child!" she sighed sympathetically whilst returning to console the distraught Laila.

"I'm sorry you've had such an awful day and lost your precious necklace, really I am, and I apologise if I seemed a little harsh on you" she said stroking Laila's head.

"So why can't you at least take a moment out of your day to show me where this nest is then? pleaded Laila tearfully.

"It's not that far away is it? All you have to do is take me there, it won't take a long. I'll climb quickly I promise!"

Donna could sense the desperation and dejection in her voice and felt indecisively torn between her heart and her commitments.

"If circumstances where different I swear I would say unequivocally yes, but today is the day of the Spring Equinox, the first day of Spring. It is a sacred time when darkness and light are equal and the land is reborn once again, I wish you could understand. This is a very important day for me and I am obliged to be elsewhere" she said. Laila's shoulders slumped and her bottom lip began to protrude slightly.

"Oh well, happy equinox" she mumbled, dragging her heels off like a wounded soul along the dusty track towards the Warren oak.

"Wait!" yelled Donna.

"Ok, ok I will get you to Broom hill!" She exclaimed in a sudden volt-face.

"It would be callous of me to turn my back on you and leave you like this in your moment of need, and after all as you say, it is the equinox".

Laila beamed.

"Really!" she said ecstatically." "I can't thank you enough; I swear I will return the favour. So which way are we going?" asked Laila eager to depart.

"Oh no my child! I won't be coming with you" said Donna with an air of amusement

"I only said I would get you to Broom hill, I didn't say I was going to take you there personally".

Laila looked perplexed. "I don't understand?" she said. "If you are not going to take me there then how will I ever find the nest?"

"With the help of a guide" replied Donna.

"A guide?" asked Laila even more confused.

Donna took Laila by the hand and smiled.

"I know someone who knows every inch of these woods better than anyone and they can take you straight to Prowlers nest quicker than I ever could" she said.

"Who?" asked Laila baffled.

"Not who, but what!" smirked Donna, and with that she cupped her hands either side of her mouth and began to make, what can only be described as a loud kissing sound.

She directed the peculiar noise towards various points on the horizon as if she was calling someone or something but nothing happened. Again and again she made the sound and still nothing. Laila began to think she was deranged until in the far distance she caught something moving in the corner of her eye. It was small and indistinct and quite broken in form against the wooded background. Only the light shimmer of reflective eyes were distinguishable, betraying its presence beneath the dense shadows of low limbed holly bushes.

And then it broke boldly loose from its concealment and out into open ground. To Laila's surprise she noticed that the creature was heading directly towards them. Initially she mistook it to be a large ginger tom cat, as its tail was long and bushy. But as it drew nearer it began to look more like a pooch before she finally realized that the creature was in fact a large dog Fox.

It appeared to glide effortlessly as it made its way across the sweeping green between the edge of the thicket to where they stood, its feet bouncing delicately to and fro across the soft turf. Laila's eyes widened with surprise. She had never seen a wild Fox in all the time she had frequented the forest and to see one ambling along as bold as brass during the day was a sight to behold.

"Come Rocco!" called Donna, clapping her hands and squatting down low, prompting the creature to sprint rapidly towards her at speed, almost knocking her over. Donna chuckled as the excited Fox licked her hand enthusiastically.

"Would you like to stroke him Laila?". It's ok, he won't bite you" Said Donna.

Very cautiously Laila lowered her hand above the Foxes head and began gently patting him a couple of times before feeling confident enough to stroke him.

Gently her fingers ran through the beautiful chestnut fur and she found it almost impossible to contain her elation.

"It's a Fox!" she beamed.

"Yes it's a Fox," laughed Donna. "His name is Rocco, I found him some years ago abandoned in Theydon wood". "His mother was hit by a car so I brought him up from a young kit".

"How awful!" said Laila sadly.

"It's ok, Rocco has a family of his own now, don't you boy!" said Donna petting the animal while looking up at Laila affectionately captivated.

"Did you know that the Fox is the cleverest and wisest of all the woodland creatures, and is considered by some to be a very sacred animal" she said. But Laila didn't seem to hear, she was far too involved in the moment.

"Are you ready then?" said Donna.

"Ready for what?" asked Laila engrossed.

"The necklace!"

"Oh yes, sorry" she said shaking her head in order to free herself from the fox's enchantment.

"Rocco will be your guide, he knows every inch of the forest, just follow him and he will take you straight to the nest" said Donna.

"You want me to follow the Fox?" asked Laila cynically.

"Yes!, he is a magnificent guide" said Donna. But Laila was slightly less optimistic, finding the whole idea of following Rocco to an obscure tree somewhere in the forest unsettling as well as profoundly bizarre.

"How does he know where I want to go?" she asked.

"Trust me, he knows where you want to go" said Donna confidently.

"But what if he does take me to the hornbeam at Broom hill, I might not even be able to reach the nest" she said.

"You will!, it's in the lowest fork of the pollard and the large holes in the trunk make it as easy as climbing a ladder. Anyhow I have seen you climb effortlessly into the crown of the Warren oak and believe me that's far more demanding" replied Donna.

"But what if the crazy bird attacks me again?"

"It won't go near you when there is a fox about. The fox is the dominant predator in the forest"

"Will it take long to get there?" asked Laila dubiously.

"Not at all, it's probably only about two miles at most from here, plus he will take you along the untrodden paths through the forest, you'll be there in no time".

"And what about getting back from Broom hill?.

"Just say 'Duir, Duir' and Rocco will guide you back to Warren pond I promise" said Donna. Laila frowned and looked apprehensively at her. She was not convinced and yet the prospect of going on an adventure through the woods with a fox was just too good an opportunity to miss.

"And you're sure I won't get lost in the woods?" she asked. Donna just smiled and nodded her head.

"Ok! Well I guess I'm ready then," said Laila. Donna knelt down in front of the Fox and held his head gently in her hands and looked deep into its eyes.

"Rocco, Huathe, Huathe!" she uttered whilst pointing east. Without hesitation the fox briskly scampered off towards the trees.

"Go on catch him up, Foxes are swift creatures and so must you be" said Donna. But Laila was still hesitant.

"Are you sure?" she asked.

"Believe me, Rocco will get you there and back safely" "Now go before you lose him" said Donna. "Will I see you again?" asked Laila ambling backwards.

"Yes I'm sure of it! Now quickly, Rocco is waiting for you, and be careful climbing that hornbeam," she shouted. "Ok, thanks!" hollered Laila racing off towards the distant woods. Donna stood and watched as Laila and Rocco disappeared into the cover of the trees. "Good luck!" she whispered softly.

Onward in earnest through the dense thicket Laila made haste in pursuit of the agile Fox. Through bramble and bracken and the unbeaten paths it lead her, whilst all the time she followed, anxious and uncertain.

"How far was Broom hill? Who was Donna?, Should I trust her? And what if Rocco ran off leaving her lost in the woods?" All these thoughts and fears filled her head.

"Shall I turn back now and just forget the whole thing?" she muttered under her breath with the constant pain of bramble scratches and stinging nettles adding to her anguish. Yet tenaciously she pushed on, crawling under and over fallen trees and squeezing through countless gaps in holly bushes. Laila always enjoyed a bit of adventure but she was getting more than she had bargained for today. "Wait for me Rocco!" she called as she tried to navigate her way safely through a rather dangerous and awkward blackthorn. The Fox paused momentarily about fifty yards in front of her before looking back insensibly. And then no sooner had she overcome the obstacle he was off again at speed.

It wasn't too long before Laila looked as if she had quite literally been dragged through a hedge backwards, and her morale began to wane slightly as the cuts and bruises took their toll. She decided that there was no need to rush anymore and stopped to rest by a fallen Beech tree to catch her breath. Brushing the loose debris from the trunk she sat down and rested her chin in her hands and began to contemplate. Pondering over her decision to embark on what seemed by now an utterly ridiculous idea. "What was I thinking?" she asked herself. "This trek to Broom hill is taking far longer than I thought. We must have easily travelled more than two miles by now".

Just then Rocco came trotting up and leapt onto the trunk beside her.

"What am I doing here Rocco?" She said stroking his neck. But he just glared at her with his head tilted to one side as if trying to comprehend what she was saying, before nudging her arm impatiently with his muzzle.

"What do you want?" she asked feeling tired and irritable. He then began barking and jumping up at her but Laila was reluctant to move as she was quite comfortable on the log. But Rocco was having none of it and persisted in agitating her by grabbing the corner of her dress and pulling it, forcing Laila back on her feet again.

"Ok Rocco! Come on let's go," she sighed rubbing her sore shins before continuing her quest for Prowlers nest. Further and deeper into the woods they went and lower set the sun in the distant sky until eventually it became nothing more than a blood red ball resting amongst the branches of silhouetted trees.

Rocco began to pick up the pace when they reached a narrow dried up brook that meandered through the Birch scrub. Even though Laila was tired the brook was a virtual path compared to the assault course she had so far endured and she found it a lot easier to keep up.

On the bank of a wide sweeping bend in the brook stood a gigantic contorted Hawthorn tree where Rocco decided to rest.

"Is this it? Is this Broom hill?" she asked wearily wandering around for signs of a hornbeam pollard while Rocco curled up in a tight ball at the base of the gigantic tree, tucking his nose between his hind leg and stomach with only his two tiny eyes visibly fixed on Laila.

"There are no hornbeams here!" she said looking around bewildered and confused.

"This is a birch thicket!".

Only the sound of a busy road nearby lessened her concerns about finding the nest. At least she was near civilization and not lost in the wilderness she thought, yet still with an underlying feeling of disappointment.

"All this way for nothing!" she said kicking a stick irately across the ground.

"I knew I shouldn't have listened to Donna" she scorned.

Laila's attention then turned to Rocco curled up beneath the tree.

"Oh I get it! You want to rest!. Ok Rocco but only for a little while, it will be getting dark soon and I want to be home before then," she said sitting herself down beside him.

Resting her back against the tree she smiled
lovingly at the dog Fox looking up at her.
"What a strange day this has been, no one would
ever believe me if I told them" she chuckled whilst
gently stroking his head.
Laila was just about to enjoy a well earned respite
when she became suddenly and inexplicably
overwhelmed by a strange vertiginous sensation.
It began with a strong tingling feeling similar to that
of pins and needles, passing up through her body
from her feet to the crown of her head and gradually
grew in its intensity. This was then followed by a
feeling of extreme nausea and giddiness, as the
forest around her appeared to spiral faster and faster
like a spinning top. Feeling as though she was about
to lose consciousness Laila laid down flat against
the ground, bringing her knees up to her chest. She
then took a few slow deep breaths and closed her
eyes. "What is happening Rocco?" she muttered
shakily.

Chapter Two

The Green man

After what seemed like nothing more than a brief moment of disorientation, Laila's nausea gradually subsided and she began to feel a lot better. But as she opened her eyes she found herself not in the dusky wood as would be presumed, but in a place of absolute darkness, where in the tenebrosity, not even a speck of light from a far off distant star could be seen, and the air hung warm and suffused with the insistent aroma of earth and mould.

She tried moving her limbs only to find them heavy and cumbersome as if restrained by gravity, whilst her skin tingled and crawled with life.

In her panic Laila leapt impetuously to her feet, breaking free from the confines of the blackness and back into the light of day once more.

Lurching clumsily across the forest floor she gasped for breath whilst spitting humus and earthworms as she retched.

"What is this?" she croaked anxiously as centipedes and arachnids expeditiously abandoned her hair and clothing, scurrying off in all directions like rodents on a sinking ship.

Shaken and confused she stood up and brushed herself down.

And then to add to her horror and astonishment she noticed that her dress was covered in fungal mycelium and the mucus trails of slugs, as if she had been buried alive beneath the earth for some considerable time.

Deeply distraught by the bizarre inexplicable happenings, Laila was keen to get out of the forest as soon as possible.

"Duir, Duir" she whimpered nervously, reciting the returning command to the wily little fox only to discover an empty space where he once lay.

"Rocco? Oh no, where has he got to?" she muttered as she restlessly searched about the hawthorn for signs of her absent companion.

The tranquil glade was cold and still and the sound of the nearby road could no longer be heard.

"Rocco! Rocco! Where are you boy?" she called with a sense of unease at being alone in an unfamiliar part of the forest, her lost voice echoing in vain amongst the boughs.

The silence was so loud that not even the peep of solitary song bird broke the hush of the muted wood.

"Come now Rocco stop playing games" she whined in her agitation, before resorting to imitating the kissing sound that the enigmatic Donna had used to summon him, yet still nothing stirred.

"Where is that silly creature?" she mumbled nervously whilst pacing up and down.

"Perhaps he has just gone off to get something to eat" she thought, trying to remain positive as well as to comfort herself.

It was whilst she was searching around for the missing fox that she noticed something very peculiar. The forest looked strangely different. So totally different in fact from what she recalled that it was as if she was somewhere else entirely. The trees seemed somehow larger in height and girth, much bigger than anything she had ever seen before. And the canopy above, which was once sparse with foliage, now appeared to explode with colour. Golden yellows, browns and crimson red leaves splashed across a buttermilk sky like paints on an artist's palette. It was a beautiful sight to behold like every English autumn but this was supposed to be March? Captivated and yet perplexed by the vision, Laila could only look up in awe.

"How can this be happening?" she thought.

"I saw snowdrops only this morning unless; I've been asleep for the past six months?. But that's impossible!. I must be dreaming!" she thought pinching herself on the arm.

"Ouch! It's real alright!" she groaned, wincing from the reality check.

"Ok these must be some kind of exotic tree that have been planted here and I've simply wandered into someone's garden by mistake. That's it!" she asserted, trying to convince herself that there was some obvious rational explanation for the strange phenomena.

Gradually the forest began to fill with light as the morning sun began to rise. She checked her watch. "7pm? But that's not right! What is going on here?, am I going mad or did I really fall asleep in the forest?"

"Oh my word! Mum and Dad will be worried sick!. Right I must find that road and get out of here" she murmured to herself before aimlessly wandering off like some desperate cast away adrift in the wilderness.

She had no idea where she was heading; she just chanced her arm that a road may appear at some point along the direction she was travelling.
"Rocco!, Rocco!" she continuously cried on her blind journey, in the hope that he may suddenly come to her aid and guide her out of the woods, but there was no sign of the little fox at all.
The further she walked the more she felt lost. Everything looked the same after a while, tree after tree, shrub after shrub it went on seemingly without end. Yet still Laila pushed forward optimistic that she would eventually find civilization, but without even the noise of a distant car to raise her hopes she grew increasingly despondent until eventually after a few hours her pace became sluggish and laboured and she finally yielded defeat beside an old fallen tree. Listless and tired she amused herself for a time by counting the different varieties of leaves that blanketed the forest floor.
Her morale had hit rock bottom by now and with no sign of Rocco or any idea where she was, Laila had almost abandoned hope of ever getting out of the forest that day. Until out of nowhere the unexpected sound of a faint voice could be heard in the distance being carried along upon the breeze. Her ears pricked up immediately and she looked about in order to determine the source of the sound.

It appeared to be coming from an area of dense holly bushes, about one hundred and fifty yards from where she sat.

So without hesitation she made her way over to investigate.

As Laila drew closer she stopped and hid behind the buttress of a tree for a moment. Peeking cautiously around the bole so as to make sure she had not been seen approaching, and that all was well before continuing. She could hear the voice was that of an individual with a deep bellowing tone who was laughing a lot and talking away intently to someone whom, from what Laila could determine had had no real involvement in the conversation. She decided to examine the mysterious voice a little further as her curiosity had got the better of her. So tentatively she made her way over. Every step placed meticulously as not to make a sound in the deathly silence. She knew the slightest snap of a twig could easily give away her presence in the unearthly hush.

Hunching over to conceal herself amongst the scrub she sneakily tiptoed up to the holly thicket at a safe distance and peered inquisitively through a small gap in the leaves. There she could only just make out the shape of what appeared to be a man who was colossal and robust. He was dressed in what only can be described as some kind of camouflage robe with twigs and leaves poking out of it in all directions, but as he had his back towards her she couldn't quite see his face.

He was permanently arched over whilst in conversation which suggested his accomplice was someone obviously small, but Laila's view was obscured so she couldn't see the other individual at all until the tall man eventually stood upright to reveal the recipient of his discourse.

"How very strange?" she thought. It appeared that his confabulations were directed towards a tiny Yew sapling growing beside a clearing.

Stepping back he shook his head seemingly agitated with the small tree, as if somehow disappointed with its taciturn manner.

And then just when it appeared he had lost patience, and was about to sit down on an old tree stump, he suddenly leapt up and began laughing loudly again.

"Ha! I know why you don't want to be moved to that clearing! It's those rabbits isn't it? You are worried that they may strip your bark he roared as if to ridicule the little tree.

"He's a Looney!" Laila thought as she watched him taunt his subject.

"Well well, I would never have thought of you as being such a weed Ioho" he said stamping his foot mirthfully.

Then after a moment of chuckling, he began whispering to the little Yew tree. Laila was intrigued by the stranger's outlandish behaviour and wanted to hear more, or at the very least get a better view of him, so she leant forward on her tip toes. But unfortunately the shrub was too high and dense, and the bold foliage made it almost impossible to see through clearly.

All she could visibly make out was his extremely long legs. So audaciously she climbed up into the shrub to get a better view. Branch by branch as stealthily as a cat she clambered up into the crown of the shrub until finally she found a slightly better angle on the glade in which the stranger was concealed. Even so she still had difficulty seeing him, as he was elaborately camouflaged to the point where he was almost invisible.

"Damn it! Stand up!" She mumbled impatiently. Yet no matter where he moved he was constantly bent over with his back towards her. She concluded that the only way she would be able see him properly was to change her position, so she decided to move gradually further out on the branch. It seemed like a good idea initially until she heard the slow creaking sound of timber under stress and noticed that the limb she was standing on was beginning to bend under her weight, so instinctively she grabbed at a larger overhanging branch for support.

"Phew, that was close!" she thought, not realising that in fact the branch she was holding onto was totally rotten. Crack! Went the flimsy limb and down went Laila still holding the rotten branch.

"What on earth!" roared the man jumping backwards with surprise as Laila came tumbling out of thin air bringing a large percentage of the holly bush with her.

She landed awkwardly as she hit the ground and twisted her leg, and so began rolling around the glade groaning in agony.

"Who are you?" the man asked. "You startled me leaping out like that!".

But Laila remained curled up in a ball on the floor.

"Arrg!I think I've broken my leg," she said in a strained agonising tone.

"Don't be ridiculous! You've hardly made a dent in the ground" he said.

"Oh, really!" Snapped Laila grimacing, whilst trying to straighten her leg.

"Here, let me help you up!" he said offering assistance.

Hesitantly she reached up before freezing in total horror at the sight that met her eyes.

There before her was a hand so gigantic and grotesque that all Laila could do was just stare at it dumbfounded.

Each of its fingers were as thick as her arm and almost as long, and the swarthy flesh was ligneous and finely cracked like the bark of a tree. Fine shoots grew like hairs across the dorsum of the hand and even the fingernails resembled the testas of acorn shells. Nervously Laila panned upwards to be greeted by a huge smiling face.

"Ahhrrgg!!!" she screamed at the top of her voice almost bursting a lung in terror. His entire face was covered in beige oak leaves that emanated in layers from his flesh. Only his nose, mouth and big round green eyes could be seen peering eerily through the foliage. Instinctively Laila tried to get away but floundered in her haste, stumbling backwards into an area of impenetrable blackthorn.

With the creature now blocking her exit she found herself cornered with no possible means of escape. All she could do was cower into a ball as the colossal figure drew nearer.

"What is the matter with you?" he asked, crossing his arms as if offended by her sudden strange outburst. He was not a man in the human sense of the word as Laila had initially assumed. In fact he was unlike anything she had ever seen before and certainly not of this world. He stood a lofty nine feet seven inches tall in height and his mighty torso and limbs were furrowed and knotty, and not too dissimilar to the boughs of an oak tree.

 Green algae stained his root shaped feet and hands, while dense bunches of leaves sprouted forth from his chest and groin.

"Help!" Laila howled.

"Help? Why are you in some kind of trouble?" asked the creature.

"Please don't hurt me!" begged Laila trembling hysterically.

"Why would I wish to hurt you? He asked seemingly confused.

"I've heard that's what monsters do to children".

"Well that's as maybe, but I'll have you know that I am no monster!" He replied, taking umbrage to the remark.

"I am a Green man!" he said proudly.

"And Green men do not harm anyone, unless provoked of course!"

"Does that mean you're not going to hurt me then?" asked Laila anxiously.

"Yes of course it does!, although I don't feel you deserve it after your puerile behaviour" he groaned.

Laila remained curled up in a ball, still unable to move with fear.

"Thank you Mr Green man, thank you" she said timidly but he refused to acknowledge her gratitude. Instead he strolled off in a huff to the far corner of the glade and sat down on his tree stump, put his chin in his hands and began denigrating Laila to his companion.

"What's this world coming to eh Ioho?" he said speaking to the little yew sapling.

"One would think that these juvenile sorceresses would have better things to do with their time, instead of playing these senseless games".

"Spying on me, then materializing uninvited like that. And then having the audacity to call me a monster! I ask you, what has become of the sacred arts?". Laila listened intently to the Green mans rants before realizing that his negative discourse was aimed at her.

"I am so sorry Mr Green man I didn't mean to insult you" she whimpered. "And I wasn't spying on you honestly." "I was just lost and I heard you talking" she said lifting her head humbly from her stoop.

The Green man looked over at Laila with a contemptuous glare.

"Oh really little witch! Do you expect me to believe that?" he said dismissively before returning to the yew sapling once again.

"See how easily it is for these young witches to lie Ioho!. "The dishonesty oozes from her lips like the sap from a birch" he scorned.

 After a few minutes Laila apprehensively rose to her feet.

"Am I free to go Mr Green man?" she asked in a hushed and humbled tone.

"I wish you would then maybe I could get some peace!" he snapped.

Never had Laila felt so scared in all her life. Here she was lost in a strange part of the forest with only a gigantic Green man for company. And to make matters worse she had put him in a really foul mood. Timidly she approached him.

"Sorry to trouble you Mr Green man sir, but could you direct me to the nearest main road please" she asked politely.

"What main road?" he asked her abruptly.

Laila looked at him bewildered.

"You know, any main road where there are cars" she said, simulating the turning of a steering wheel. But the Green man looked none the wiser, and just stared disdainfully at her.

"What are you talking about?" he asked.

Realizing that he may not be familiar with any roads in his neck of the woods Laila tried a different approach.

"Do you know how far Warren pond is from here?" she asked.

"Never heard of it" he replied.

"Surely you must know it, there's a huge oak tree there that you can climb inside".

"I told you I have never heard of it" he said raising his voice. "Anyway the nearest pond to here is around thirty miles in that direction" he said pointing into the wild dense brush.

"Thirty miles!" Laila cried. "But that's impossible, how could I have travelled that distance in such a short time?" she said, placing her hands on her head in disbelief.

"It's quite obvious to me!" said the Green man.

"Is it?" asked Laila bemused.

"Yes it is you little witch! You appeared here by the use of magic of course. How else could you have discovered a Green man in the forest?" he snarled accusingly.

Laila appeared puzzled by the remark.

"I just heard you talking" she said.

"I don't believe you!" he roared.

"It's the truth I swear it!" she exclaimed shaking in her shoes.

"Then explain to me how it was that you passed through the forest undetected by the trees unless by the use of witchcraft or some other form of sorcery".

Laila shrugged her shoulders. "I'm sorry but I don't understand what you mean?" she said.

The Green man got up off his stump and looked down at her suspiciously as she flinched beneath his imposing frame.

Running his fingers through his long leafy beard he lifted his head in a proud yet supercilious manner. "It is totally impossible for anyone or anything to find a Green man in the woods. We commune with the trees so our awareness and vision are ubiquitous. The trees inform us to the whereabouts of an intruder walking through the forest at a vast distance yet they were oblivious to your presence, now tell me why is that?" he demanded.

"I have no idea?" sobbed Laila. "I have no idea about anything at the moment. I wish I knew what was going on, really I do! She said dolefully, before slumping crestfallen on the ground.

"One minute it was spring and I was over at Warren pond and the next minute its autumn and I'm lost and alone in a strange part of the woods".

The Green man initially offered her no solace. He just stood there stubbornly aloof, but gradually his rigidity began to slowly wane as he sensed the genuine dejection in Laila's disposition, and couldn't help but feel sympathy for the sorrowful wretch.

"I apologise if I appeared callous" he said awkwardly.

"But surely you understand that if you did not arrive here by the use of magic then how else could you have possibly got here?, you must have some recollection?"

Laila shrugged her shoulders. "All I remember was the big hawthorn tree and after that, I'm not quite sure" she sighed. The Green man fell back onto his stump as if suddenly overwhelmed by her disclosure. His eyes appeared glazed and distant as he stared blindly lost in thought.

"A spirit door!" he whispered under his breath.

"I'm sorry?" said Laila snapping him from his reflection

"A hawthorn has not grown in this part of the world for well over six hundred years" he said mournfully.

"But I saw one only a few hours ago?" said Laila "And no more than a few mile from here".

The Green man nodded his head

"I know the tree of which you speak" he muttered getting to his feet and standing for a moment in cogitation.

"There is something I want you to see" he said
walking off. "Come, follow me".

Laila nimbly scurried along in the wake of the lofty
wooden giant without objection or query.

Even though she barely knew the curious
miscreation she began to feel strangely at ease with
him. For beneath his terrifying facade she sensed a
gentle soul who meant her no harm. And anyhow,
she knew that if he had meant her ill he wouldn't
have tolerated her thus far.

"What do you call yourself?" asked the Green man
as they traipsed through the brushwood.

"I'm a human" she replied. To which the Green man
gave a chuckle.

"I had gathered that, but do you have a name?"

" Oh yes! It's Laila".

"Well Laila, I am Jack, Jack Green" he said.

"Pleased to meet you Jack" she said breathlessly
struggling to keep up with his long bounding
strides.

The conversation though brief and informal didn't
really continue much further than that for the
duration of the journey, as Laila found the task of
talking and running, far too challenging, and
decided t it was best to concentrate on keeping pace.

As they traversed through the brush the rain started
to slowly fall, burnishing the autumn leaves and

creating a picturesque spectacle of kaleidoscope painted trees, which helped divert Laila's attention from the grim cold flurry that began to gradually hamper their jaunt.

Eventually Jack stopped by an area of birch wood, soon followed by the weary Laila puffing from the trek.

"What is it Jack?" she asked, stopping to catch her breath. "What is it you wanted to show me?"

He said nothing as he stood there sombre amongst the birch trees.

"I recognise this place" she said looking around.

"Yes! This is where the hawthorn tree was". "But where has it gone?" she asked.

"The hawthorn tree that once grew here Laila was felled many centuries ago" he said pointing his long sprig like finger at the remnants of an old tree stump arising from the bend of a weed infested brook.

It was clear that the tree that once grew there had long since perished and all that remained was a worm eaten stump, with bracket fungi sprouting from every corner.

A latticework of tangled bramble stems grew all about, almost shrouding it from view. Laila looked around in dismay

"But surely this can't be the place" she said. "There must be some mistake, maybe this place just looks the same!".

Jack then pointed mournfully towards a series of fresh footprints leading away from the stump. Laila immediately fell to her knees in absolute shock and horror at the vision. The footprints were hers.

"No! Please, No! This can't be happening!" she screamed hysterically before bursting into tears.

Jack knelt down on the muddy earth beside Laila and tried his best to console her.

"It's ok" he said feeling a little inadequate. Laila looked up at him with tears rolling down her cheeks.

"What's happening to me Jack where am I?" she sobbed.

"I'm afraid I don't know if I can answer that Laila" he said in a low voice.

"I want to go home" Laila cried.

"You will!" said Jack "You will!".

Gently he lifted the listless Laila from the cold wet ground and carried her off to an area of dense conifers to shelter her from the driving rain. Laying her down on a bed of soft dry moss he covered her in dry bracken and lit a fire close by.

"Rest now Laila" he said stroking her head delicately. "I will take care of you".

"I wish I knew what was going on Jack" sniffed Laila looking thoughtfully up at the sky.

"I wish I knew too Laila, it does not make sense to me either" he said perturbed.

"One thing I do know for certain, there are strange energies at work here, I feel it in the air and in the restless whispers of venerable trees".

Laila's eyes began to fill with tears. "I wish I could see my Mum right now" she whimpered.

"Do you think I will ever get to see her again?"

"Don't talk like that Laila!, of course you will!, Jack will see to that!" he said loud and resolutely.

Comforted by his assurance Laila managed to crack a smile.

"Thank you Jack" she said.

"Don't mention it". Now get some rest" he said prodding the embers with a stick.

Eventually Laila drifted off to sleep as the autumnal fog settled in the dusky wood, leaving only the lonesome crooked figure of a Green man lit up amongst the tenebrous looming pines that held aloft the harvest moon.

The next morning Laila awoke early to the sound of bird song echoing like an enchanted aria through the tranquillity of the woods. The air was brisk but for the warm blaze of the campfire that cracked and crackled brightly beside her. "Morning Laila!" said Jack bursting the peaceful lull with his deep bellowing tone, causing her to almost leap out of her skin in surprise.

"Oh! Good morning Jack" she said with hand on heart. "I'm sorry if I look a little startled but I was kind of hoping that this had all been just a bad dream" she said.

"Well it soon will be Laila because I'm going to take you to see a friend of mine by the name of Yan Overton who I am confident will be able to help you get back to where you belong".

"Really? Who is Yan Overton?" she asked sitting up excitedly.

"Never mind that, first you must build up your strength". Here I have collected some food for you" he said passing her a handful of apples.

"Thank you!" said Laila biting into the crisp green fruit.

"How are you feeling today?" he asked concerned.

"I'm fine" Laila replied putting on a brave face.

Just then a robin flew down and landed on Jack's shoulder followed by a tiny wren. They fluttered frantically around his face and head pecking diligently at his leafy locks.

"Look Jack! You have birds on you!" said Laila with astonishment but Jack seemed almost blasé about it, and sat there totally unconcerned by the excitement around him.

"I am friends with all life in the forest" he remarked casually.

Laila beamed, "What a wonderful creature a Green man is" she thought.

"When you feel ready to leave Laila we will head towards Leo's weir. It's quite some distance from here so I suggest you ride upon my back for most of the way as the terrain can get quite muddy and uneven at this time of year, and it will be much quicker too" he said, to which Laila agreed.

After breakfast Jack got down on to all fours while Laila shinned up onto his hip so as to clamber on to his back. She put her arms tightly around his thick wooden neck and ever so slowly he began to stand upright. "Comfortable?" he asked.

"Yes" Laila replied.

She always enjoyed being up high and was feeling quite excited about the prospect of the journey ahead.

"Ready? Now hold tight" he said before striding expeditiously off into the woods with the diminutive Laila clinging on to his timber frame like a gangling fruit.

As they made their way beneath the versicoloured crowns, Jack got to talking about the hawthorn trees.

"All the ancient hawthorns were felled many centuries ago in this part of the wood during an era known as the Banishing" he said.

"The Banishing, what's that?" Laila asked.

"The Banishing was a time of change, a purging of old practices and beliefs. The ancient trees that were once venerated were now considered a threat to the formation of a new ideology, so they were cut down then taken away to be burnt".

"How can a tree be a threat? trees are good for everyone" aren't they Jack?" asked Laila perplexed.

"Yes they are Laila but trees are extremely powerful entities too. You have to understand that there are invisible forces at work which shape our world and those who were attuned and understood the workings of this energy were now seen as heretics. So with the hawthorns destroyed, these so called primordial dissidents were forced into exile". Laila looked puzzled.

"I don't understand a word you're saying? She said.

"Can you repeat that in English?"

"I'm Sorry forgive me! Yes you're right it does sound a bit confusing. It simply means one thing Laila. That nothing is sacred in this world anymore" he grumbled resentfully.

"Was there nothing you or anyone could do to stop it?" she asked.

Jack smiled, "The race of humans is too vast and ruthless .Not even a creature as big as an Ogre could stop them!" "An Ogre? That's like a Troll isn't it?" asked Laila.

"Yes they are not too dissimilar to a Troll but Ogre's are native to this part of the world" he said.

"You make it sound as if they're real" she laughed.

"Well maybe that's because they are!" replied Jack.

"You are funny Jack, everyone knows that Ogres aren't real!" she said.

"Oh really is that a fact?" he replied with a smirk.

They covered quite some distance through the forest that day before Jack decided to stop for a short break by the edge of a steep ravine.

Settling upon the high ridge overlooking the rustic mosaic of tree tops Laila sat in silent serenity, entranced by the magic of the beautiful empyrean landscape that stretched out below her.

A vast shimmering lake dominated the heart of the valley like an effulgent sapphire.

Herds of roe deer lapped undaunted by the water margins while in the sky flocks of waterfowl descended upon the lake, drawn in to the beauty and fertility of the lush oasis.

"What is this place?" she asked.

"Oh it's just one of the wilder parts of the forest" said Jack grinning with pride before suddenly and inexplicably letting out what can only be described as a loud "Choo!" sound for no apparent reason, or so it seemed.

It was as if he was attempting to falsify a sneezing sound which Laila found rather bemusing.

A moment later the water in the centre of the lake began to swell as if triggered by Jacks sudden outburst.

The movement appeared to have been caused by some weird subsurface implosion.

The violent compression generated tremendous waves which crashed violently upon the surrounding lakeshore like a miniature tsunami, destroying the earthen banks and vegetation whilst flooding the forest margin close to the lake. The water fowl instantly took to the wing and the deer scattered nervously back into the cover of the woods. Laila watched in wonder as the strange anomaly gradually receded back to its source, dragging all manner of debris towards a swirling vortex.

Then all of a sudden emerging from out of the depths of the lake and slowly rising high above the trees appeared a Creature so immense that it completely shadowed its surroundings.

"This is no ordinary forest!" said Laila a gasp.

Jack meanwhile swiftly descended the deep ferny slope down towards the lake.

"Come on Laila! What's the matter? I thought you said they were fictitious!" he laughed "Now that's what you call a swamp Ogre," he said pointing up at the giant beast and chuckling with excitement. But Laila could only gape in wonder at the incredible sight.

Like some gigantic Jurassic relic redeemed from the dawn of creation it sat, hunched over in the muddy depths of the lake. Its ashen soaked flesh running alive with water bugs and blood worm churned up from the disturbed silt. The coarse hide was thick and ridged like greisen rock.

Immense boulder round shoulders and strong muscular arms lifted pondweed from the water like hydraulic cranes, a personification of pure strength and power.

Its jaw was solid, square and under slung to allow two protruding ivory white tusks to appear either side of the mouth from behind its lower lip. Its eyes, ears and pug shaped nose where quite insignificant in relation to its size. But what it lacked in features it made up for in bulk.

"It's alright Laila, don't be scared, come on!" said Jack beckoning her down but Laila was justifiably cautious. If this creature became jittery or decided to suddenly turn nasty there would be nothing on earth to control it she thought. Even the formidable Green man appeared meagre in comparison.

"I'm ok I'll stay here and watch for a bit" she said timorously stooping down below the fronds of bracken.

"No I want to introduce you to him, he is my friend, he won't harm you I promise, come down" he insisted.

After some consideration and a lot of pleading from Jack, Laila reluctantly followed him down towards the shore of the lake, all the time keeping her eyes fixed apprehensively on the giant Ogre, just in case she had to make a quick dash for cover.

"Swamp Ogres love old lakes and ponds but unfortunately there aren't that many Ogres left in the world these days," said Jack, as they carefully descended through the steep slopes of slippery ferns.

"I've known this particular Ogre for quite a number of years now, I call him Fenndeor. He's really a gentle giant believe it or not".

When they eventually reached level ground at the base of the declivity they began to make their way around the lake towards where the Ogre sat. The ground was soft on the bay where the water had previously reseeded. Fine sand, shale and freshwater mussel shells cluttered the banks like rockweed, alongside the incongruous roving footprints of a young girl and a Green man. The muddy black water lapped onto the shoreline disrupted by the movement of the giant beast as it churned up the lake bed in search of food.

When Laila and Jack strolled into the Ogres vision it growled deep and loud as if to assert its territory, its stagnant breath belching forth a thick smog from its nostrils that hung for a time like fine web in the cold air of the misty lake.

Jack and Laila stopped close to the edge of the water line and looked up at the gigantic entity.

He didn't really pay them much regard following his initial growl and resumed masticating vast quantities of pondweed.

That was until Jack decided to start making the strange sneezing sound again.

"Choo! Choo!" he went immediately grabbing the Ogres attention.

"Shush!" said Laila distressed "Please don't do that Jack you'll startle it!".

"Don't be silly Laila I know what I'm doing, it's the noise that Ogres make when they call to each other," smiled Jack.

Laila trembled uncontrollably as the huge creature began slowly making its way towards them. It moved sluggishly on all fours through the water in a kind of ape like gait, and to a certain extent it was very similar in form.

Very top heavy across the chest and shoulders with arms almost twice the length of its hind legs.

Laila and Jack were forced to scamper backward from the shoreline to avoid being soaked by the incoming swirl.

"Hello Fenndeor my old friend?" said Jack calling up to the enormous beast, his stentorian voice echoing like a drum around the stillness of the lake.

The Ogre lowered its huge head towards them inquisitively while Laila briskly concealed herself behind the Green mans legs.

Jack began to stroke Fenndeor's chin, causing the great Ogre to emit a loud Choo sound with delight, the blast ruffling Jacks leaves and almost knocking him off of his feet.

"He is happy to see us Laila," said Jack trying to gently free her tight grip from his leg.

"Don't be impolite, say hello to him" he said looking down at Laila recoiling around his ankles, but she was far too terrified to move, preferring to remain hidden for the time being. Losing his patience the Green man turned around and grabbed her by the scruff of the neck with his powerful timber hands.

"Allow me to introduce my friend Laila," he said lifting her swiftly from her feet and holding her up high in front of the Ogre like a rag doll. Laila kicked and wiggled to free herself from Jacks grip but he was much too strong.

Fenndeor meanwhile stared intriguingly at the tiny person through his small dark menacing eyes before sniffing her face. Immediately she became limp with fear, only mustering up enough energy for a small squeak.

"It won't eat me will it?" She whimpered under her breath.

"No I told you Ogres only eat pond weed that's why they inhabit lakes, ponds and rivers. People often associate Trolls with living under bridges when in fact they are really confusing them with Swamp Ogres feeding on the blanket weed that gets caught up on the pilings.

"That's interesting," she mumbled nervously as the giant Ogre began licking her leg. It made her feel a little nausea's as its mephitic breath had the overwhelming odour of stagnant mud.

"Can you put me down now please Jack?" she asked timidly.

"Oh yes!" he said forgetting himself.

Once her feet were safely back on terra firma she began to feel a little more at ease.

"Do you think he'll let me stroke him?" she asked, to which the Ogre replied by lowering his mighty head right in front of her.

Jack laughed. "He understands every word you're saying, he just doesn't have the ability to articulate as you and I do" he said. Laila giggled excitedly and reached up on her tip toes to stroke his chin. The Ogre closed his eyes and made another loud Choo! Sound.

"You've made a friend for life there," said Jack and they both began to laugh.

Laila was relishing her encounter with the Ogre, and although Jack was too, he knew they had a more pressing engagement.

"We really should be think about heading on to Leo's weir now Laila" he said.

"Aw! Do we have to go now?" she asked looking disappointed by the transitory nature of their meeting.

"I'm afraid so, we still have some way to go" he replied.

Reluctantly Laila nodded "Ok" she said before turning to the gigantic Ogre. "Goodbye Fenndeor it was really wonderful meeting you". The Ogre sounded off with another Choo! Before slowly receding out of sight beneath the murky waters of the lake.

"Wow! That was amazing, I've just been stroking an Ogre!" Laila beamed. "My Dad will never believe me" She said, and then sudden sombre expression fell upon her face.

"I miss my Dad".

"Well let's get you home so you can tell him all about it then" said Jack trying to lift her mood.

They travelled through some beautiful parts of the forest on their way to Leo's weir. By now the autumn sun was high in the sky lighting up the enchanted forest.

"I love being in the woods amongst the trees," remarked Laila on their journey. "I know it sounds daft but it makes me feel alive, do you know what I mean?"

"Of course I do Laila it is a wonderful magical place. It is as much a part of me as I am a part of it and that's why I take care of the trees in the forest".
"You care for the trees? In what way?" asked Laila with interest.
"We Green men are the custodians of the forest. Our purpose is to assist nature in order that the forests will flourish".
"That's a wonderful thing Jack, to know your purpose in life". "I wonder what my purpose in life is?" She pondered whilst gazing up at the clouds.
"Your purpose should be to discover your purpose" he said sagaciously leaving Laila deliberating for a while.
"I noticed you talking to a small Yew tree yesterday, can you really talk to trees" she asked.
"Sure I can, it was the trees that told me the whereabouts of Fenndeor."
"That's amazing!, In fact this whole place is pretty amazing" said Laila cheerfully.

A few miles down the road she began to feel lethargic.
"How far is it to the weir?" she asked, as her arms began to ache from hanging onto the big Green man.

"Not that far, why do you wish to take a break?" he asked.

"Yes please" she said wearily.

Gently Jack lowered Laila down beneath the branches of an elm.

"Can I walk from now on Jack?" she asked rubbing her tender shoulder.

"Of course but I don't think we will make it to the weir before nightfall as it gets dark early at this time of year and we need to cover a lot of ground".

"I promise I will walk as fast as I can, it's just that holding onto you for so long tires me more than walking".

"Sure, whatever you want" he said with a smile.

So Laila and the Green man relaxed for a while beneath the shade of an elm in the dream like solitude of silence, with only their thoughts and the twitter of bird song for company.

An hour passed quickly by before Jack rose to his feet and caressed his long leafy beard.

"Are we fit and ready then?" he asked.

"Ready when you are" she said with renewed vigour and so off they went to the weir.

Chapter Three

Lev, Tuk and Volk

After a short walk through the shady underbrush they came out upon a wide muddy track that resembled a bridleway running off through the trees. It was pitted and uneven, and rain water had accumulated in the deep furrows that ran throughout its entirety. Tall beech and hornbeam trees flanked either side, creating a grand avenue that took on the appearance of a nave. Like a magnificent gothic cathedral their limbs stretched up high to support a fan vault ceiling of intricate branches overhead.

"I hope it's not far to the weir?" said Laila trying to avoid the numerous pools of mud.

"It's not that far," said Jack who unlike Laila made no attempt to avoid them, contently trampling merrily on through the quagmire. The pace was fairly slow as he had to stop frequently to wait for Laila, who tiptoed daintily along the narrow undisturbed perimeter of the track.

"I'm sorry if I'm slowing you down" she said trying to free herself from yet another bramble stem. But Jack never complained once, instead he offered to carry her on his back again to which she declined due to her stubborn pride.

On and on they plodded along the unending track. With every corner they turned another awaited, and when they reached the end of that they were greeted with much of the same. With no sign of the weir Laila eventually began to feel dispirited.
"Are there no roads in this part of the woods? How much further now Jack?" she asked.
"Not far!" he replied.
"But you told me it wasn't far hours ago" she said scraping the thick mud from the soles of her shoes with a small stick. "Could you be a bit more specific?" she asked.
Jack paused and scratched his leafy locks. "Err, about ten miles," he said casually, as if ten miles was nothing more than a short saunter , whereas Laila on the other hand was not so nonchalant.
"Ten miles! Are you joking!" she cried. "We'll never make it there before nightfall".
"Yes I know" he smiled cheerfully.
"What!, you mean to say you knew all along?".

"Sure! We Green men know everything about seasonal sunsets".

"But why did you tell me that it wasn't that far to the weir?" she asked in dismay.

"Because I didn't want to dampen your spirits, and also I rather hoped you would have moved a little bit faster to be honest," he said.

"But I'm only a small person Jack, I'm not a horse!".

"That's a shame, because if you were we would have easily been there by now," he chuckled but Laila was not amused.

"So what happens now?" she asked peevishly folding her arms.

"I recommend we set up camp here for the night, it will be dark in a couple of hours and we can make an early start in the morning. There's a nice area of level ground a hundred yards ahead which will be ideal," he said squelching off again.

"Hang on!" snapped Laila. "You're not telling me that we have to sleep in the forest again are you?".

"No, you're the one who will be sleeping, we Green men don't need sleep".

"But Jack its freezing out here in the woods!. And to tell you the truth this place gives me the creeps!".

"Don't worry! I'll take good care of you" he replied and set about collecting dead wood en route to the camp.

 Once they had arrived at the designated area, Jack immediately began creating a living space for Laila by clearing away the wet leaves and deadfalls that littered the ground.

He then he lifted her up high and set her down in the branches of a large hornbeam.

"Right! You wait here while I go and collect some more wood" he said.

"Why do I need to be up here?" she asked bewildered.

"Because wolves can't climb trees," he replied.

"Wolves!" exclaimed Laila.

"It's ok there's nothing to worry about they are quite a considerable distance away, and besides once I get a fire going they won't come near. Now you stay there" he said before vanishing like a shadow into the hazy sylvan dusk.

"Don't be long!" She called feebly after him.

There was a cold snap in the air and the indigo sky was beautiful and clear, but for Laila who sat trembling in the eerie twilight there was nothing to behold but the gloom, as all about her the forest stirred with unfamiliar sounds.

"Is that you Jack?" she would whimper every time she heard a noise, only to realise that it was nothing more than the wind in the trees and her overactive mind.

Slowly time ticked by and the night grew closer and ever colder. Laila watched disquietly from her perch as the sun finally sank below the horizon. Jack had been gone for quite some time and doubts to whether he would even return began to trouble her thoughts, until suddenly out of the blackness there came a loud crashing sound like a falling tree, startling Laila and almost dislodging her from her roost. Moments later Jack appeared with his arms fully laden.

"Here we are!" he said vivaciously dropping a huge pile of branch poles and brushwood onto the ground. Laila gave a huge sigh of relief.

"Phew! It's you Jack, you gave me a such a fright!".

"What are you worried about?" he asked.

"What am I worried about? What do you mean?" she gasped. "You said there were wolves in this forest".

"Yes that's right but as I said before they are miles away, and anyway you have nothing to fear while I'm around" he laughed throwing her a couple apples.

"But I didn't think there were any wolves left in the wild?"

"Maybe where you come from, but around here there are plenty of them, as well as the odd bear or two".

"There are bears as well?" gulped Laila.

Jack walked over to her and put his big strong hand gently on her shoulder.

"Listen to me Laila, no bear or wolf can harm you while you're in the forest with a Green man, trust me" he said, putting her mind at rest.

He then began constructing a shelter from the bits and pieces he had collected from his foray.

His skill at manipulating natural materials was amazing and within no time at all he had constructed a very impressive shelter for Laila to sleep in. It was circular framed construction with straight deadwood poles encircling a narrow entrance. The roof and walls were overlaid with brushwood and leaf litter to a depth of around two feet, giving it an almost tumulus appearance.

"Your dwelling awaits your inspection madam" said Jack lifting Laila back down from her high branch. She quickly crawled inside on all fours excitedly before peering out of the entrance. The floor inside the shelter was covered in a thick bed of dry bracken, which gave it a really cosy feel.

"This is wonderful Jack!" she said with a big smile.

"I'm glad it meets with your approval," he laughed.

"I'll build a fire around here," he said piling some kindling a short distance from the entrance of the shelter.

"The heat will make the camp nice and warm for you tonight without setting it alight".

The moon shone brightly over the trees that evening and a fire was soon briskly a roar. Laila gazed intently at the flickering flames as they danced over the embers while Jack sat in the umbrage of the trees and beyond the reach of any stray sparks igniting his foliage.

"Here's some food Laila. I know it's not much but it should appease your appetite until morning" he said passing her some oatmeal looking biscuits he had made from grinding wild nuts into a paste and baking them beside the fire on a flat stone. Laila nearly bit his hand off with hunger.

"Slow down they are still hot, you won't appreciate the flavour" he said.

"I can't help it I'm starving!" she mumbled whilst spitting biscuit crumbs all over him.

The slate grey smoke from the fire spiralled and billowed up into the ether as Jack looked up in wonder at the millions of stars overhead.

"What a beautiful evening for a sky ramble" he remarked.

"What's a sky ramble?" Laila asked.

"It's when you lay on your back on top of a hill or in a field or anywhere where your peripheral vision is not obscured and look up at the night sky and imagine your roaming through the stars" he said with a far away glare.

"I've done that!" said Laila with a smile.

"It's strange" said Jack thoughtfully.But whenever I sky ramble on a night like this and I look out into the vastness of space it makes me realise just how insignificant any troubles I may have really are. Here I am, a conscious living being smaller than a grain of dust on a tiny planet looking out into infinity; it gives me an odd sense of euphoria".

"You say the strangest things sometimes Jack" smiled Laila affectionately.

Jack was in essence a child but to look at his him you wouldn't think it.

In the dim glow of the fire his appearance seemed intimidating and almost macabre as the flittering light from the fire threw ever-changing shadows on his foliate features. And yet bizarrely Laila felt totally safe in the company of this terrifying looking creature in the darkness of the woods. But even in the presence of something as wonderful as a Green man she still longed to be somewhere else.

"I can't help thinking about my parents, they're probably worried sick about me" she said staring pensively back into the embers again.

"You would get on well with my Dad Jack, he knows everything about plants and trees. He's always telling me the names of things and what they can be used for. I guess that's where I got my love of nature. And my Mum, well she is just so kind and loving. But then aren't all mothers" she said glancing over at her quiescent companion.

"Do you have parents Jack?"

"Not in the same respect as you. My parent happens to be one and the same" he replied prodding the embers.

"What do you mean? She asked.

"It's complex" he said with a frown.

"If you don't want to talk about it I understand" she said staring dolefully into the flames.

Jack looked at her sitting there wistfully and pondered for moment.

"Eight hundred autumns have passed since my emergence into this world" he sighed.

"I was once nothing more than a tiny acorn believe it or not, formed upon the branches of a great oak growing by the banks of the river Connit in the Grayweald.

Late one season I dropped from my peduncle into the turbulent river below and was washed downstream for many miles before finally coming to rest upon the gravel bar of a shallow bay. There amongst the shale I was picked up in the mandibles of a hungry Jay foraging for food along the margins. It took me back along the course of the Connit with the intent of burying me in its store, but whilst in flight, North of Allington downs it inadvertently dropped me into a magical pool known as Swallow spring. It was there upon the muddy margins of the pool where I began to germinate, but instead of growing into an oak tree as nature intended I became a Green man, and well, that's about it really" he said dolorously.

"What about your family?" asked Laila with interest.

"Again I don't have a family in the same way as you do. But I do have a lot of siblings; in fact my parent gave birth to two thousand four hundred and sixty three acorns that year".

Laila burst into laughter. "Did they all become Green men too?".

"No I am the only one of my kind unfortunately".

"What do you mean unfortunately?".

"Well I should have been a tree but due to thaumaturgic circumstances beyond my control I became a Green man" he replied sadly.

"I think you're wonderful Jack, at least you're different, at least you can walk about! I have never seen any tree do that!".

"Sure I can do that, but I am still a tree at heart and by nature. I often dream that one day I will stay in one place and put down roots and then maybe grow into a magnificent oak and watch the world go by".

You are strange Jack!" said Laila giving way to a huge yawn. "I feel quite worn out now! Do you mind if I lay down for a bit?" she asked whilst having a well earned stretch.

"Of course I don't mind, you get some rest. We can set off at first light tomorrow, that way we can exploit the short daylight hours".

"Ok! Well Goodnight Jack" said Laila crawling into her shelter.

"Goodnight Laila, sweet dreams" he smiled.

It was dawn when Laila awoke the next day. She stuck her head out of the shelter before rubbing the sleep from her eyes. The fire was still burning away happily but Jack was nowhere to be seen. Torpidly she crawled outside and went and sat down on a big old log by the heat of the flames. It was absolutely freezing and the sun was only just beginning to rise. "Jack!" she called, but there came no reply, and so she called again, and still there was not a sound. So she got up and decided to go and look for him, but she didn't have to search far as he was standing a few hundred yards away talking intently to a copse of Birch trees and laughing loudly as usual.

As she approached he turned around with a big smile.

"Here she is! Good morning Laila did you sleep well?" he asked.

"Yes fine thanks" she replied looking somewhat dishevelled and unkempt.

"I have some good news for you!. The trees tell me that the track to the weir is safe from wild beasts".

"Great!" she yawned.

"I thought that would put your mind at rest" he smiled.

"So when can we go then?" she asked.

"Soon, but first let's break down the shelter and return the encampment to the forest unaltered" he said picking up a birch bark container filled with muddy water.

Laila grabbed the container and took a huge sip before cringing with disgust.

"Yuk! That's awful!" she wrenched.

"That's not for you to drink, that's for putting out the fire" he chuckled.

When they returned to camp Laila had some crushed apple juice and woodland biscuits for breakfast and then smartened herself up by brushing her knotty hair with a juniper sprig whilst Jack cleared away the fire and shelter. He was so meticulous that once he'd finished, it looked as if no one had ever set foot there.

"Now that's what I call a job well done!" he smiled looking over his shoulder as they made their way back along the bridle track towards the weir.

And then suddenly out of the blue he began sniggering for no apparent reason, or so it appeared to Laila, until he explained the cause for his sudden outburst.

"Forgive me Laila but I just remembered something amusing".

"What is it?" she asked.

"The Birch trees thought you were my offspring as they have never come across a human in this part of the forest before" he laughed.

"That sounds great! I would love to be a Green girl" she smiled. "And then I'd be able to talk to trees as you do Jack, it must be wonderful,".

"It's quite easy talking to the trees; it's just the interpretation that's the difficult part".

"What do you mean?" asked Laila intrigued.

"Well they can understand us obviously as we possess a voice that is audible but they have to communicate via the use of external forces such as air currents for instance in order to speak to us. By harnessing the wind they can communicate by either creaking their boughs or rustling their leaves". Laila was amazed.

"So you mean to say that when I'm walking through the forest and I hear the rustling of leaves it means the trees are talking?"

"Well Yes! But you also have to take into consideration that it might be just a blustery day in which case it can sometimes make it quite challenging to decipher the articulation from the overall ambient noise".

"And you understand these noises?" asked Laila amazed.

"Sure I do! It's often very subtle like the motion of a single leaf, so you have to look and listen carefully".

Laila looked around at the tall trees that lined the edge of the track with a whole new fascination.

"Can I try talking to a tree Jack?" she asked.

"Be my guest," he said. "Pick a tree you would like to speak to and I will interpret".

Laila inspected a few trees until eventually selecting a small leafed lime. She gazed bashfully up at Jack.

"This is really strange" she said.

"What do you mean?" he asked.

"Well I'm always talking to trees, like my friend Mr Tree over at Warren pond but for some reason I feel a little bit embarrassed. I'm not sure what to say?".

"Why not try saying hello, I find it's usually a good starting point!" he grinned.

She took a moment to compose herself before speaking.

"Hello, how do you do my name is Laila!" she said curtsying politely. There then followed a brief silence as she waited in anticipation of a reply. Watching intensely every leaf and branch Laila stood motionless. And then there was a sudden yet almost indistinct movement, as a light breeze caught a few fine twigs high in the crown but nothing really discernible. Curiously she turned to Jack who had a huge smile on his face.

"What is it?" she asked.

"The lime said it is very pleased to communicate with your kind".

"Really?" she said ecstatically.

"Yes! Though merely a translation you understand. Trees obviously don't adopt the same formal expressions as humans, but basically that is what it said" he replied. To which Laila instantly leapt around clapping her hands with excitement.

"I can speak to trees!" she yelled and Jack began to laugh.

"Well done Laila you're learning how to be a proper Green man, or should that be Green girl. When we get to the weir I will introduce you to some really interesting crack willows" he said.

"That sounds great I can't wait! Oh and don't forget your friend Yan too" she said skipping joyfully along the track. "Of course that goes without saying. As soon as we get to the weir we can collect enough provisions for the journey to Yan's house" he said.

Laila's mirth immediately ceased as her gaiety turned to confusion at Jacks unexpected remark regarding his friend Yan.

"Collected enough provisions? Does that mean that Yan doesn't actually live by the weir then?"

"Oh my word, no! He lives nowhere near it" said Jack casually.

Laila couldn't believe what she was hearing.

"Forgive me Jack? But I thought you were taking me to see Yan?".

"That's right I am!" he smiled.

"So why are we going to the weir?" she asked.

"Because the weir is by far the best place to set up camp for the evening, plus we can stock up on what we need". Laila kicked the ground in frustration.

"Evening!, Camp! Please Jack, not another night in the forest! I want to go home don't you understand I've had enough of sleeping in the woods!. You promised you would help me" she said overwrought, and with that sat in a defiant huff on the side of the track. Jack stopped mid stride before wandering back over to her.

"Hey come now Laila, I said I was going take you to meet Yan and that is what I intend to do" he said kneeling beside her and rubbing her back reassuringly.

"So how far is his house from the weir?" she asked.

"Oh, not that far" he said in a slightly disingenuous tone.

"You keep saying it's not far but how far is not far?"

"Well, give or take a mile with undulating terrain and also taking into consideration river crossings, I would say about, a two hundred and fifty miles". This striking revelation made Laila feel even worse than before.

"But I reckon if we pick up the pace we should arrive there in about two weeks" he said, trying to lift her morale but without success, because no sooner had he spoke she just started crying.

"Cheer up! It's not that bad! We will be there before you know it, you'll see" he said with a smile.

"Oh yeah! And how are we going to do that, fly there?" she blubbered.

Jack paused and looked thoughtfully up at the sky for a moment before rising sharply to his feet and holding his finger triumphantly in the air.

"That's it Laila!, why didn't I think of it earlier" he said shaking his head. "Yes! We can fly to Yan's house!".

Laila wiped her eyes and looked up at him puzzled. "Fly? But how?" she asked.

"On a broomstick Laila that's how" said the Green man audaciously.

"But flying broomsticks aren't real, are they?" asked Laila squeezing his hand.

"Of course they are Laila! I'm surprised at you. I have witnessed thousands of witches in flight and believe me it is a wonderful spectacle to behold, although they do tend to prefer flying mostly at night these days in order to avoid attracting attention to themselves".

"But what keeps them up there?" asked Laila totally captivated.

"Hazel! that's the magic wood," he said looking around, before suddenly disappearing off into the scrub, and returning seconds later with a small 'Y' shaped sprig of hazel.

"Here you go" he said handing it to Laila, who had no idea what was expected of her.

"Now hold the two forks tightly with your hands up turned and keep them level, now ever so slowly walk over there" he said pointing to the opposite side of the track. Laila felt slightly abashed but did as she was asked.

Carefully she made her way across, each step slow and measured and then when she neared the other side of the track, the sprig suddenly leapt up out of her hands as if by magic, making her jump back with surprise.

"Jack roared with laughter. "You found it then!" he said.

"Yes! But what is it?" Laila asked.

"It's a called a dragon path" said Jack. "It's an invisible current of earth energy that witches use as flight paths". "They run in straight lines across the land and this particular one runs from here to virtually Yan's front door" he said punching the air with excitement.

"I still don't get it? She said.

"Let me explain" said Jack picking up the sprig from the ground. "Hazels are the only shrubs that react this way to dragon paths. They have the ability when under stress to repel the earth's terrestrial magnetism" he said in an erudite manner.

"Slow down" said Laila. "What does terrestrial earth thingamajig mean?"

"Well basically, dragon paths and broomsticks act similarly to the opposite poles of magnetite. They push each other away, and as the besom or broomstick is obviously lighter in mass than the earth then the potential energy is forced upwards thereby creating lift".

Even though it sounded a bit discombobulating Laila was quite impressed.

"I still don't understand what all that means Jack, but it sounds amazing!. And have you flown a broomstick before?" she asked.

"No never, but I know how they work, and there's always a first time for everything" he said grinning from ear to ear. "Now hang on!" said Laila stepping back dubiously.

"You don't really expect me to get on a broomstick with someone who has never flown one before do you? It's far too dangerous".

"There's nothing to worry about I have pretty good idea of what to do" he said looking up at the clouds.

"No! There is no way I'm getting on a broomstick with you Jack!" exclaimed Laila resolutely.

"Well I suppose we'd better start walking then" he remarked brashly before strolling off down the track. "Only another two hundred and forty five miles to go".

"Wait!" called Laila after him, "let's not rush off just yet!, let me think for a minute. Maybe it's not such a bad idea after all but answer me this Jack, how safe is it?"

Jacks smiled. "It's safe Laila trust me, have I let you down yet? He asked.

Laila shook her head.

"Anyhow witches have been flying along dragon paths for thousands of years without incident" he said trying to give his point some gravitas but Laila was not convinced.

"Yes but you're not a witch".

"Maybe not, but at least I understand the mechanics. Plus I have watched witches fly on numerous occasions and it doesn't look that difficult. Anyway Laila what would you prefer, walking for fourteen days or flying for a few hours?"

Laila stared vacantly in deliberation before gazing up in the air.

"If you don't like it we can always come back down and continue on foot" said Jack.

"Ok let's give it a go then" she said reluctantly.
"Great! The first thing we need to do is make a besom and I know just the place where we can get one" he said picking her up and putting her on his shoulder, before wandering off the track and into the undergrowth.

They hadn't wandered far into the woods before they came across a huge hazel growing in a clearing amongst some larger standard trees. Jack began to speak with the shrubs about his intentions and asked for consent to collect some timber to which the hazel agreed. So with his adept skill he removed a long thick straight limb from the base with a flint axe that he had knapped from a large cobble.

"Can you help me collect some brush wood Laila," he asked pointing at the thin twigs that sprang forth from the main stem of the shrub.

Carefully she began breaking off the smaller branches and within no time had accumulated quite a considerable stack.

And when they had finally collected all the materials they required for the besom she felt quite spent and slumped down on the pile to rest.

"I won't be a moment Laila, I'm just going to get some water for the hazel, so if you want to take a short break here that's fine" said Jack walking off into the dense thicket.

"Can I come too?" she asked.

"Sure! If you like" he replied.

En route to the water source Jack removed a small branch from an elderberry bush and began forcing a thin straight length of hazel through centre of it.

"What's that for?" asked Laila watching him gouge out the pithy core.

"It's a straw," he said blowing through it to clear out any loose debris.

"What do you need a straw for?".

"You'll see soon enough" he replied.

They eventually arrived by the edge of a mire in an area of low growing scrub.

"Perfect!" said Jack kneeling down and pushing the straw into the stagnant goo.

"Whatever we remove we replace, it's the way we do things in the forest" he said.

"What do you mean?" Laila asked.

"Well the hazel gave us the materials to build our besom and so we must return the favour by watering the hazel as a way of saying thank you" he said before putting his lips around the elder stick.

There was a loud gurgling sound as he drew forth the water from the bog.

"Yuck! How can you put that in your mouth?" she asked but Jack was unable to reply as his mouth was full to almost bursting point.

So with bulging cheeks he had to make his way back to the hazel grove in total silence whilst Laila spoke garrulously about her matted hair and filthy shoes.

Back at the hazel, Jack began to expel the water he had collected around the roots of the shrub like a hose until the ground was thoroughly soaked.

"Right! Now that's done we're ready to make the broomstick," he said wiping the sediment from his chin, much to Laila's disgust.

They gathered up the brushwood and hazel pole and made their way back to the track where Jack set about diligently making the besom. He used strong willow bark as cordage and whittled the pole into shape using his flint axe.

When he had finished it was very impressive and also colossal in size.

"What do you think?" he asked.

"It looks great Jack but isn't it a bit large?" asked Laila whilst pacing up and down and inspecting the giant besom.

"It's designed to carry both of us that's why" said Jack laying the huge broomstick carefully on the ground close to the area where Laila had earlier located the dragon path.

"There's just one more thing we must do before we can fly" said Jack handing Laila a collection of withered purple plants.

What are these for?" asked Laila.

"Wolf's bane!, Witches use it to rub on their skin before flying, it makes them feel lighter apparently so you must do likewise".

"Aren't you going to rub some on too?"She asked dubiously examining the plant.

"I don't need to because I'm made of wood just like the broomstick" said Jack. Laila gazed at him and then again at the flowers in her hand.

"Oh alright then" she said and rubbed some onto her arm.

"Ok Laila that's everything!" said Jack standing astride the giant besom.

"Let's go then," he said lifting the front of the pole up between his legs.

"Where do I sit?" asked Laila.

"Just climb onto my back and put your arms around my neck".

"But my arm feels a bit numb after rubbing that plant on it" said Laila worried.

"It's ok, that's what it's supposed to do!" he said.

"Right now come on Laila lets reach for the sky!" he roared with excitement.

Laila clambered up on to his back whilst Jack shuffled sideways with the besom between his legs until eventually he was straddling the dragon path. And then to their total amazement nothing at all happened.

"I'm beginning to think that there may be more to this than just magnetism" said Jack. "Perhaps the witches also use some kind of telekinesis".

"What's telekinesis?" Laila asked.

"It's the power to move an object with your mind. Now let's try it together Laila, I want you to concentrate really hard on the broomstick".

So Laila and Jack both stood there fixed attentively to the spot for a few minutes staring at the broomstick and willing it with all their might to fly yet nothing happened.

"I don't think this is going to fly Jack to be honest" said Laila.

"We mustn't give up now Laila, come on, concentrate a little harder!" he said.

So once again they stared and stared and stared some more and just then when it seemed that it was all in vain the besom began to suddenly vibrate gently and rise upwards. "It's working" yelled Jack elated.

The brush wood lifted initially and then levelled out before Jack felt his feet gradually leave the ground.

He wobbled about a little bit at first whilst trying to locate his centre of gravity on the narrow pole.

Up and up they levitated like magic until they were floating way up high in the clouds.

"Whoa! Don't look down" said Jack anxiously. But Laila couldn't resist a peep at the trees tops far below and nervously increased her grip around his neck.

The bridle track beneath them now appeared as nothing more than a small dark narrow squiggle in a landscape of autumn gold that stretch out around them for miles.

"Why aren't we moving?" asked Laila, trembling like a leaf.

"I don't know?" mumbled Jack, who was equally as petrified. "I'm not quite sure what creates the forward motion?"

"Do you know how to get us back down then?" Laila asked.

Jack shrugged his shoulders. "Erm? No not yet" he said. "Maybe if I leant forwards a bit then that might get us down" he said shifting his body weight tentatively a few degrees towards the front of the besom. This did not create the effect of decent but instead it set the broomstick in motion and off they flew.

"Wehey! We're moving Laila!" laughed Jack as the broomstick soared across the sky. It rapidly began to pick up momentum and within no time they were rocketing along at such a speed that the trees below seemed almost a blur. Only the horizon remained fixed in the distance.

A flock of Brent geese scattered in flight beneath their feet as they zoomed by.

"This is incredible!" yelled Laila at the top of her voice as the cold icy wind blew hard against her face, causing her cheeks to smart numbly and her eyes to stream.

"Look at that Laila!" said Jack also having to shout to be heard above the whistling howl of the wind, as they passed over Leo's weir.

Far below they, could see the white surf from the waterfall bubbling up like a boiling kettle followed by the violent swirling currents whipping up the weir pool. Tall crack willows on the banks moved in the breeze as if to wave as they passed by.

"Looks like we won't need to stop there now!" he laughed.

"I feel like I'm dreaming Jack. I've never had so much fun in all my life" exclaimed Laila.

 "I know exactly what you mean, it's amazing!" he hollered, as the leaves on his face fluttered erratically in the air. "Look at that!" and "Look over there!" was all they could say to each other on their flight as they watched the spectacles of nature pass below them. Herds of roe deer ran through the forests and foxes chased each other across the multi coloured patchwork of fields. Distant pastel mountains home into view on the horizon as the landscape became gradually more and more rugged.

"That's where Yan lives," said Jack pointing to some far off silver Mountains.

"Oh really? That's great!" said Laila almost frozen solid from hanging on to him.

"And what is that Jack?" she asked pointing to a tiny black speck in the distant sky.

"It's probably a buzzard, there are quite a few in this area" he said squinting his eyes to focus. But as the speck grew in size it became apparent that it was not a buzzard at all but something far more menacing.

"Oh no! It's a witch!" he yelled as the figure of a woman dressed in long black robes and raven hair came hurtling towards them at speed. Laila quickly clambered down from his neck and stood balancing precariously on the besom, terrified in case the witch saw her.

The witch began waving her fist angrily and started shouting at Jack.

"Get out of my way! This is a one way ley" she screeched furiously.

Just then when it looked as if a collision was imminent Jack made a sharp banking manoeuvre narrowly avoiding a head on crash.

"Get off the ley line fool!" yelled the witch as she sped by. Meanwhile Jack struggled desperately to regain control of the broomstick as it spun through the air with Laila trying to cling onto him, but her arms and fingers were too numb to grip and she eventually lost her hold and tumbled head first from the broomstick.

"Help! Jack!" she screamed as she plummeted from the sky towards the earth.

"Laila!" yelled Jack as he spun off into the clouds still clinging on to the besom.

Fortunately for Laila she landed in an area of swampland which softened her landing. But even so the impact temporarily knocked her unconscious.

She was slightly delirious when she eventually came too and assumed she was still asleep in her bed at home,
awakening from some surreal dream about Ogres and Green men on flying broomsticks.

That was until she heard the mumbling sound of unfamiliar voices talking around her, and the cold sensation of water on her back before realising that she was in fact lying down, not in her bed but in some putrid smelling swamp. She instantly sat bolt upright and found herself sitting on her backside in the middle of a wide barren marsh, filled with mossy pools and outcrops of sedges, and there in front of her stood three short gaunt figures. Immediately they leapt back at her sudden movement. They were quite small in comparison to Laila, about two thirds her height and their skin was indigo blue. They were also very similar in appearance to each other. Long hooked noses and pointed chins gave them an almost crescent moon shaped face. Their greasy long hair was black, thin and scraggly and draped around long pointed ears. Laila noticed that their thin wide mouths were lined with small razor sharp teeth like piranha fish and each wore a black cloth hood with long liripipes hanging down at the back. Brown tunics covered the torso and were fastened at the waist by a thick black leather belt with spear shape daggings at the hem. Their slate grey tights and peaked leather shoes were sodden with bog mud and each of them carried a long spear which they pointed aggressively at Laila.

"It must be a witch that slipped from its broomstick, that would explain why it fell from the sky," said one of the creatures with a short black spiky beard. "No surely it's got to be a giant fairy whose wings broke off when it hit the ground," said the smallest of the three. "Don't be silly Volk! It's much too big to be a fairy".

"Whatever it is let's kill it and eat it!" said the largest with a sinister smile.

"No Tuk! We are not going to kill it, we can sell it, we'll get more for it alive" said the one with the beard.

"Isn't it an ugly looking thing, just look at that vile little snout and those horrid blunt white teeth" said the small one using his spear as a pointing stick.

"Leave me alone!" said Laila pushing the spears from her face with the palm of her hand.

"It talks!" said the small one with surprise.

"Who are you? And what do you want?" asked Laila.

"We were pondering the same question of you. Are you a Witch, a Sapien or some kind of giant Fairy?" asked the bearded one.

"I'm neither, I'm a girl, you know a human" said Laila.

"The bearded one smiled wickedly. "Did you hear that Tuk? We have got ourselves a Sapien".

"A Sapien! Let's kill it now Lev!" said the biggest of the three trembling with excitement.

"Who's a Sapien? I didn't say I was a Sapien I said I was a human" said Laila.

"So it calls itself human" he said rubbing his long pointed chin. "Human, as pertaining to mankind, intelligent, sympathetic, merciful and humane" he scoffed sarcastically before cackling with laughter. "That's the kind of typical arrogance you'd expect from these vulgar creatures, to refer to themselves as some kind of empathetic supreme being, yet in reality they are by far the cruellest and most destructive of all creatures to walk the green earth" he said raising his voice. And with that he turned around sharply and hit Laila hard across the back of her head with the blunt end of his spear.

"Ouch!" She cried "What did you do that for?"

"Because you're a Sapien and I hate Sapien's more than anything in this world" he replied with a snarl.

"Why do you keep calling me that? I've no idea what a Sapien is?" said Laila rubbing her sore head.

"A Sapien is what you are stupid!" said the small one joining in the abuse and hitting her violently across the arm with his spear.

"Ouch! Stop that!" she said angrily.

The bearded one then began to walk slowly around her with his arms folded imperiously.

"Let me explain! You revolting creature. A Sapien is not too dissimilar to a caged animal, such as a domestic chicken for example. It has wings and yet it has totally lost the ability to fly. A Sapien is a domesticated cultivated creature that has lost its wild spirit and turned its back on the natural world," he said mordantly while his companions chuckled menacingly.

"But why do you hate them so much?" she asked.

"Because they are pernicious creatures with no respect for life or the forest, they're nothing more than an ecological disease" he said raising his voice again with rage. Laila felt uneasy as if she was in some way responsible for his disdain.

"But not all of them can be bad" she said.

The bearded one made no comment, but just stared at her with contempt in his eyes

"And what are you if you don't mind me asking?" muttered Laila nervously.

"We are Goblins of course! Stupid!" said the big one lashing out at her with his spear. Laila quickly curled up into a ball in order to protect herself from an imminent beating.

"Calm down Tuk!" said the bearded Goblin restraining him. "She doesn't understand, she's a Sapien, remember?". The large Goblin looked quite disappointed at being deprived of the opportunity to strike her, yet never the less he did as he was told. Then the bearded Goblin walked up to Laila and prodded her in the stomach with the butt end of his spear.

"You probably refer to us as hellion no doubt".

"Hellion?" said Laila unfamiliar with the term.

"What are you deaf Sapien?" said the small Goblin rearing up to strike her but this time Laila was ready for it. As soon as the spear came down towards her she put up her arm to block it and then as quick as a flash seized the shaft with both hands pulling the small Goblin towards her and punching him straight on the nose as hard as she could. He tumbled backwards holding his face, whilst knocking over the bearded Goblin like a skittle. The larger Goblin then growled furiously and charged at her plunging his spear deep into her thigh. Laila let out a piercing scream as the cold steel ripped into her flesh and she rolled around frantically trying to pull it free. By which time the other two Goblins were on her like a shot, grabbing her fingers and forcing her arms up behind her back.

 She fought furiously to get them off by trying to bite and head butt them but as she tried to stand up she found she couldn't, as the nimble Goblins had bound her arms and feet together with rope.

"She's a feisty one!" said the smallest Goblin wiping the blood from his nose with the back of his hand.

"She sure is Volk," said the bearded Goblin pulling the spear from her leg and applying a clump of sphagnum moss on to the wound whilst Laila yelled in pain.

"You really are stupid creatures you Sapiens" he sneered as Laila lay face down in the muddy swamp gasping for breath. She was so tired and in so much pain she could hardly move.

"Right Tuk! You grab the cart while me and Volk take care of the Sapien," said the bearded Goblin.

"Get up you turkey you're coming with us" said the small Goblin pulling Laila up off the ground with the assistance of the bearded Goblin.

"My leg!, I can't move" groaned Laila as the warm blood ran down her thigh.

"You will do as you're told" said the little Goblin putting a noose around her neck. The bearded Goblin cut the bindings from her legs but kept her hands tied behind her back.

"Now don't try anything silly or I'll set Tuk onto you again" he said pointing to the big Goblin who had wandered off a short way ahead of them pulling a large wooden cart behind him.

"Come on move!" said the small Goblin tugging on the noose around her neck like a leash.

So mercilessly Laila was forced to limp along behind them like a lame dog as they lead her off through the marsh with the bearded Goblin taking up the rear of the group, his spear pointed at Laila's back all the way. She felt so low as she hobbled along through the cold stagnant mud and pined for her mum and dad. She also hoped that Jack would appear and come to her rescue. Yet the hope of seeing anything other than midges on the swamp seemed pretty optimistic.

Chapter four

A journey into the unknown

Bitter was the wind that blew across the barren morass that day, as they made their way up to higher ground. The terrain became rugged and the gradient steep as the low lying woodlands began to diminish in size behind them, now consisting only of small clumps on an ever expanding horizon. Colossal grey boulders lay strewn across the open ground like gigantic sheep on a hillside, grazing on the rich green carpet of moss and coarse grasses that covered the slopes. The wooden cart shuddered and creaked as it bounced off the uneven track that wound its way up the hill. Roughly hewn slate steps ascended the dewy acclivity making it slippery and awkward to walk on, causing Laila to lose her footing occasionally along the way, almost twisting her ankle.

"Where are you taking me?" she asked anxiously.

"Never you mind, just keep moving," said the bearded Goblin prodding Laila sharply in the back with the tip of his spear.

When they reached the top of the ridge they stopped to survey the rolling downs.

"Look there it is down there Lev!" exclaimed the largest Goblin pointing eagerly to the valley below.

A glistening silver stream could be seen meandering through the alder trees that lined its course.

"Right, let's get down there and set up!" said the bearded Goblin excitedly.

As they descended the slope towards the stream, the rushing water could be heard gushing fiercely upon the wind.

The stream was wild and swift and cascaded down through the valley, dropping steeply in places and creating beautiful picturesque pools of white water. Once they arrived on the bank they followed the watercourse downstream for a distance until they finally found a suitable area sheltered from the wind beside a dense group of trees.

"This will do!" said the bearded Goblin. "Put the cart over by that rock and get the rods out Tuk," he said to the biggest of the group.

"Right, you sit there!" he said pushing Laila violently backwards onto a large boulder.

"What do you want me to do Lev?" asked the smallest Goblin putting his spear down and rubbing his hands together.

"I want you to stay here and keep guard and make sure the Sapien doesn't try to escape Volk" he said picking up his spear and passing it back to him.

"Oh, Ok Lev" he mumbled subserviently.

The bearded Goblin and his larger associate then proceeded to make their way down to the water's edge with a couple of split cane fishing rods in their hands.

"You fish that swim up by the eddy Tuk and I'll cast upstream towards the fallen willow" said the bearded Goblin whilst baiting his hook with what appeared to be a large pink shrimp.

The small Goblin couldn't hide his frustration as he stood there and watched enviously at his cohort's casting their baits into the turbulent swell.

"You seem ruffled" said Laila cautiously attempting to make conversation with the sorrowful rogue.

"Do you want to fish too?" she asked

"Shut up!" he snapped.

"Sorry" she whimpered, cowering nervously.

He leant his spear carefully up against a tree and sat down on a large rock before resting his long dejected chin in his hands. An uncomfortable silence ensued as he sat in dour observation of his companion's pleasure, before turning to Laila with frown.

"Yes, actually I do want to fish" he said glumly.

"Maybe they will let you have a go later".

"No chance!" the Goblin replied abruptly.

"Oh, why not?" she asked.

"Because Lev said I have to stay here and guard you" he said pointing his finger at the bearded Goblin. "It's just not fair!" he grumbled.

Even as his captive she could see how morose and disappointed the little Goblin was and couldn't help but empathise.

"Who is your bearded friend? He does seem to order you about quite a lot if you don't mind me saying?" remarked Laila tactfully.

"Yes I know he does. He's my uncle Lev, he's very kind believe it or not and extremely clever too, oh and also a fantastic angler". When uncle Lev's got a rod in his hand you're guaranteed a feast" he smiled proudly.

"And your other friend?" she asked.

"That's my brother Tuk. He's as strong as a wild boar and as gentle as a butterfly but he's not that good at fishing. To tell you the truth I think my uncle Lev just lets him fish just to keep him quiet" he chuckled.

As he began to speak endearingly of his kin his malevolence towards Laila began to wane.

"So how did you come to fall into the swamp?" he asked. "We all saw you tumbling from the sky like a stone; I was surprised you survived the fall".

"You wouldn't believe me if I told you" said Laila shaking her head.

"Try me!" he said.

 Laila paused for a moment to recollect her thoughts.

"Well, I was on a broomstick with my friend Jack who happens to be a Green man, when all of a sudden we nearly had a crash with a witch who was flying towards us. Anyway I fell from the broomstick and that's about all I can remember really, it all went a bit blank after that".

The Goblins eyes lit up in wonder. "Wow! You mean to say you have actually seen a Green man?" he said nearly falling backwards from his rock in total amazement.

"Sure! He's my friend," said Laila.

"I've always wanted to see a Green man but I hear they are impossible to find" said the Goblin.

"That's because they communicate with the trees and the trees warn them of intruders in the forest" said Laila who had by now become a bit of an authority on Green men.

Just then they heard Lev shouting.

"I've got one on!" he yelled as his rod arched against the strain of the fighting fish.

The line raced across the surface of the water as the fish headed towards the safety of a fallen tree.

"Tuk bring that landing net!" he called as the big Goblin came running up.

"I told you my uncle Lev was good" said the small Goblin clapping his hands and jumping up and down with excitement.

"He certainly is smiled Laila.

"It's a twenty pounder Volk!" shouted the large Goblin lifting the landing net clear of the water to reveal a huge salmon almost as big as himself.

"Well done Uncle Lev!" shouted the little Goblin.

"That's a good fish isn't it Sapien?" he said turning to Laila with a huge smile on his face.

"Yes it is," she said.

"Sorry! what is your name by the way?" he asked.

"Laila" she replied.

"I'm Volk".

"Well how do you do Volk!. I would normally say that I'm pleased to meet you, but under the present situation I am not pleased. Not pleased at all I'm sorry to say".

"I understand" he replied.

"But I am Sorry about punching you though" she said contritely.

The small Goblin rubbed his nose and laughed.

"Don't worry about it" he grinned.

"I don't blame you; you were just trying to protect yourself, I would probably have done the same".

"So what were you all doing in that smelly swamp?" asked Laila.

"We are moss croppers" he said.

"What's a moss cropper?" she asked.

"It's what we do for a living. We collect the sphagnum moss from the swamp, and when we have filled our cart we take it back home to our village to sell. We love the taste, it's a real delicacy where we come from" he said wiping the drool from his lips. "But never mind us, tell me how you come to meet a Green man?" he said with great interest.

"Well, it began when I went down to Warren pond one morning.....".

But before she could finish the bearded Goblin came marching up with a furious expression on his face.

"What on earth do you think you're playing at!" he yelled making the little Goblin almost leap out of his skin.

"What is the matter with you Volk? Are you stupid? I knew I shouldn't have left you here to guard the Sapien," he said throwing his rod to the ground with rage.

"What have I done Lev?" asked Volk nervously unaware.

"What do you mean, what have I done? You've been holding a conversation and laughing with this disgusting Sapien! I saw you from over there! Have you lost your mind?" he shouted, "Right get out of here and do something useful. Go and collect some wood for the fire before I lose it, I'll take over from here" he said, trying to kick the little Goblin up the backside before he scurried off.

He then turned to Laila and pushed his spear up close to her face.

"One more word from you and we'll bury you here!" he said angrily.

Laila was so terrified she just lowered her head passively away from the tip of the spear without uttering a word. Lev then bound her feet together.

"I wouldn't try escaping," he said. "You won't get far, and even if you got as far as the swamp, the wolves would get you so I suggest you stay put and do as you're told if you know what's good for you". And with that he picked up his rod and returned to the river, looking back over his shoulder at Laila with a hostile glare.

As the evening light began to fade, Lev and Tuk ceased their fishing exploits as it became too difficult to see their floats in the darkness, so they prepared the fish they had caught earlier beside the campfire.

"How did you get on Tuk?" asked Volk returning from his timber forage. Lev began laughing loudly.

"I didn't catch anything!" said Tuk sadly.

"Yes you did!" said Lev giggling. "You caught the bottom of the river a few times remember?"

"Yes very good Lev! Thanks for reminding me" Tuk mumbled miserably.

That evening whilst the Goblins sat around the fire laughing at Tuk's inability to catch anything, Laila sat alone in the bitter cold shadows with only their silhouetted backs for company. It was at this moment she felt that things couldn't get any worse. There they were laughing and joking and eating huge amounts of salmon and bread while she had nothing at all to eat, and the delicious smell from the food was beginning to torment her hunger. But then she noticed Volk look over his shoulder at her a couple of times before glancing uncomfortably back at his Uncle Lev.

He then coughed deliberately to get his uncles attention.

"Lev, don't you think we should give the Sapien some food?" he said timidly. Lev and Tuk both started to laugh as if to dismiss the suggestion as nothing more than a joke.

"No chance Volk!" said Lev.

"Yeah! Why should we give a Sapien anything other than a slap around the face brother?" sniggered Tuk with his mouth full of food.

Volk turned and looked over at Laila once again shivering in the darkness, and then at them scoffing their faces by the fire.

"Well you said we were going to sell her right?"

"Yes that's right!" said Lev.

"Well we won't have anything left to sell by the morning will we? Because she isn't going to last the night if we don't at least give her something to eat" said Volk. "Wouldn't you agree Tuk?" he said in an attempt to win his brothers alliance in the discussion.

"Yes he's got a point," said Tuk nodding his head at Lev. The decision was now in Lev's hands as usual. He looked a little reluctant at first but agreed that it had to be done.

"Alright alright!" he scowled. "Here! Give her some food and get a blanket from the cart; we wouldn't want it to freeze during the night would we?. Oh yeah and grab my violin too while you're there, I'm in the mood for some music".

Volk leapt to his feet. "Thanks Lev!" he said trying to contain his delight.

He rushed over to Laila with a plate of food and a beaker of water and put them on the boulder next to her before pulling out a knife from under his belt and severing the bindings from her hands. The relief was amazing, for the first time in ages she could actually move her arms again.

"Thank you Volk!" she said smiling at the little Goblin whilst rolling her stiff shoulders back and forth.

"That's ok, I'll get you a blanket now!" he said scampering off to the cart.

Lev watched him from beside the fire.

"Your brothers not like you Tuk" he said. "He is weak of heart".

"What do you mean?" asked Tuk.

"Well look at him! Rushing around like a menial to that Sapien. He actually cares for it!". Tuk looked over at Volk running up to Laila with a blanket in his arms.

"It won't be for long, once we've sold it he'll forget about her" he said turning his eyes back to watch the flames in the fire. "Anyway Lev I forgot to ask, who will want to buy this Sapien from us? I mean who are we going to sell it to?" he asked.

Lev sat up and rubbed his hands together.

"I know just the place and they will pay a good price too" he said with a beaming smile. Tuk just looked blankly at him.

"The stockyard of course!" he said.

"Brilliant!" said Tuk licking his lips. "Hey but don't tell Volk until we get back home, we don't want him getting upset".

"Why should he be upset? He will get a fair cut of the earnings like the rest of us" said Lev.

"Yes I know that! But he's a bit of a sensitive soul that's all" said Tuk.

"Sure whatever you say" said Lev before calling Volk back to the fire.

"Hey Volk! Are you going to stay with that revolting Sapien all night or are you going to join me and your brother for a bit of music?".

Volk swiftly hurried back carrying an empty plate and Lev's violin under his arm.

 "Sorry, I was just waiting for Laila to finish with her food" he said.

"Its Laila now is it?" said Tuk sardonically.

"Never mind all that Tuk!" said Lev raising his voice. "Let's play some music I'm getting bored of

all this pathetic Sapien talk" he said greasing his
bow.

"Well that's not what you were saying earlier" said
Tuk getting annoyed.

"Will you leave it out Tuk!" growled Lev with a
stern glare. "Can we play some music now please?".
Tuk got up and started walking off.

"Where are you going?" asked Lev.

"To get my bodhran from the cart if that's alright?"
he replied in an agitated tone.

"What's up with him?" asked Volk.

"Oh I don't know? Just in one of his silly moods
again I suppose" said Lev dismissively, and began
playing his violin softly. Volk pulled out a tin
whistle from under the blanket he was sitting on and
began accompanying him until Tuk returned to the
fireside with his bodhran.

He sat down but didn't join in for some time as a
silent protest. But eventually he succumbs to the
music and starts playing along. Laila watched and
listened intently as the three Goblins played the
most beautiful music she had ever heard. She
wrapped the thick woollen blanket that Volk had
given her around herself and curled up on top of the
boulder and closed her eyes while the magical
music sent her off into a deep sleep.

She began dreaming that she was back home by the Warren pond with her mother and father and the sun was shining brightly. She could see herself climbing up high into the branches of the noble oak and laughing as her father beckoned her down. And then as she turned around to climb higher she came face to face with Prowler who screeched and flapped his wings in her face.

In her fear she tried to clamber down as quickly as she could to get away but slipped and fell to the ground. As she hit the ground she suddenly awoke, startled and with her heart beating rapidly.

"Your awake then?" said Tuk appearing over her. "Get up you filthy creature we're getting ready to go" he growled and kicked her sharply in the ribs.

"Where are we going?" she asked as he leapt down from the boulder.

"Get up and shut up!" he said walking away.

Just then Volk came over with some water.

"Are you ok?" he asked.

"No!" she said rubbing her side "Where are they taking me?"

"We are heading up into the mountains" said Volk.

"What do they want with me?, and why are we going up into the mountains?" she asked anxiously.

"Don't worry you'll be all right!" he replied. "Just drink up quick before I get in trouble".

"Come on Volk! Bring the Sapien with you, we need to get a move on!" shouted Lev while loading the cart.

"My uncle said you don't need to have your feet bound anymore" smiled Volk while cutting the rope from her ankles.

"That's sweet of him" said Laila sarcastically.

It was early morning and still quite dark when they left the stream and the clouds hung thick in the sky with just the pale moon breaking through.

The mist filled the valley making everything cold and wet. Laila slipped a few times on the damp grass as they made their way back up in to the foothills. She was tired and afraid of what fate might have in store for her.

Even though she had made a connection with Volk she knew that it was Lev who would ultimately decide her fate.

"I'm sure I overheard him say that he was going to sell me, but to whom?, and for what? She pondered anxiously. "Where are you Jack?" she muttered despondently under her breath as she followed the Goblins up into the foggy mountains on what could only be described as a journey into the unknown.

The mists began to clear as they ascended into the mountain but the climb became gradually more strenuous as the path grew steeper and steeper and

Lev ended up having to help Tuk out with the wagon in places. They paused occasionally to catch their breath and discuss the route before moving on again. Volk was ordered to take up the rear of the group in order to prevent Laila from escaping back down the mountain but there was no chance of that. Not only was she limping from a deep spear wound but Volk continuously questioned her about the Green man.

"So how tall are they?" he asked, panting all the time for breath, in the high altitude.

"They are huge!" said Laila as tall as a Rowan but not quite as big as an Ogre".

"How do you know how big an Ogre is? Have you seen an Ogre too?" he asked with wonder.

"Yes my friend the Green man introduced me to one called Fenndeor" she said feeling quite blessed with her encounters.

"That's amazing!" said Volk.

Just then Lev stopped and snapped at them angrily "Shut up you two!" he said. "Especially you Volk, I've already warned you once about talking to the Sapien!"

"Sorry Lev" muttered Volk timidly.

By now they were high in the mountains and could see all around for miles.

"Looks like storm clouds over there Lev!" said Tuk pointing away towards the far off horizon. The distant sky shone like a dark silver grey veil and a faint rumble could be heard upon the wind.

"That's not coming this way! It's heading south Tuk" said Lev confidently.

"Well we had better head down to lower ground in case it changes direction, we don't want to get caught out on the mountains in that do we?" said Tuk.

"Don't worry Tuk! Even if it did come this way by the time it got here we should be well over the summit and making our way down the other side. Now come on, the longer we stand around here debating it the better our chances of getting caught out" he said pushing onward.

As they made their way up towards the top of the mountain they began to increase the pace. The summit was still a long way off and the wind was beginning to feel cool and breezy.

"This is stupid! We won't reach the summit before that storm arrives and it is heading this way I'm telling you!" exclaimed Tuk stopping with the barrow and staring at the dark looming sky. "I say we find some shelter now before it's too late!"

"What is your problem Tuk?" said Lev annoyed.

"We have travelled this route for years on the moss

runs and you know as well as I that we are near the top, so why look for shelter back down the track when we can shelter in the caves on the other side? Come on and stop panicking" he said. But no sooner had he spoke then a few specks of rain landed on his nose.

It started to drizzle lightly, which initially was of no real concern to the group as it remained steadily like that for a while, by which time they had covered quite a lot of ground. But then the wind started to pick up in strength and the air became suddenly suffused with the strange scent of wet grass before the real deluge struck. It started with a deafening thunderclap that shook the mountain and then the sky opened up.

"Run for the caves!" howled Lev in the downpour whilst desperately trying to help Tuk shift the cart which had its wheel caught in a deep rut. Laila immediately came limping to their aid and helped them push it free.

"There's the summit!" yelled Lev, shouting to be heard over the roaring torrent. "Run for it!"

So Laila and the three Goblins made a final dash for the top of the mountain.

The storm was fierce and the incline was at its steepest, yet with their energy almost spent they still managed to get to the other side without being blown clean off the mountainside. A short descent from the summit revealed an outcrop of granite cliffs littered with caves.

"At last!" gasped Volk with relief as they stumbled into one of largest of the caves before collapsing on the floor in sheer exhaustion.

The cave was huge inside. As big as a concert hall with a vast network of smaller caves and tunnels leading off in all directions from the main chamber. Long spiked stalactites hung from the roof, dripping into reservoirs of clear water below. The constant ripples distorting the smooth surface of the water and fragmenting the reflected paintings that dominated the cave walls. Laila was intrigued by the primitive images all around her. The crude paintings depicted hunting scenes as well as what appeared to be Goblins with spears battling mythological creatures. Just then Volk appeared beside her looking like a soaked rat.

"What do you think of the paintings?" he asked as she stood in awe of the rock art.

"I've seen pictures of cave paintings in books before but I have never seen anything quite like this" she said gently touching the images with her fingertips.

"What is this picture of? It looks like Goblins

hunting giants" she said naively. Volk shook his
head.

"No this is not a hunting scene Laila, it is a painting
of a huge battle that took place many centuries ago
in a valley called Ura, about one hundred and fifty
miles south of Puo Landum where the Goblins
fought the Sapien hordes".

"And what is that? It looks like some kind of
winged lizard" said Laila pointing towards the
image of a huge reptilian creature that took up most
of the cave wall.

"That is Geborga the dragon who fought off the
invading Sapiens. He was created by a magical
priestess named Isla" said Volk proudly. Laila found
the story fascinating and wanted to know more.

"And who was this magical priestess?" she asked
inquisitively. But before he could answer Lev piped
up.

"Shut that Sapien up Volk! She is doing my head
in!" he said angrily.

"Sorry Lev" said Volk pressing his finger softly
onto Laila's lips while giving her a reassuring smile.

Tuk stood by the entrance to the cave and watched
the driving rain outside while wringing out his
waterlogged waistcoat before throwing it violently
on to the floor in fury.

"This is all your flaming fault!" he said shouting at Lev.

"Don't you talk to me like that!" said Lev getting to his feet and walking over to confront Tuk.

"I'm not responsible for the damn weather!"

"We could have avoided it though, couldn't we?" said Tuk prodding Lev firmly in the chest with his index finger. "But no! You had to push on and now we are all going to die in this cave of hypothermia," he grumbled.

"Will you shut up Tuk for one minute?" said Lev kicking Tuk's damp waistcoat across the cave.

"We aren't going to die because we are going to build a fire!".

Tuk just glared at Lev for a moment before walking over to the cart.

Putting his hand inside he pulled out a couple of soaking wet logs.

"And how do you propose we start a fire with these?" he said sarcastically holding them up before dropping them on the floor. Lev put both his hands on his head and slumped backwards against the wall of the cave.

"I don't know? I just don't know?" he said agitated.

Volk then appeared like a beacon of hope from the back of the cave, his arms laden with dry deadwood.

"This should burn quite nicely though! Shouldn't it Uncle Lev?" he said smugly with a big grin. Lev and Tuk's faces lit up with surprise.

"Where did you find that?" asked Tuk running over to help him with the wood.

"About a year ago when we last camped here I remembered I had collected so much firewood that I ended up storing a load in the back of the cave".

Tuk threw his arms around Volk and gave him a strong embrace.

"I knew my little brother was a genius" he said with a smile.

"Well done Volk!" said Lev rubbing his head.

Tuk then immediately began building a fire a few feet from the mouth of the cave whilst Lev and Volk collected the rest of the stored timber. Laila meanwhile just sat and watched quietly shivering at the back of the cave.

Once the fire was underway they huddled around it so as to dry out their damp clothes. The steam belched like a fog from their sodden garments, making it appear as if they were sitting there alight.

"Come and dry your clothes Laila!" said Volk forgetting himself for a moment and beckoning her over.

"Stay right where you are Sapien!" said Lev pointing menacingly at Laila, causing her to freeze in her tracks. Volk's face dropped.

"Why can't Laila join us Lev? After all she did help us with the cart didn't she?" he said.

"I won't share the company of my fire with that lesser being!" he replied sternly.

"Oh it's your fire now is it?. If I remember rightly your fire consists of a few wet logs in that cart over there, this is Volk's fire and he has the say about who shares it!" said Tuk jumping to Volk's defence.

"What is this? Have you both forgot who you are?" said Lev amazed. "You are Goblins and she is a Sapien, our sworn enemy!"

"But Laila's different" said Volk.

"There is no such a thing!, A Sapien is a Sapien!" said Lev defiant in his resolve.

"Forget it Volk," said Tuk sneering at his Uncle.

"He never listens to anyone but himself that's why we are in this mess in the first place"

"You've changed your tune Tuk! I thought we both agreed we were just going to sell the Sapien not socialise with it!" said Lev.

"Yes but it wouldn't hurt to let it at least dry its clothes would it?" said Tuk shaking with rage.

"Why are you getting uptight Tuk? You hate these creatures more than me!. And if I can just remind you, it was you who suggested we kill the Sapien when we first discovered it in the swamp the other day" said Lev.

That was the final straw for Tuk, he could not contain his anger anymore. He grabbed Lev by the scruff of the neck and lifted him clean off the floor. "Yes! Well maybe I should have killed her back then when I had the chance, after all she's only going to be sold for slaughter anyway" he said.

 Volk stumbled back in shock.

"Slaughter! You mean we are going to sell her as meat?" he said in horror.

"Well done Tuk!" said Lev, and with that he kicked Tuk hard in the stomach. Tuk doubled over from the blow before leaping on top of Lev, and within no time the two Goblins ended up in a nasty brawl, ripping each other to pieces like wild dogs.

"Stop!" yelled Volk as he tried in vain to break up the fight. Meanwhile Laila was beside herself with terror at the realisation of her impending doom.

She had overheard every word, and the fear of being slaughtered for food brought on a feeling of extreme nausea.

"They're going to kill me! I have to escape, I have to get out of here!" she thought, looking around at the tunnels leading off in all directions.

So while the Goblins were preoccupied with fighting each other she quickly made her escape.

Creeping off to the rear of the cave she began to venture down into one of the numerous tunnels. Even though she had no idea where it was leading to, she just knew she had to get away.
Further into the dark she went until the sound of the Goblins feuding became nothing more than a distant echo.
By now there was no visible light and she was travelling blindly through the cold blackness.
 Manoeuvring slowly and cautiously with each step, she made her way deeper into the abyss, keeping tight to the side of the tunnel by feeling her way along the cave wall.
Meanwhile Volk noticed her disappearance.
"Where's Laila gone?" he said immediately bringing an end to the brawl.
"I knew I should have tied that Sapien up!" cursed Lev wiping the blood from his nose.
"She must have heard you talking about selling her for food and slipped away whilst you were fighting" said Volk looking concerned.
"Well she couldn't have got out through the mouth of the cave so she's got to be down one of the

tunnels" said Tuck walking over to the fire to pick up a burning branch.

"But what way did she go?" said Volk looking at all the numerous tunnels that littered the chamber like a piece of Swiss cheese.

"We'll have to split up! She wouldn't have got far" said Lev passing out the spears "Volk! Grab yourself a torch from the fire and take that tunnel there!" said Lev pointing towards a dark hole at the back of the cave. "Tuk you take that one and I'll take this one" he said and with that they swiftly dispersed.

Soon Laila began to hear the Goblins voices growing louder down the tunnels as they came in search of her.

"Come out Sapien? There's no escape!" she heard one of them say menacingly in the distance. Her heart began to race as the fear of being caught gripped her. In her dismay she began to panic and hastened her pace, stumbling and banging her head as she went.

Whilst floundering in the darkness she became increasingly aware of an obnoxious scent arising from within the tunnel. It was so strong it almost made her gag. The temperature grew warmer too which Laila found very disconcerting. As she moved on a little further, the stench grew stronger and in the blackness she could hear deep bellowed breathing and the sound of something moving. It was then she realised she was not alone.

Laila froze with fear as she heard whatever it was in the tunnel coming closer. It stopped right beside her and there was a moment of tense silence before the creature in the darkness let out a shrieking roar that shook her to the bone. Laila immediately screamed with terror as her trembling legs gave way and she fell to the ground. But just then when it seemed as if her fate was sealed the tunnel suddenly began to fill with light as a tiny figure carrying a torch appeared from out of the blackness.

"Laila! Stay still!" said Volk as the light from his burning torch revealed the creature in the dark.

The flame flickered in its cold black eyes while the shadow of the beast filled the cave. Its huge scaly head was like that of a dragon with vicious razor sharp teeth. Its body resembled a large serpent, but with two large muscular legs protruding from its flanks. It screeched and roared while it flapped its membranous wings and clawed the ground, tormented by the intrusion of the burning light. Lowering its long neck it lifted its wings high and prowled slowly and menacingly towards the invasive glow as if hunting its prey.

"Run Laila! Get out of here!" said Volk looking understandably terrified at the site of the gigantic beast that now loomed over him. Laila quickly made her way towards the entrance to the tunnel keeping her back pressed against the wall.

"I'm not leaving you here alone!" She screamed.

"Just get out of here! Do as I say!" he said waving his torch to and thro in an attempt to distract the creature from Laila.

The creature snapped angrily at the light.

"Get rid of the torch!" shouted Laila.

Volk slowly backed away from the advancing beast until he found himself cornered.

"It's only interested in the fire! Get rid of it!" she yelled in frustration. With that Volk threw the burning branch with all his might across the cave with the creature turning and bounding after it.

"Run!" yelled Laila holding out her hand.

Volk sprinted towards Laila in the dim light and the safety of the tunnel exit as fast as he could.

"Phew that was close," he said gasping nervously as they ran towards the faint lights emanating down the tunnel from Lev and Tuck's distant torches.

But no sooner had they left the cave; there came a loud thudding sound right behind them. All of a sudden Laila could hear Volk yelping.

She turned to look for him but it was too dark to
see.

"Laila help me!" he cried from beyond the
darkness. Laila ran back screaming.

"Volk! Volk!" she shrieked, running blindly in
search of her friend.

Within seconds Lev and Tuck had appeared lighting
up the cave once more.

In the corner they could see the huge creature with
Volk wriggling frantically in its Jaws.

"It's a Wyvern! And it's got Volk!" roared Lev.

 Tuck let out a desperate scream and with no
consideration for his own safety ran straight at the
beast, plunging his spear deep into its chest. The
Wyvern screeched and reared up from the blow,
dropping Volk from its mouth. Then Lev came
running over waving his burning torch in front of
the Wyvern, shouting and hissing as loud as he
could to draw its attention away while Tuck picked
Volk up from the floor.

Then Lev threw his spear with menace at the
Wyvern as it took to the wing.

It flapped around for a while, crashing into the walls
and roof of the cave with its long dark wings before
flying off down one of the tunnels.

 Lev ran over to Tuck who was kneeling beside Volk
and stroking his head.

"How is he" asked Lev.

"It looks bad" he said staring up at Lev with a vacant glare of desperation on his face.

"Let's get him out of this place" said Lev putting his hand onto Tuk's shoulder. Laila's eyes filled with tears as she watched Tuk ,the once ferocious Goblin reduced to whimpering child as he gently picked up his little brothers limp body from the ground and carry him off down the tunnel.

"You hang on in there little brother, Tuk is going to take care of you now and make you better you just wait and see" he said as the tears rolled down his cheeks. When they got back to the cave entrance he laid Volk carefully down beside the fire on a blanket.

Volk was shivering uncontrollably and sweating. Tuk began mopping his head with a damp cloth.

"I'll get some more firewood!" said Lev dashing off.

Rapidly Volk's condition grew worse as he slipped in and out of consciousness. His eyelids began to hang heavy and he could only partially open them. Tuk lifted his head to pour water on his lips, his hands trembling all the time. "You're not going to die! I won't let you, do you hear me Volk? You and me are going home tomorrow and I'm going to tell the village how brave you are" he said sniffing emotionally after each word while cradling his brother like a baby in his arms. Just then a small tear left Volk's eye and slowly rolled down his face and his shivering suddenly ceased..

"Speak to me Volk! Don't leave me, please speak to me Volk!" said Tuk anxiously embracing him tight to his chest. Lev returned from out of the darkness at the back of the cave with more firewood.

Tuk turned and looked up at him before bursting into tears. Lev's heart sank;

"He's dead Lev" said Tuk and began wailing hysterically from the extreme pain of his broken heart.

Lev dropped the wood onto the ground at his feet and threw his arms around Tuk.

"Come now!" were the only words he could muster as he fought back his own tears. Laila stood to one side of the cave observing the woeful scene while sobbing uncontrollably herself. Then she made her way slowly and cautiously towards Tuk. "I'm so sorry" she said kneeling beside him. He glanced up at her before leaping on her like a wild cat and pinning her down on the floor.

"This all your fault!" he roared while trying to strangle her. Laila could hardly talk and gasped for air, but just then Lev came to her aide and pulled Tuk off.

"What are you doing?" screamed Tuk, shouting and crying at Lev whilst holding his uncle up against the cave wall like a toy doll with his immense strength. "It was the Wyvern that did it Tuk not the Sapien," he wheezed. "Volk's liked the Sapien remember?" Tuk just looked at him vacantly as if trying to comprehend what had happened before lowering Lev gently back on to his feet. Laila lay on the floor wincing and rubbing her sore neck apprehensively watching Tuk approach her. She expected him to turn on her again but he ignored her. Instead he shuffled by as if she wasn't there.

Like an empty soul he made his way towards Volk. Bending down he picked up his brothers body and carried him to one side of the cave and lay him down before covering him up with a blanket. He then went and stood by the entrance of the cave with his arms folded, silently looking up at the sky in deep grief, not moving or speaking just watching nothing for almost an hour. Lev never spoke during this time either; he just stood solemnly by the fire and fed the flames contemplatively before walking over to Tuk with a beaker of wine.

"Here drink this," he said.

"I'm not thirsty," said Tuk staring into space.

"Come and rest by the fire then" said Lev softly.

"Yeah I will, just give me a minute," he said wiping the tears from his eyes.

Lev patted him reassuringly on the back before returning to the fire.

Laila was also feeling grief stricken by what had happened and sat with her head in her hands on the floor. She had lost her only friend and ally, and the only person who would take care of her. She put her hand in her dress pocket and pulled out the crumpled remnants of the purple flowers that Jack gave her before they flew on the broomstick. She examined them carefully and began gently teasing them back into shape as best she could. Then ever so quietly she crept over to where Volk's body lay and placed them on his chest. She then picked up his blood soaked hand and held it tightly. Floods of tears dripped from her eye like falling rain on to his cold skin, each warm tear seeming to glow in the dull gloom of the cave.

"Get away from him!" roared Tuk, startling Laila and making her drop Volk's hand in terror.

 He then ran at her like a charging bull and threw her up against the wall.

"I wasn't doing anything!" yelled Laila in terror.

"You will die for what you've done you cursed Sapien," said Tuk furiously.

"Calm down Tuk!" said Lev trying to restrain Tuk who by now was like a creature possessed. But it was futile as Tuk was just too powerful for him.

"Please don't hurt me!" screamed Laila.

"You are dead meat Sapien!" roared Tuk.

"Leave her alone!" yelled a voice from behind him. Straight away there was silence and no one moved as if they had been turned to stone.

"Why can't you just leave her alone?" said the voice again from the back of the cave. Tuk slowly turned his head to see who was making the bold remark. And there, out of the shadows like an apparition stepped Volk.

All Tuk and Lev could do was stare aghast in disbelief.

"What's the matter with you? Why are you looking at me like that?" asked Volk confused.

Lev walked up to Volk and took him by the hand and examined him thoroughly for cuts and bruises. "How can this be happening?" he said in amazement. Volk looked at Lev with an addled expression.

"Will someone tell me what's going on here?" he asked. Tuk released Laila gently from his grip and walked over to Volk and put his arms around him.

"I have no idea what's going on and I don't care, all I know is I love you little brother and I'm glad you're alive" he said smiling.

"Of course I'm alive! I was just asleep over there when I heard the commotion".

Lev walked over to inspect the blanket where Volk's was laid to rest.

He then made his way back to Volk and lifted up his waistcoat before prodding and rubbing his skin.

"What's going on? Hey stop that Lev!" said Volk pushing him away. Lev shook his head.

"There's not so much as a scratch on him" he said gawping at Tuk. "And the blankets clean too".

"But it was soaked in blood?" said Tuk.

Just then Volk's piped up. "Hello everyone! I'm here!, will someone tell me what's going on?"

Tuk took his brother by the hand and looked him straight in the eye.

"Don't you remember the Wyvern Volk?" he asked.

"Wyvern? What Wyvern?" he replied, looking rather bemused.

"You were killed by a Wyvern when you tried to save the Sapien".

"Yes that's right!" said Lev. "The creature had virtually disembowelled you and you lost a lot of blood". Volk's looked at his stomach. There was no sign of anything.

"Is this some kind of joke?" he asked, but they just looked at him with glazed expressions on their faces.

He then looked at Laila.

"Is this true?" he asked.

Laila nodded her head.

"But how do you explain the fact that there are no signs of injury anywhere on my body?"

"I can't explain it at all? It's totally impossible, it's as if it's happened by magic" said Lev before turning to Laila. "Magic! Wait a minute," he said pointing at her. "You were the last person to be with him!".

"So it was you!" said Tuk marching up to her.

Laila cowered in fear as he approached. But when he got up close to her he kissed the back of her hand and bowed his head.

"Please forgive us Laila for what we have done to you" he said.

Laila looked confused. "Err? Sure!" she said. Then Lev walked forward.

"There is nothing I can say to you Laila that can express my deep shame, please will you join us for a drink by the fire?" Laila was as dumbfounded as the Goblins to Volk's miraculous recovery but she knew it was better to go along with it than end up in an abattoir.

141

"Yes I would like that" she said looking over to
Volk who had a beaming smile on his face. Tuk
went and fetched some wine and Lev put down the
best blanket for Laila to sit on. They topped up their
beakers and Lev proposed a toast.
"Here's to Laila, our sister!" he said and with that
they raised their beakers and drank to her health.

Chapter five

Grasmont Castle

That evening the Goblins serenaded Laila with a wonderful medley of jigs and reels before tiring the stars with anecdotes of their many moss cropping exploits. But for the Goblins who had lived a fairly modest existence, Laila's stories were by far the most compelling.

"So you're telling me that the people from your lands travel about on horseless carts?" said Lev astounded.

"That's correct!" replied Laila.

"That's amazing!" they all gasped.

"If you ask me I reckon you arrived here from another world not another land" said Tuk, to which Lev and Volk both agreed.

"To tell you the truth I have no idea where I've come from, where I am or how I got to be here? I honestly thought that this was all a dream but yet I can still feel and taste things".

"One thing's for sure, you're here for a reason, everything happens for a reason" said Lev.

"But for what?" asked Laila.

"I'm not sure, but if we can help you we will" he said looking at Tuk and Volk who gave a unanimous nod.

"Well I remember my friend Jack the Green man telling me about someone he knew called Yan Overton who might be able to help explain all of this, and maybe get me back home" said Laila.

Lev stood up suddenly and began walking up and down repeating Yan's name under his breath.

"I know that name!" he said scratching his head. Then he stopped and his face lit up.

"Of course! I know Yan Overton! How could I forget?" he beamed.

"What! You mean to say you know him?" said Laila excitedly.

"Well I wouldn't say I exactly know him personally but I've heard a lot about him".

"He is a wizard who resides in the silver Mountains West of Lhansburg".

"A wizard!" exclaimed Laila.

"Yes! One of the last remaining wizards of his order apparently". Laila couldn't believe her ears.

"I feel as if I'm in a fairy tale, what with Wizards, Ogres and Goblins" she laughed.

"Actually we would prefer to be called your friends!" piped Tuk.

"Sorry! Yes, Friends I mean," said Laila correcting herself.

"I believe you might be right Tuk! Perhaps I did arrive here from another world, because until now I thought that all these characters were just myths".

The Goblins started to laugh.

"The world you come from sounds more like a fairy tale to me" chuckled Volk.

"I'm sure it does!" smiled Laila walking over to speak with Lev who stood contemplatively at the cave entrance.

"Do you think you would you be able to show me the way to Yan's house?" she asked him timidly.

Initially he seemed quite taken aback by the request and appeared almost hesitant at first but agreed to help her as best he could.

"Sure Laila! We'll show you the way. It's some distance from here and in the opposite direction to where we want to be heading but a true friend is always there when you need them. We will set off for the silver mountains at first light tomorrow" he said. "We had better get some rest now as it's quite an arduous journey".

 Laila lay down beside the fire and covered herself with nice warm blanket and watched the glowing embers slowly fade. This was to be the best night's sleep she had in what seemed like ages and the idea of meeting a real wizard was thrilling. "I hope Jack will be there at Yan's house?" she thought before drifting off to sleep.

As usual the Goblins were up bright and early loading the cart.

"Good morning Laila!" said Tuk handing her a beaker of hot blackberry water as she opened her eyes to the new day.

"Thank you" said Laila sitting up to drink. She was still weary but the warm cordial soon helped perk her up.

"That was delicious" she said handing back the empty beaker.

"Glad you liked it" he smiled.

"We're ready when you are Laila!" said Lev. "The rain has eased off for the time being so the sooner we get going and exploit this break in the weather the better".

"I'm ready" she said keenly before getting up to stretch.

"I've put some hot water and a sprig of soapwort in a basin over there for you to wash with" said Volk.

"That's very kind of you!" she said feeling humbled by their courtesy and relieved at the thought of a wash.

After she had freshened up they left the cave and made their way down the mountain. It still felt cold and damp and the morning breeze gave Laila a slight shiver.

"Here! Put this around you" said Volk passing her a blanket.

"Thank you Volk!" she said gratefully.

Although it had rained a lot the previous night, only sparse remnants of the downpour were apparent. The sky was now dissected by snow white clouds of cumulus drifting overhead like ships in the blue. It could quite easily have been a beautiful spring morning if it were not for the sight of migrating geese and the inclement chill in the air. The rain had dispersed into the numerous streams that ran down the mountainside. Only the damp grass and mossy pools that filled the pits and troughs indicated the presence of the previous night's deluge.

"It's quite amazing how quickly the weather changes here!" said Laila looking up at the sky.

"Yes amazing" mumbled Volk aloof.

He seemed troubled, as if something was bothering him.

"Laila! Do you mind if I ask you a question about yesterday?" he said with an agitated frown.

"Sure! What do you want to know?"

"Well, it's about what happened with the Wyvern. I was just wondering if it was true that you brought me back from death."

Laila glanced ahead to see if Lev and Tuk were within earshot. Fortunately they were trundling some distance away pulling the noisy wooden cart behind them.

"To tell you the truth Volk, I really have no idea how you were healed? It was a miracle. I was as surprised as your brother and uncle to see you alive again" she said.

"But Lev and Tuk told me that you were some kind of sorceress?"

"I'm no sorceress I'm sorry to say; I'm just your average girl. I don't have any magic powers whatsoever, but if that's what they want to believe then that's fine with me" she said.

Volk looked almost disappointed by her admission.

"I rather hoped you were" he said.

"It shouldn't make any difference what I am. Whatever happened in the caves back there we should just be grateful for" she said patting him gently on the back.

He looked up at her grinned.

"Yes you're right!" he said, "It's not what you are but what you do that matters".

"Well said Volk!" smiled Laila.

"After all when you think about it, I was nothing more than Sapien to you before you got to know me and now we have become good friends. I think it just goes to show that we Sapiens can't all be bad". Volk looked a little bemused.

"Yes I suppose you're right but I've never really given it much thought before to be honest" he said.

They trudged on a bit further down the mountain before eventually pausing on a wide plateau to rest. The view was outstanding as the clouds eventually dispersed to reveal the mountainous panorama.

"That's where we are heading," said Lev pointing towards the distant lustrous silver mountains that reached up into the sky.

"It doesn't look far!" said Laila.

"I know it doesn't look that far but it's quite deceptive. What looks like only a short distance in the mountains can take an eternity to get to due to the steep nature of the terrain".

"How long do you think it will take us to get to Yan's house?" asked Laila.

"It's quite a long way down" said Lev looking over the edge at the sheer drop below. "And once we reach the bottom then we have to ascend up the other side. If it was flat I would say about a day's walk but under these conditions I would estimate about three, maybe four" .

"Three or four days!" Said Laila disheartened.

"Hey hang on a moment! What about the Alder falls?" piped Tuk.

"Oh yes! Good thinking Tuk I forgot about them" said Lev.

"What's Alder falls?" asked Laila.

"It's a steep ravine that you can cross via a rope bridge. It's a short cut through the mountains" said Tuk.

"That's sounds perfect!" said Laila. But Volk didn't seem quite so enthusiastic with the idea.

"Personally I would much rather we went down the mountains the long way" he said sitting down upon a rock as if ashamed by his suggestion.

"Why do you say that Volk?" asked Laila puzzled.

"He's scared of the rope bridges" chuckled Tuk.

"Well I don't know why you think it's so funny Tuk! You're the one who has to pull the heavy cart across" replied Volk annoyed.

Tuk's face dropped as he realised the implications of his brother's statement so swiftly retracted his proposal.

"We shall continue our course down the mountain," he declared. But Lev was having none of it.

"Hold your horses Tuk! I think you're forgetting yourself" he said. "I am the elder here and I say we're going to Alder falls, and anyway it was your initial suggestion".

"Yes but me and Volk prefer the long route so you're outnumbered Lev!" said Tuck defiantly.

"You're forgetting something else Tuk, Laila doesn't want to walk across the mountains for four days so the vote is split, which means in this situation, I being the elder have the deciding vote, and I say we are going to Alder falls!.

"But how are we going to get the cart across?" asked Tuk.

"With great difficulty no doubt but I would rather do that than spend another four days clambering around on this ruddy mountain" exclaimed Lev. Tuk wasn't at all pleased, and went off to sulk by the edge of the track with his back towards the group. Lev looked at Laila and raised his eyebrows and then gave a deep sigh.

"I don't know," he mumbled before resting up against a large stone.

There was a brief awkward silence before Volk decided to calm the tension with some music on his flageolet. He played slow and soft and with such feeling that it almost sent them into a kind of trance. The music complemented the breathtaking surroundings, weaving tranquillity amongst the group like a magic spell.

When he had finished Tuk rose to his feet and stretched out his arms.

"Shall we go then?" he said looking at Lev.

"Where to?" asked Lev.

 "Alder falls of course!" replied Tuk and with that he picked up the handles on the old wooden cart and made his way off down the bumpy track. Laila looked at Lev with a big smile on her face.

"Come on! I believe you have an appointment with a wizard" he said with a grin.

As they traversed the mountain ridge Laila questioned Volk as to why he was so reluctant to cross the falls.

"I suffer from vertigo" he said looking embarrassed.

"We all have our fears there's nothing to be ashamed of" said Laila putting her arm around his shoulder.

"But Tuk and Lev are brave and fearless whereas I'm just…" Volk paused before continuing his sentence. "Never mind! It doesn't matter!" he said getting a little emotional.

"Hey now let me tell you something!" said Laila sensing his dejection. "I saw the bravest Goblin that has ever lived stand up against a huge Wyvern in that cave back there, so if it's bravery we're talking about then you're the bravest by far".

Volk simpered coyly.

"I forgot about that" he said.

"Anyway, there's nothing brave about being fearless" remarked Laila.

He stopped for a moment to reflect on what Laila had said as she carried on down the path. Then a huge smile began to grow on his face.

"Yes! You're right!" he laughed and scurried on after her.

They soon arrived beside a steep ravine that was linked by long roped walkway. A thin narrow path ran perilously close to the rock face that led them towards the bridge. Laila looked down at the rolling river far below as it twisted and gouged its way between the heart of the mountain.

"It's a steep drop" she said stepping back from the edge nervously.

"Don't worry Laila I'll cross with you" said Volk holding her hand reassuringly.

Stepping carefully on to the walkway Lev tested the bridges rope supports that spanned the ravine for any weaknesses

"Ok Tuk, you're first!" he said trying to disguise a smirk.

He was amusing himself with the look of terror in Tuk's eyes as he slowly pulled the cart onto the bridge. The ropes began to sag and creak under the weight of the cart and Tuk's legs wobbled uncontrollably as the bridge began to sway.

"Hurry up Tuk!" said Lev laughing as the overcautious Tuk crossed the bridge tentatively.

"Shut up!" said Tuk who was in no mood for jokes. The slats were old, split and worn with age and looked as if they had seen better days.

The Bridge spanned about thirty metres from one side to the other and Tuk ran the gauntlet of being first as usual. It was a tight fit for the cart and he struggled all the way across as the wheels occasionally got caught on the rope trusses. After a white knuckling twenty minutes he eventually arrived safely on the other side. "Come on then!" he called, with an element of relief in his voice.

"Well at least we know the bridge is safe to cross if it took the weight of Tuk and the cart" said Lev turning to Laila and Volk.

"I suggest that Volk go next".

"Why can't we all go together?" asked Volk.

"Because my dear nephew these bridges are extremely fragile and unpredictable so it would be safer that we go one at a time. And anyway, you and Tuk are the slowest so the sooner you two are over the better" said Lev chuckling and patting Volk gently on the head.

"Laila and I will follow you shortly".

Volk looked even more terrified than his brother Tuk when he approached the bridge. His hands trembled as he held onto the thick rope rail, all the time staring ahead with trepidation.

"It's ok Volk just don't look down" said Laila egging him on. He took a deep breath and closed his eyes before gently stepping onto the wooden slats.

"Come on Volk you can do it!" shouted Tuk from the other side of the bridge as his little brother crossed nervously with one eye open, freezing every time the bridge swung. Inch by inch he made his way slowly across with Tuk singing his praises after each step.

It seemed to take forever before he got to the other side but when he finally made it he couldn't contain his jubilation and leapt about like a March hare. Not just because he was safely across but because he had faced his biggest fear.

"Are you ready then Laila?" asked Lev.

"Erm? I must confess I'm a little nervous!" she said looking over the edge. "I'll go next then!" he said pushing her to one side.

"Unlike you and my nephews I have no fear of rope bridges" he said with a conceited smile.

"I will be over there in no time then you can follow up at your own pace". And with that he trundled off quickly and confidently across the bridge.

Now came Laila's turn.

"Come on Laila, it's safe!" called Volk. But Laila was feeling far more anxious than she thought she would as she stepped onto the bridge for the first time. Gently the ropes swayed from left to right as she shifted her weight from one leg to the other. The stream below could be seen between each slat, making her feel dizzy with vertigo. Volk beckoned her from the other side of the bridge.

"Don't look down whatever you do! Just keep your eyes on me!" he said reaching out his hands. Laila done as he asked and remained focused on him all the way, but then suddenly halfway across she heard a loud snapping sound, before the bridge rails totally collapsed.

"Laila!" yelled Volk as she stumbled over the rail. Luckily she managed to grab one of the floor trusses and hung precariously by one arm over the ravine.

"Help!" she screamed as she dangled helplessly from the rope.

"What are we going to do?" asked Tuk turning to Lev for guidance, only to find him recoiling dubiously whilst trying to conceal a knife behind his back. Tuk then noticed the bridge support had been cleanly severed.

"It was you! You cut the bridge!" he said in shock.

" Now take it easy Tuk, I had to do it, don't you see? The Sapien isn't a sorceress at all! I heard her tell Volk" said Lev nervously shaking from the fury in his nephew's eyes. Tuk grabbed Lev violently by the throat.

"You've gone too far this time" he roared clenching his fist but Volk quickly pulled his brother off.

"We have to save Laila!" he yelled frantically.

 Laila meanwhile tried in vain to pull herself back up on to the partially collapsed bridge by hooking her leg over one of the rope supports, but unfortunately she failed to muster enough energy to lift her own body weight.

"Hold tight! I'm coming for you," said Tuk crawling out onto the bridge.

"I can't hold on any longer!" screamed Laila as her grip began to gradually loosen, with only her fingertips preventing her from falling. Tuk desperately tried to get to her as quickly as he could. Clambering in and out of the collapsed bridge supports whilst trying to avoid shaking her loose.

"I'm coming Laila, hold fast" he kept saying as he crawled nearer.

"Hurry Tuk!" called Volk anxiously, but it was too late. Just as Tuk was about to grab her, Laila let out a terrified scream. Losing the energy to hold on any longer she fell from the bridge.

Everything appeared to move in slow motion as she dropped from the sky. All she could see was Tuk and the bridge against the skyline, hopelessly reaching down and calling her as she moved further and further away from him and closer to the river below. Moments from her life flashed before her eyes, but strangely her fear began to subside as she accepted her fate.

The last thing she was aware of was hitting the water with an almighty splash.

Silence and darkness followed before she could discern the sound of rushing water and the sensation of severe cold all over her body.

"Am I alive?" she wondered as she opened her eyes and looked up at the bright sky. Hesitantly she moved her arms around and could feel the soft sand and water around her.

"I must have survived the fall!" she thought getting to her feet.

Laila had been washed up onto the shoreline of an eddy just out of the main flow of the river. A thick wild forest bordered the edge of the river on both sides as far as the eye could see. Laila looked around for the Goblins. "Volk! Lev! Tuk!" she shouted whilst wandering along the sandy shore, but in her heart she knew her cries were in vain. Once again Laila found herself soaking wet and abandoned in the wilderness.

She began to follow the course of the river downstream to see where it would lead her.

The river was wide and muddy coloured with rolling rapids and no visible means of crossing. Navigating her way along the bank was hazardous and difficult too as rough boulders blocked her path and she was forced to clamber around quite a lot.

Laila had only travelled for a short while when she noticed some peculiar looking steps ahead of her leading up from the river's edge and into the dense forest. And there alone at the foot of them sat a small dog fox staring back at her.

"Rocco!" she called running as quickly as she could towards him. But he disappeared, briskly ascending the stairway into the woods.

The steps were by no means natural or crude earthen cuts, but dressed blocks of the finest granite. And each step was exact in its dimensions. They looked almost out of keeping in relation to their wild untamed surroundings yet to Laila they represented civilization and she wasted no time following the fox up through the forest. She felt slightly apprehensive as she climbed the long winding stairs, as she had no idea of what to expect at the end of them but she also realised that she had no other choice but to take that chance.

The forest was thick and lush as if summer had arrived early. Fronds of young ferns sprouted in every conceivable gap, and whole sections of the stairway were overgrown with brambles and nettles, suggesting that they had not been in use for some considerable time. As Laila reached the final flight she could see they lead out to a clearing where the ruins of an old stone castle could be seen. It was a tall dark eerie looking place.

Sections of the walls were missing and nature had reclaimed most of it. There was no sign of life other than a few jackdaws that had taken up residence in the castles turrets. In the uneasy silence she peered out from the safety the woods.

Grabbing a long stick to defend herself from any wild animals she may encounter she inquisitively approached the castle to take a closer look.

Making her way towards the main entrance she could see the drawbridge was down, spanning a boggy overgrown moat that ran around the whole circumference of the ruins. Stepping onto the bridge she glanced up at the two huge cylindrical towers that loomed over her.

"Hello! Is there anyone one home?" she hollered nervously as her voice echoed around the walls, but there was no reply. Assuming it was safe she entered cautiously to investigate. Stepping into the heart of the building she noticed that there was no roof on the castle and the sky could be seen from within. All internal floors above the main hall were absent too and the only visible decor was the long grass that covered the ground and the ivy that scaled the walls.

Who ever had inhabited this place she concluded had long since gone. Not even the remnants of everyday utensils remained.

Laila climbed up one of the castles many spiralling staircases to the top and looked out across the forest. It was surrounded by wild meadows that were probably once well grazed pastures. And on the fringes the oak woods stretched off far and wide.

She spent some time exploring the remains of the castle to see what she could find. The labyrinth of stone corridors and rooms were cold and bare and over each door arch a grotesque carving of a gargoyle hung, staring menacingly back and unsettling her in the now diminishing daylight. It was getting late and she needed to get her head down for the evening so she looked around for somewhere to sleep. Luckily Laila had come across a long thick drape rolled up in a small alcove during her explorations around the castle. It was a dirty moth eaten curtain but to Laila it was going to be her blanket for the evening. She collected some dry grass from around the castle grounds and made a bed in the corner of a recess overlooking the great hall. She selected it due to its vantage point.

If any intruder came into the castle that evening at least she would see them before they saw her which made her feel a little safer in such unfamiliar surroundings.

The dusk soon arrived and visibility dropped as well as the temperature. The moon was bright which allowed her to see at least some of the great hall in the fading light.

She was so cold yet still managed to slip in and out of sleep, dozing off for fifteen minutes only to awaken again from the chill.

This went on for some time, until around midnight she noticed a strange mist appearing. It was similar to fog yet it crept across the moat like a living smoke being drawn into the castle from outside. The peculiar thing about it was the way that it almost seemed to glow in the darkness as if it were alight. This began to unnerve Laila so she sank slowly beneath the drape, but what happened next was totally unexpected.

As if by some ethereal force the fog began to transmogrify and divide, and then take on the shape and form of what appeared to be people. Just the basic shapes at first and then becoming gradually more and more detailed like an apparition. They were dressed in archaic medieval clothing and they moved around busily as if preparing some kind of banquet. Objects too began to appear from within the mist from carts to cutlery to livestock. Even the ruined walls of the castle began to reappear around her as if time was rewinding before Laila's very eyes, reverting to a moment in history when the castle was a bustling community. Beautiful tapestries adorned the ceiling joists and children chased each other up the stairwells.

Instead of feeling scared Laila was mesmerised. She couldn't believe what she was seeing and was fascinated by every detail. Everyone was smiling happily and getting on with their daily business when all of a sudden a small child ran up towards where Laila was huddled up and looked right through her as if she wasn't there. "Hello" said Laila politely, but the child just looked around as if she was looking for somewhere to hide and scampered off again down one of the corridors. Laila was confused yet curious by the child's actions and decided to follow the little girl. She turned into one of the rooms and disappeared out of sight "Hello?" called Laila searching the room for the little girl but there was no sign of her. The room was full of clothes and linen hanging up on cords from the walls like some kind of laundry room. Then from behind her appeared four children of similar age. They ran around the room giggling and looking for their friend but they never even noticed Laila standing there. So Laila walked over to one of the children and tapped her on the shoulder gently to get her attention. But as Laila touched the girl her hand passed straight through her body. She stood back in shock.

"They must be ghosts, they can't see me?" she thought as the children scampered off again. But then a voice behind her made her almost leap out of her skin.

"What are you doing in here?" said a large rotund man standing in the doorway and staring angrily at her. Laila froze as he bowled up to her but instead of talking to her he began talking to the little girl who was hiding behind Laila in the laundry room. "Come on I've been looking everywhere for you" he grumbled and walked straight through Laila and over to the small girl. Seizing her by the arm and taking her off back down the corridor. Laila stood a while in the room, trying to take in all what was going on before deciding to mingle about amongst the spirits of the castle. It was as if she had travelled back through the vestiges of time to when the castle was in its peak. Exploring every nook and cranny and every jar on every table right up to the brightly coloured tapestries, all demanded her attention. She would pause constantly to run her eye over the detail of some of the most mundane objects.

To bear witness to this magical event was a wonderful privilege that could not be passed upon fleetingly by one so inquisitive.

After investigating every room in the upper section of the castle Laila made her way down the narrow stone spiral staircase into the great hall with its bustling hive of activity.

Invisibly she wandered amongst the shadows observing the daily lives of the castle's inhabitants, listening intently to everyday conversations with an almost obsessive interest. Up and down the great hall she wandered until she found herself walking out of the main entrance of the castle and onto the huge timber drawbridge that traversed the moat. It was a bright sunny day outside the castle, which puzzled Laila as only an hour or so earlier it was dusk and she was sleeping. But after all her strange adventures and experiences, such bizarre phenomenon became almost commonplace and she never gave it that much attention. As she stood on the drawbridge she noticed that it wasn't just the time of day that had altered. The once weedy overgrown moat she had passed earlier now ran deep, clean and free of debris. Small children fished with crude rods along its margins while others swam happily further along. Jumping in and chasing each other as they enjoyed the beautiful sunny afternoon. A wide area of low grazed grass encircled the castle's grounds and stalls were set up outside. Traders sold their wares and the scent of hot bread filled the air. Page boys tended to the horses while their masters conversed in small groups beside the main entrance. Laughing loud and boisterously amongst themselves. The atmosphere although very busy was one of peace and serenity and for a moment Laila felt a sense of great joy. But all this was soon to change when for no apparent reason or so it seemed to Laila, everyone cowered simultaneously and appeared startled, scared and confused. It was as if some invisible force or distant sound had shattered their tranquillity. Everybody stood fixed to the spot and stared in the same direction to what appeared to be the source of their concern. At first Laila was quite bemused by the reaction of the people. Whatever it was they heard was inaudible to her and of no significance. Yet the overwhelming look of fear on their faces indicated that something was amiss, something terrifying which made Laila feel uneasy. Suddenly the children began to panic and raced off screaming into the safety of the castle. Falling over obstacles in their desperation to escape from whatever it was they feared.

"Run for your lives!" yelled the knights as they drew their swords and stood their ground shoulder to shoulder defensively. Laila was confused by the sudden pandemonium and her instincts forced her to take refuge as quickly as possible. She limped briskly towards the entrance of the castle just as the drawbridge was being raised.

"Wait!" she cried but it was too late. The drawbridge was raised beyond her reach and she could only watch helplessly as it slammed shut. Meanwhile the trees in the woods began to sway violently and the wind picked up as if a storm was about to rage. The horses began to leap restlessly on their reins and yet still Laila had no idea what it was that was causing the anomaly. But whatever it was she didn't wish to wait around to find out so decided that it would be wiser to leave while she could. Making her way to the opposite side of the castle she ran into the forest as quickly as her legs could carry her, wincing all the way from the wound in her thigh. Behind her she could hear the commotion at the castle forcing her to increase the pace until she was almost sprinting. Not looking back or pausing for breath she raced through the forest before losing her footing and tripping head over heels onto the ground with a thud. When she clambered back on to her feet to brush herself down she noticed that it was now totally dark in the forest with only the moonlight filtering through the dense canopy above. It was as if someone had suddenly switched the lights off, or she had suddenly awoken from a bad dream. No longer could she hear the cries from the castle and the air was silent again. The uneasy chill of the dark forest was no consolation from the chaos of the castle. Blindly she fumbled through the thick brushwood, walking head first into low branches and thorny brambles. She had no idea where she was going but followed her instinct to keep moving. She hadn't travelled very far when in the distance she heard something heading towards her at speed. As it drew closer, so the sound of snapping timber grew louder. Instinctively she dived for cover between the roots of a nearby tree. Curling into a tight ball and not moving an inch. She hoped that whatever it was would pass her by but to no avail. The noise drew nearer and nearer until it stopped almost immediately beside her and ceased to move anymore. Opening one eye slowly she looked up to see a gigantic figure looking down at her. It was tall and dark and seemed indistinguishable against the trees as it stood silhouetted against the navy blue sky, while its eyes seemed to glisten menacingly in the moonlight.

Chapter six

Yan Overton

"And what do we have here, is it a rock or a root?" a snickering voice remarked from out of the bleak grim stillness of the trees, and one that sounded familiar to Laila. She looked around again curiously from her concealment just as the lustrous moonlight began to illuminate the face of the strange figure in the darkness.

"Jack, it's you!" she cried leaping to her feet and launching herself straight at the huge timber giant in a loving embrace before shedding a few happy tears.

"It's ok Laila; I'm here now you're safe. I have searched for so long to locate you" he said, softly stroking Laila's hair comfortingly while she remained latched onto his leg in a vice like grip. She wasn't going to lose him again after all she had been through.

"What happened to you Jack? Where have you been? I was captured by Goblins and was nearly killed falling from a rope bridge and, and..."

"Slow down Laila!" said Jack interrupting her hysteria in mid sentence.

"I am aware of your exploits with the three Goblins my dear Laila; I have been kept abreast of your movements by the trees beyond the marsh. They informed me some time ago of your whereabouts, so I tracked you for the first day or so but lost you when you ascended into the mountains".

"You see, the alders that grow beside the river where the Goblins fished that afternoon told me that you were heading towards the Gamolham Mountains. But there are no other trees to speak of growing up on the mountain side other than some hardy young blackthorn growing in the foothills, so I was unable to track you from that point onwards"

"It wasn't until you had reached Grasmont castle that I had any hope of finding you, and then the most astonishing thing happened. You seemed to disappear from sight for what seemed an eternity" he said lifting her up in the air and placing her gently onto a bough at eye level.

"So what happened to you Jack?" asked Laila wiping the tears from her eyes.

"The last thing I recall was the broomstick" said
Jack whilst fingering his leafy beard thoughtfully.
"I held onto that broomstick for all I was worth and
I can tell you it wasn't a pleasant flight. I was spun
around and around like a sycamore samara for mile
upon mile but I could do nothing to control it.
Eventually my luck changed for the better. The
dragon path I was on ran close by a large lake, so I
seized my opportunity"
"What did you do?" Laila asked.
 "I let go of the besom".
Laila's eyes widened.
"Was it a long drop?" she asked.
"Well yes I was quite high up at the time, just above
the trees, but unfortunately I fell into the shallow
end of the lake".
"Have you broken anything?" she asked looking
concerned.
"Only some reed mace growing in the margins who
weren't too pleased I can tell you!" he smiled.
There was a short silent pause before they both
burst into laughter.
"You are funny Jack and I'm so pleased you're here
with me again" said Laila happily.
"Right, well let's get you warm! A fire is called for
me thinks and then when you have rested we will

head off as soon as your fit" said Jack snapping some deadwood from a nearby tree.

"Where are we going?" Laila asked.

"To see Yan of course" he replied.

"The wizard?" piped Laila enthusiastically.

Jack stopped at once from collecting wood before slowly turning around.

"And what makes you presume that he is a wizard?" he asked suspiciously.

"The Goblins told me!" she said. "Well that's what he is after all, isn't he Jack?" she asked. Jack didn't reply straight away. He just stood there quietly for a moment as if choosing his words carefully.

"Well yes I suppose he might be" he said with some reluctance.

"But we won't mention wizards anymore if you don't mind as they prefer to remain anonymous" he said abruptly concluding the subject, before constructing a bow drill for the fire. Laila just shrugged her shoulders in acknowledgement and said no more about it as it obviously seemed to be a bit of delicate subject from Jacks reaction.

Within a few moments a fire was burning, with Laila and Jack sitting snugly by the warmth of the flames.

"Tell me about the castle back there Jack, its haunted isn't it?" she said.

With an absent glare he looked up at the sky.

"Oh Grasmont?" he mumbled. "No it's not haunted it's just been abandoned for centuries".

"Why was it abandoned? Who lived there?" she asked inquisitively.

"From what I have heard, it was an autonomous self contained community called the Verax tribe. No one really knows what happened to them, it's a mystery, an enigma that not even the noblest trees could answer" he said in a low voice. Laila looked thoughtfully at him and then looked back into the heart of the fire.

"I know what happened to them Jack" she said. "I was there and I saw everything, the last moments of their lives played out in front me".

Jack suddenly snapped out of his pensive mood and looked over at Laila with an astonished frown.

"But Laila, no one knows what happened to the Verax, they disappeared centuries ago".

"I swear I saw what happened with my own eyes Jack! I saw the ghosts of the castle as clear as I see you now.

I saw the pictures on the walls and the children playing in the halls" she said raising her voice passionately. "They were destroyed by some sort of storm!" Laila's affirmation and unexpected outburst instantly had Jack's full attention.

"A storm you say? But that is totally impossible." He said dismissively

"There has not been a storm strong enough to destroy a castle since the days of the Banishing. Maybe you were tired and imagined it Laila. Tiredness can do that, and after all you have been through quite a lot" he said trying not to sound too condescending.

"I know you don't believe me Jack but I know what I saw!" she said throwing a hand full of leaves on to the fire as a gesture of her exasperation.

"I have no doubt that you may possess the ability to see the shadows of past events Laila but no ancient tree has ever mentioned a great storm, and I can only go on what the learned trees have told me".

Laila took a deep breath and sighed"

Yeah I must have been tired!" she said in a sardonic tone. Laila was in no mood for confrontation and resided herself in the knowledge that she knew better. Jack sensed her indignation so attempted to lift her morale with some positive news.

"Yans house is not that far from here Laila" he said pointing in an easterly direction. We can make a move there whenever you're ready".

"Really? That's fantastic!" she beamed, looking up at the morning sun that began to fill the darkness with light again. She also noticed that Jack seemed to have altered somewhat in appearance.

"Jack! You look different from when I saw you last?" she said walking towards him for a closer inspection. "Ah! That's because I am coming into my early growth" he smiled. "My foliage is getting greener now that the season is progressing. Laila touched his thick leafy face.

"It suits you Jack, it makes you look younger" she said.

"Why thank you Laila" he said standing up to bow politely.

"Right! Shall we dispense with the fire and proceed to Yan's?" he said.

"Sure! That sounds like a great idea, I'm feeling much better now that I've had a rest" she said rubbing her face.

After dousing the fire they gathered themselves up for the journey ahead.

"How far is Yan's house from here?" she asked, concerned that Jack may be taking her on yet another one of his mammoth jaunts.

Jack chuckled loudly. "Still the ever inquisitive Laila" he said. "Well don't worry your pretty little head, we should be there by midday" he smiled.

The woods became gradually thinner as they made their way through the brake, with fewer mature trees and only the odd elder or silver birch scattered throughout the clearings before eventually they walked out onto beautiful open downland.

Small green copses floated upon the swirling golden meadows that surged beneath the wind like restless waters in a gale, whilst skylarks rejoiced at the advent of spring.

"This is wonderful!" said Laila as they strolled along the narrow path that ran beside the meadow. Jack stopped along the way and leant against the old post and rail fence that ran along its perimeter.

"Yes it is truly breathtaking Laila" he uttered as he absorbed every inch of the scenery.

"I'm amazed that spring is here already".

"Don't you have a winter in this place?" she asked casually, whilst picking a daisy from the short grass sprouting from the verge of the path.

"Winter has been and gone" Smiled Jack as they moved on.

"Has it?" asked Laila looking puzzled.

"Yes and now spring is in the air and the rebirth of all life is once again upon us".

"Wow that's crazy! Time does fly here, I feel as if I've only been here a short time and yet a whole season has passed me by, but then nothing surprises me anymore" she said trotting to keep up with Jack who was merrily bounding along ahead of her.

The journey to Yan's house was to become more of a guided walk for Laila than trek as Jack babbled on continuously about the names and uses of the numerous plants they encountered along the way.

"Ah! Here's another interesting specimen" he said stopping to admire a small chequered bell shaped flower. "It's called a snake's head fritillary after its resemblance to the flesh of that splendid reptile the snake".

As much as Laila enjoyed the beauty of spring flowers she was becoming gradually less attentive and eager to get to Yan's house.

"Yes it's very pretty Jack but hadn't we better get a move on?" she asked.

"What's the rush?" he said, It's only over there!"

Jack pointed to a small cottage perched upon the brow of a hill at the foot of a silver white Mountain. It was a quaint looking place surrounded by trees with smoke puffing from its chimney.

"What are we waiting for!" shouted Laila pulling on Jacks hand excitedly.

"Slow down Laila I wanted to show you some interesting lichen growing in this boggy ditch over here" he said excitedly. But just as he turned around to show her the marvel she was off, hobbling briskly up the path and laughing loudly.

"See you there!" she shouted.

"Hey wait for me!" called Jack in hot pursuit.

After around a hundred metres Laila stopped to catch her breath just as Jack came walking up.

"I assume from your rather hasty retreat young lady that you find my talks on flora somewhat dull?" he said with a smirk.

"No Jack you are very interesting but can we talk about plants after we have spoken to Yan? If you don't mind" she replied politely.

"Ok Laila I understand" he smiled as they made their up the track towards the cottage.

Once they had reached the brow of the hill the cottage appeared almost indiscernible by the numerous trees that encircled it. If it wasn't for the dilapidated fence and the drifts of informally planted geraniums, one could be forgiven for thinking there was nothing there.

They followed the fence along a well mown verge until finally they came to an archway covered in clematis, where a wooden gate that had seen better days hung precariously on its rusty hinges. It had a crude plaque nailed to the arch that read 'Dial House'.

Jack had to step over the arch as he was far too big to walk beneath it.

Laila looked around at the colourful clooties that hung from the branches of the trees as they walked up a slippery cobbled path towards the cottage. The building was old and rustic and the sagging tiled roof was covered in ivy. It was a symbiosis between man and nature, as each one fought for its own space yet neither conceding to the other. Just then beyond the vegetable patch at the end of the building a figure of a man appeared pushing a wheelbarrow full of compost.

"Yan!" yelled Jack loudly before running up to him and lifting him up in the air like a small child.

"Jack! You old rotten stick you!" laughed the man leaping onto the wooden giant's neck in an embrace.

"What brings you here?" he smiled as Jack carefully lowered him to the ground.

"Well to see you of course Yan" he said.

"Really? Well this is indeed a welcome surprise" he beamed.

"And also to see if you could possibly help out a friend of mine?" said Jack pointing at Laila standing demurely with her arms behind her back a few yards down the path.

"Yan may I introduce you to Laila. I met her recently whilst planting Yew sapling's in the forest. "Pleased to meet you Laila, I'm a very old friend of Jacks, and any friend of Jacks is a friend of mine" he said walking over and shaking Laila gently by the hand. She felt a little nervous of him at first but smiled back courteously.

"Pleased to meet you too" she said.

He wasn't quite how she imagined a wizard to be; in fact he looked more like a vagrant in appearance. There was no long white beard or pointy hat. Not even a crescent moon symbol embellishing his attire.

Instead his white hair was long and matted as if a brush had never touched it in months and grey stubble covered his weathered looking face. His clothes were black and shabby and his boots were covered in thick mud.

"Come my friends and rest your weary limbs" said Yan leading them to a large wooden bench situated on a flat mown area of the garden.

"Would you like some tea Laila?" he asked, rubbing his hands together.

"Yes please" she replied taking her seat at the table.

"And I will make some lovely mud for you my dear Jack" he smiled before wandering off into the house.

"He is not how I thought he might be" said Laila quietly under her breath.

"Don't be fooled by appearances Laila, he is extremely wise and powerful" said Jack reassuringly.

Seconds later Yan appeared crossing the lawn, carrying a wicker tray loaded with cups and saucers and an old cracked teapot.

"Here we are" he said putting the tray down and pouring a cup of tea for Laila.

"And here's yours Jack" he said placing a large mug of the blackest mud in front of the Green man, who wasted no time in gulping it down. Laila looked on in disgust as he wiped the foul black goo from his lips.

"That was delicious Yan" he said.

"Oh it was nothing really I just soaked some old compost through a strainer and the rest was easy as they say" he laughed.

"Right so what can I do for you Jack" said Yan stirring his tea meticulously.

"Well as I said you earlier it's not actually me but Laila who needs your help" he replied.

"And there was I thinking you came all the way out here to visit your old friend Yan because you missed me so much" he quipped while winking at Laila wryly.

"Well yes that as well but it's more than just a social visit Yan. You see, Laila needs to get back to where she belongs, to a place called the Warren pond and I thought that you being such a learned person you would be able to assist her in that quest" he said disquietly.

Yan looked at him with a puzzled gaze and then began to chuckle uncontrollably.

"Well well, I'm disappointed in you Jack; you mean to say that you come all this way to ask me for help in finding a pond? Yet if there is anyone more adept at locating a pond in the whole of this land it would be a Green Man. For crying out loud Jack, you have the ability to converse with trees, have you lost your mind?" he said leaning back in his seat and rolling his eyes in disbelief.

"Yes I know I could, and I would under normal circumstances but this is entirely different" replied Jack agitated.

Yan was intrigued and leant forward on his seat.

"How different?" he asked. Jack seemed almost uneasy in disclosing what he knew and looked around as if he needed to check that no one was listening in on him. He then looked Yan in the eye and whispered under his breath.

"Laila arrived here through the spirit door of an ancient hawthorn"

Yan looked back in astonishment.

"Are you sure?" he asked. "I thought they had all but vanished".

"I'm sure of it! Everything Laila has told me I know to be true. The strange circumstances surrounding her arrival and the fact that she knew the exact location of an ancient hawthorn is proof enough to me. But that's not all! She appeared in the forest totally undetected by the trees, now how do you explain that? Asked Jack. Yan scratched his head and pondered for a moment.

"Jack, I need you to do me a favour. I want you to use your arboreal ubiquity, so as to warn me of any undesirables that may be lurking anywhere nearby, it's vital that no one overhear our conversation".

"Sure!" said Jack and wandered off to talk with the trees in the garden. Yan then turned to Laila with a concerned look in his eyes.

"In order for me to help you Laila you will need to tell me everything from the beginning! Don't leave out any detail as it is imperative that I understand exactly how you came to find this place" he said placing both hands on her shoulders. Laila happily agreed and told Yan the whole story from leaving her house in the morning to Prowler stealing her necklace and falling asleep beneath the hawthorn tree. And when she had finally concluded her tale Yan jumped to his feet and punched the air euphorically.

"That's it, that's it! I understand now, it all makes sense!" he said in a moment of joyous realization.

"Understand what?" asked Laila oblivious.

"Well there have been rumours afoot recently regarding a rare hawthorn and Prowler coming in to the possession of the legendary magical necklace known as the Brisingamen. I must confess I didn't believe it at first but this proves it"

"What's the Brisingamen?" asked Laila.

"Now don't play games with me Laila!. You know the necklace I'm talking about. The one you had belonging to the goddess Freyja" he said sternly waving his finger at her.

"Who's Freyja? That necklace belonged to me! I told you it was given to me by my Dad?" she said.

"Then we must get the necklace back as soon as possible, so that you can return it to him and consequently to Freyja" said Yan gripping her arm tightly.

"Ouch you are hurting me!" said Laila pushing him away and storming off down the garden a short distance before halting dead in her tracks and turning around angrily.

"Listen Yan! I honestly don't know what you're talking about but let me just say this. Unlike you I'm not that bothered about the necklace anymore, I just want to get back home to Warren pond. I only came here because Jack told me that you might be able to help me but all you seem to be interested in is my stupid necklace!"

Yan shook his head.

"I'm sorry you feel that way Laila but you obviously don't realise the consequences of your actions. By giving the Brisingamen to Prowler you have inadvertently put the power of the jewel into the hands of Lhanna".

"I never gave my necklace to that magpie, he stole it from me! And who on earth is Lhanna?" snapped Laila who could no longer contain her frustration.

"You mean to tell me you have no idea who Lhanna is?"asked Yan astonished.

"No! I don't! And neither do I know who Freyja is or why you keep on calling my necklace the Brisingamen?" she replied despondently before running over to Jack.

"Oh Jack what is happening here?! I don't know what he is talking about? Please just get me out of here and take me back to the forest.

Just then Yan walked over and took her gently by the hand.

"Please forgive me Laila, for my reckless behaviour I really didn't mean to upset you, I'm sure this is all very confusing for you" he said apologising humbly.

"Of course I will help you get back to Warren pond. Come, sit down and finish your tea, I've got some homemade biscuits I would like you to try. I baked them fresh only this morning".

Laila was distressed and annoyed and in no mood for tea but she was also starving hungry and the thought of freshly baked biscuits quickly quelled her vexation.

Yan went off into the house and returned moments later with a tray of steaming biscuits.

"Enjoy!" he said as Laila began filling her face.

"These are amazing! I've never tasted such delicious biscuits in my whole life" she said polishing off the tray. Yan sat back in his chair contentedly.

"I'm glad you like them" he smiled.

"So when are you going to take me back to Warren pond? I don't mind leaving tomorrow if that's better for you" said Laila mopping the crumbs from her plate. Yan shifted restlessly in his seat and poured himself another cup of tea.

"I know you may find this impossible and almost ridiculous to believe and I don't wish you to think for a second that I am trying to insult your intelligence Laila, but you have to trust me when I tell you that the Warren pond that you are searching for no longer exists, in this world anyhow" he said veraciously. Laila stared blankly back at him. " What do you mean Warren pond doesn't exist? That's impossible, where has it gone? It couldn't have just disappeared!".

"It exists in another time and place beyond this".

"What's that supposed mean? I don't understand?" she said getting addled.

"Ok let me elucidate. There were once many ancient hawthorn trees throughout the earth called world trees which were sometimes referred to as spirit doors. They were called this because they acted like doorways into other worlds, their roots and branches passing into the many alternative dimensions. Shaman and witches use them to travel to these other worlds on spiritual journeys. Now you remember you told me about that afternoon when you felt nauseas and fell asleep beneath a hawthorn tree up in Theydon woods?, Well what you didn't realise is that you were not in fact falling asleep at all, but experiencing an altered state of consciousness whilst passing through one of the spirit doors into another world, this world!. Don't you see? That explains why in your eyes the seasons appeared to change almost instantaneously" he exclaimed endeavouring to explicate the inconceivable.

"I realise that conceptually you may find that difficult to accept but you need to realise that there are many worlds beyond the confines of your own, and far beyond the realm of human perception. Microcosms within macrocosms, in an infinite number of parallel universes" he said passionately lifting his arms aloft to the sky.

Overwhelmed and shocked by such an astounding revelation, Laila was completely nullified and just sat there without uttering a single word as if emotionally depleted.

Whatever tormented her thoughts she remained reticent to express, leaving Yan supping his tea in the uncomfortable silence that ensued. He knew she would need a moment to come to terms with what he had told her, and could sense her dejection yet made no attempt to console her, as he felt it better to be reserved rather than to offer feckless words of solace.

Laila got up slowly from her seat and wandered across to the other side of the garden towards where an old wattle fence stood and gazed out into the surrounding fields in quiet contemplation. "Tuk was right!" she muttered timorously to herself.

It was a beautiful scene from the garden, full of flower meadows and distant mountains that helped soothe her wretched soul like a magical remedy.

"It's a lovely view isn't it?" said Yan wandering over.

"I often stand her and look out across the fields myself."

"Yes it's lovely, you're lucky to have such a wonderful view from your garden" said Laila solemnly pining for the view of her own garden.

"I realise this all seems a bit crazy, but you are obviously here for a reason and I believe that reason must be for you to return to your world with the Brisingamen".

"I told you Yan, it is not the Brisingamen, it's just a necklace my Dad bought me for my birthday, why don't you believe me?"

Yan shook his head,

"No Laila it simply can't be, you don't understand! Prowler would never pass through a spirit door in search of the Brisingamen unless he knew of its exact whereabouts!".

"Maybe he made a mistake then?".

"I very much doubt that someone with his sagacity would make that kind of mistake"

"But he's only a bird!" she scoffed".

"He may have appeared in the form of a bird to you Laila but in this reality he is a nefarious shaman by the name of Ibora. He used the power of anifornum to transform himself into the guise of a magpie in order to steal the necklace. You have to realise we are dealing with a very powerful and ruthless individual here".

"Well if he wants to go to so much trouble just to steal my necklace then he can have it! I don't care about it anymore; it's brought me nothing but bad luck. All I want to do is go home. Will you help me Yan? Surely you must know the whereabouts of a spirit door?" said Laila distraught.

"Yes but it's not quite that simple Laila. You see Prowler is still in possession of the necklace and regardless of whether you believe it to be the Brisingamen or not is irrelevant, we just can't take the risk. The fact is, it cannot remain in this world otherwise the repercussions could prove catastrophic. I will do everything in my power to help you get back home, but not without the necklace in your safe keeping".

"But how will you get it back?" she asked.

Yan chuckled "Free your mind of the how Laila and focus on the when, the universe is drawn towards positive thoughts. It's only a matter of time before you're back at Warren pond you have my word. The most important question right now is, are you hungry?"

Laila nodded her head enthusiastically. "I'm sure you would like to wash too" he smiled.

"Yes please Yan, I' haven't had a proper wash for so long I can't remember what it's like" laughed Laila.

"Well I had assumed you weren't the type who would normally rub thick mud onto their tights" he quipped.

"Ok, well I will start making some lunch while you make yourself comfortable and I will ask Jack to show you where the facilities are. I've got some Verbascum oil in the bathroom for you to put on that wound of yours as well" he said as they strolled back over to the table where Jack was sitting contently grooming his new green leafy locks.

Jack looked up as they both strolled into view from across the other side of the garden.

"I thought you had run off and left me" he said with a smile.

"Well we were thinking about it but the trees would have given us away" laughed Yan before putting his hand on to the giant Green Man's shoulder.

"Would you be so kind as to show Laila where the bathtub is? I have filled the cauldron with boiling water so there's enough for a bath".

"Sure!" he replied getting to his feet.

"Follow me Laila" said Jack, ushering her towards the house.

"I'm going to make some food soon" called Yan.

"Oh, and Jack! Could you show Laila the spare room overlooking the meadow; she can sleep in there tonight".

"Ok", replied Jack.

"Are we staying here tonight?" asked Laila.

"Well if Yan thinks we should then we should" said Jack. "I saw him talking to you over by the fence, did he offer any words of advice?" asked Jack inquisitively.

"Well I learnt a few things about how I got to be here but as far as getting me back home he said he'll let me know later".

"Yan will sort it out Laila I'm sure of it" smiled Jack before crawling on his hands and knees to get through the door into the house.

The door from the garden lead into a small kitchen with a high ceiling just high enough to accommodate the huge Green Man who stooped awkwardly to move around. The clay floor was cracked and uneven and the walls were crudely plastered. Timber support beams crisscrossed the building given it an almost organic skeletal feel. A large library lead off from the kitchen, its slanted shelves filled with books on three sides and a black cast iron fireplace vacating the fourth.

"This is the living room as well as the library" said Jack sitting down on a long wooden bench with a coarse cotton mattress laid across it.

"I'm afraid I can't go anywhere else in the house as the rooms are far too small for me to manoeuvre in but if you go through that door and follow the stairs up you will find the bathroom, first door on the left. And the room opposite is yours" he said fumbling through the vast tomes that crammed the shelves. Laila made her way through the twisted wooden door leading out of the library. Lifting the latch she found herself in a hallway with rickety stairs leading off of it. Every step up she took seemed to creak and groan under her weight as if it was about to collapse any minute. Walking into the bathroom she felt relieved at the sign of a bath tub. Bolting the door behind her she began to pour hot water from the cauldron into a long wooden tub and stirred the water until it cooled slightly before submerging herself in it up to her nose. For the first time in what seemed like months she felt totally content to just simmer.

Chapter seven

Lhanna and Isla

In the tranquil peace of the garden Yan was digging up some carrots from his vegetable plot in preparation for lunch while Jack looked on in quiet contemplation.

"So what do you think Laila's purpose is in coming here?" he asked curiously.

"That I am not quite sure about as yet my green friend, but if she is the custodian of the Brisingamen as I believe we have established; then we must do our utmost to return it to her".

"Do you think she might be a fledgling witch?" he asked.

"I very much doubt it. No, she is just the unfortunate victim of circumstance I'm afraid. I realise that her passing from one alternative dimension to another would appear shamanic, and you would of course be forgiven for thinking she was a witch, but she seems totally oblivious of anything regarding the power of the necklace and is convinced that it has no significance at all. And yet it was the magic of the Brisingamen that lured her here in the first place, and it shall be that which returns her I hope" he said optimistically.

"Are you sure it's the Brisingamen Yan?. It just seems odd that she would have unwittingly been in acquisition of such a mythical jewel".

"I realise it's a paradox, and if I didn't know better I would probably disregard it as pure conjecture, but the fact that Ibora recently acquired the necklace has removed any doubt from my mind".

"But how will you get it back now that Ibora has it?" asked Jack.

"That my friend is the question" he replied as he strolled off toward the house with his basket of vegetables.

Inside Laila sat by the open fire wrapped in a long brown robe she had found in her room which totally swamped her.

Her damp clothes hung on a string like Christmas decorations from the hearth.

"I see you found something smart to wear" smiled Yan as he entered the library.

"Yes, I hope you didn't mind? I just thought it would be a good time to wash my clothes as they were as desperate as me to get clean".

"Not at all my dear Laila, you are my guest and I want you to make yourself at home, in fact I insist" he said stepping back into the kitchen.

"I'm going to make us a nice bowl of pottage for lunch, how does that sound?"

"Oh wow hot food!" she said with a big grin on her face.

Jack crawled in through the door on all fours and sat in the corner almost filling the room.

"Have you had a look at the books?" he asked.

"No not yet" said Laila eyeing up the bulging shelves of dusty volumes that surrounded her.

"Look! Here's a book on the Brisingamen that you might find interesting" said Jack passing her large leather bound book from the shelf with runic symbols on the cover. She looked back at him vacantly.

"If you don't mind Jack I would rather not right now" she said politely. Yan sensed her discomfort from the kitchen and quickly seized the opportunity to change the subject.

"I hope you like onions Laila as I'm really quite chuffed with my crop so far".

"Oh yes thank you Yan" she said.

"Do you like gardening?" he asked.

"Well I've not really done much in the way of gardening but I'm sure it must be nice to see things grow and eat them".

"Yes its really rewarding, I think there is a book in there about growing vegetables that you may find of some interest with some rather detailed illustrations". Laila just smiled warmly,

"It's ok Yan, if you don't mind I'm happy just to watch the wood burn on the fire for now" she said.

Yan entered the room a short time later with a wooden board containing a large brown bloomer and some mouldy looking cheese.

"Have some bread and cheese for starters Laila, the pottage will take a while to cook. This should hold back the hunger pang" he said before placing it onto the circular timber table that took up the middle of the library.

There was a moments silence as they tucked into the bread and cheese before Laila spoke up.

"You mentioned someone called Lhanna back there Yan, who is she?"

"Someone you wouldn't like to cross" he promptly replied. Laila looked at him puzzled.

"Forgive me Laila I keep forgetting you are new here, and that to you this is all a bit incomprehensible"
"Let me tell you what kind of person we are dealing with here" he said disquietly gazing out at the sky before drifting off with his musings like the clouds that floated by the window. "I will start from the beginning".

Many centuries ago the world was once free from hate and war, and the energy of life and all living things like the mountain streams flowed unhindered throughout the land. There was a time of relative peace and tranquillity in the great forests of the earth until the day of the occultation, when the Moon eclipsed the Sun and cast the world into shadow. The celestial union between the Sun and moon bore forth its fruits upon the womb of the great Earth mother in the form of two baby girls. They were delivered into this world from the depths of the cold mountain lake of Glaslyn, where they were discovered one morning upon the pebbled shores by a hedge witch named June who was out collecting water from the mountain streams. She took the girls in and cared for them as if they were her own and taught them the magic of the old ways.

As the seasons passed the girls grew and so did their power. Being divine daughters of the Sun and Moon their magic was limitless and before long they learnt to develop their inherent powers, manipulating matter or anything they so desired.

Isla was altruistic by nature and used her powers to heal. Seeking out the sick and injured of the world, finding fulfilment in helping those in need. Yet her sister Lhanna was the polar opposite. She was imperious and sadistic and found pleasure in domination and the acquisition of wealth.

On the day of their eighteenth birthdays the girls parted company from their guardian June, and went their separate ways.

Isla headed into the Grayweald, a vast forest in the north, to live amongst the creatures and inhabitants of the forests while her sister Lhanna went off in pursuit of opulence.

It wasn't long before her search lead her to the city of Firgen in the land of Vercia. A magnificent stronghold situated between two mountains with huge red granite walls that ran forever, encompassing a towering citadel. Beautiful bright coloured banners flew from every corner and the black slate roofs of the houses cluttered the bailey like a lake of jet. Lhanna gazed intently at the vision before her. This was a city of plenitude, this was her city.

The next morning at sunrise she stood outside the walls of the city and threatened to tear them down and destroy the homes of all the occupants inside unless the ruler of Firgen knelt before her and declared her its Queen. At first the people of the city mocked her demands, regarding her threats as merely the rants of a lunatic, until they experienced the strength of her wrath.

The once huge impenetrable stone walls of the city crumbled like sand as the mountains began to shake. People fled in fear of their lives as their homes began to collapse around them.

In desperation the king of Firgen sent forth his armies against the evil sorceress but they were no match, for her power was immeasurable and she simply cut through them like a scythe.

After two days of desperate resistance they finally laid down their arms and surrendered, pledging their allegiance to their new Queen whilst their King knelt before her begging for forgiveness and for his life.

Lhanna drew forth the king's sword from its scabbard and took off his head with one clean swipe

and held it aloft as a gesture of her might and intolerance and proclaimed herself sovereign.
"Oh no! That's terrible!" Laila gasped. "How could she do such a thing when the king had surrendered?" "Because my dear Laila she has no heart or feelings for anyone but herself. It is a common trait in avaricious people".

"From that day forth she subdued the people of Firgen, ruling over them with an iron fist, and in her arrogance even changed the name of the city to Lhansburg after herself.
Yet still this was not enough to appease her desire. Her appetite for power grew even stronger. So she created an army, the likes of which had never been seen before in this world and sent them forth to expand her empire. Taking lands from the seven great kings and all who those did not acknowledge her as supreme sovereign by force. One by one great empires fell to her armies until she had all that she could behold.
 Well almost all. There was one place she did not possess, the vast territory in the north known as the Grayweald, and the more one desires the less they are content. Lhanna was a megalomaniac and always wanted more and now her eye was on the north.

The race of Goblins inhabited most of the
Grayweald which covered many thousands of miles.
They were dissected into small kingdoms run by
various tribes. Some lived high in the mountains
and others in the wooded lowlands. They were all
that stood between her and total domination. Her
desire to invade the Grayweald became intense.
Rich in timber and minerals as well as agricultural
land meant she couldn't ignore it any longer, and
the Goblins were a divided nation and so no match
for her armies. But they had a huge deterrent, and
that was her sister Isla. Isla was a good friend of the
Goblins and respected and protected their symbiotic
existence within the Grayweald.

 She was also the guardian of the Grayweald and its
inhabitants, and would never allow any harm to
come to them. She had heard mutterings of her
sisters warmongering but avoided confrontation in
the interests of peace.

But as time passed, Lhanna's rapidly expanding
empire began putting an immense demand on their
Queen for the Grayweald's resources and she knew
it would be only a matter of time before she would
have to face her sister Isla.

This prospect concerned Lhanna slightly, as Isla
was a far more powerful an adversary than any she

had ever encountered in her campaigns for empire. And also she hadn't spoken a word to her for many years. How could she avoid conflict with such formidable opposition she wondered? Make them your ally of course!.

So Lhanna immediately set about devising a series of malicious deceptions in order to achieve her objective. Firstly she began by setting fire to her own wheat fields and farmlands, accusing the Goblins as being the perpetrators.
Through fraudulent propaganda she incited a culture of resentment and indignation towards them. This would give her a valid justification to invade the Grayweald. Yet instead of sending in a huge force she dispatched only a small unit of conscripted soldiers to be martyrs to her cause on what can only be described as a suicide mission. Their subsequent annihilation at the hands of the Goblins would prove to be the final catalyst for war".
 "But I don't understand?. Why would she send in her own soldiers to be killed?" asked Laila puzzled.
"Because they were merely pawns. Don't you see Laila; she could have quite easily sent in her entire army and taken the Grayweald without much resistance, but that would have appeared to her sister Isla as an act of aggression. This way any

response by Lhanna could not be condemned and would only be seen as legitimate retribution. So now that all the elements were in place Lhanna rode out into the forest in search of her sister and future ally.

Arriving by a lake in the woods she tethered her horse to a tree and from out of nowhere Isla appeared.

"Lhanna! It is wonderful to see you here; this is indeed a pleasant surprise! I have not heard from you for so many years" said Isla embracing Lhanna gently.

"I have missed you too Isla and I have spent far too many long night thinking about you and wondering what you were be doing" said Lhanna with a smirk of devious insincerity. Stepping backwards she studied Isla for a moment.

"My you have grown into such a beautiful flower" she remarked.

"You are too kind Lhanna" said Isla flattered.

"Come now Lhanna I'm sure you have travelled far, I insist you join me for food and wine and we shall catch up on lost time" said Isla joyfully pulling Lhanna's hand like a gleeful child. But Lhanna did not share her enthusiasm; instead she just stood there with an expression of deep sorrow on her face.

"I'm afraid I cannot Isla as much as I long to. You see my people are in desperate need of me and I fear the more I delay them the graver their fate may be".

Isla looked confused. "What people and plight are you referring to?" she asked.

"Since we last spoke I have become Queen of a peace loving nation, and therefore I am responsible to my people.

"But what brings you here to the Grayweald?" asked Isla concerned.

"I came to seek your help in this my hour of need. I know time has separated us but I knew that the only person whom I could turn to when I needed them most would be you my sister" said Lhanna in an anxious tone.

"What is it you ask of me Lhanna, you know I will do all that I can for you".

Lhanna paced up and down as if to compose herself. "We are on the brink of a war that seems unavoidable. I have done all that I can to bring about peace in the land but my efforts have been in vain and I have no other choice but to turn to our closest allies for support" she said. Isla was shocked.

"But who would attempt such a hostile act?" she asked.

"The Goblins!" replied Lhanna.

Isla shook her head in disbelief.

"No! That is not possible, they are a peaceful race! They are my friends, it is not in their nature".

"Oh but it is!" said Lhanna.

"They killed my soldiers and set fire to our crops without provocation, leaving many starving. What am I to do, pretend it never happened?"

"Do you want me to negotiate a treaty with the Goblin for you?" asked Isla.

"No! I want you to unite with me sister against this vermin who threaten peace in our world and destroy them".

Isla gasped.

"I'm surprised you do not know me better Lhanna to suggest such a thing!" I could never harm anyone especially the Goblins. And from what I've heard on the wind it is your belligerence that threatens peace in this world she said raising her voice.

"Come Isla, if we unite we could have the entire world in our hands and no force in the land could stand in our way, just imagine it!" said Lhanna passionately.

"And what Then?" asked Isla.

"We sit alone and distant upon our conceited thrones, content in our indifference to the world? Caught up in the endless cycle of desire that

enslaves the very soul to a life endless suffering?
"No Lhanna! Keep your plutomania! It has no value here!" she said in disgust.
Suddenly Lhanna let out a scream of fury and frustration.
"So that's how you want it to be then is it Isla? Refusing to help your one and only sister!" she roared.
"And there I was giving you the chance to be somebody in this world, to rule alongside me and share my wealth and power. And yet all you want is to live here in this dank, inhospitable forest caring for these paltry creatures! What a fool I've been to have considered you a threat, when all along you were nothing more than a slave to the weakness of your compassion!.
Well I'm glad you wish to remain neutral as I intend on sending in my armies before the Samhain to crush your precious Goblins, and there is nothing you or they can do to stop it! After all as you said in your own words, you couldn't harm anyone, remember?" laughed Lhanna as she mounted her steed.
"Enjoy your peace, while it lasts!" she said before galloping off into the forest leaving Isla standing alone by the lake.

That evening when the moon was full, Isla contacted the Goblins, summoning their chieftains, known as 'Daloch''s to a meeting on top of a tall hill called the Mount where they were informed of their fate.

"Can you not do anything to help us?" asked one of the chieftains by the name of Gordaloch.

"I'm afraid I cannot take up arms to the determent of others regardless of your plight" she replied.

"But you are the custodian of the Grayweald and you possess great power, why can you not at least save the forest?" asked another Daloch.

"I swore to my stepmother June that I would only use my power for good, such as healing, that was my promise and I cannot break that. It is time for you all now to unite as one and win the battle you face for peace and for the Grayweald".

Gordaloch bowed his head low. "Even if we unite we are still no match against such a huge force. We won't be fighting for the Grayweald; we will be fighting for our very existence".

"I promise I will do all I can for you but I cannot harm them" she said and left the Daloch's in conference up on the Mount while she made her way to Lake Glaslyn to deliberate.

There by the shores of the lake she sat in quiet meditation for four days requesting guidance from the earth.

Meanwhile riders were dispatched from Lhansburg to all four corners of the kingdom with orders from Lhanna, to advance upon the Grayweald.

Forty eight hours later the might of her elite army headed north toward Goblin territory, reinforced by supplementary legions en route until a vast endless expanse of polished steel ran like a tsunami across the land. An unstoppable force intent on genocide with Lhanna riding up front on a huge white horse, dressed in a beautiful red velvet dress. She had no need of armour or a shield as she was impenetrable to the sword or arrow of any Goblin warrior.

Lhanna loved a battle, enjoying nothing more than to see her enemies fall to their knees submissively, while her army of subordinates gave their lives in her honour. This was the thrill that drove her lust for war.

On the eve of the Samhain the two sides converged at a place called Ura valley. The Goblins lined the valley ridge in their thousands and so had the strategic advantage but they were dwarfed in number by Lhannas army who totally flooded the valley below. Gordaloch sounded his horn and the

Goblins let loose a volley of arrows that almost blackened out the sun. Hundreds of Lhannas men fell as the arrows rained down on them.

"Forward!" Lhanna cried and the mighty war machine began to move, advancing in huge quarter distant columns towards the ridge.

Slowly step by step they began to climb the slopes up towards the Goblin line, as wave upon wave, they fell under fire. Clambering over their dead they pushed on tenaciously in their hundreds of thousands. No matter how many arrows flew they just kept on coming like a wall of shields until eventually the clash of Goblin swords rang out across the valley.

The Goblins were quickly overwhelmed by the advancing tide and were hacked down like scrub. Few survived the first day of the battle and those who did were forced to retreat into the mountains.

"Where are you Isla?" cried Gordaloch as he watched in vain as Lhanna's merciless army raised his villages to the ground.

Isla was at Lake Glaslyn when the battle of Ura valley raged, oblivious to the Goblins plight.

Rising to her feet on the day after Samhain she held her arms aloft in a moment of realization.

Picking up a small quartz pebble from the ground she uttered an incantation before hurling it far out into the centre of the lake.

The stone broke the mirror smooth surface of the water with an almighty splash, shattering the silence of the mountain air as it echoed through the gorge like a drum. Gradually the ripples emanating from the impact dissipated upon the shore followed by a moment of calm that seemed to last forever.

Just then a tiny solitary bubble of air appeared on the surface of the water, followed seconds later by another and yet more until eventually the whole of Lake Glaslyn appeared to boil furiously.

Suddenly the lake exploded skywards as if a volcano had erupted at its heart turning the mountain sky into a raging storm while all around water fell in torrents. Isla took refuge from the deluge by scampering into the recess of a large bolder, waiting for the downpour to subside.

As quickly as it began the crescendo receded leaving only the delicate pitter-patter of water droplets. She crept cautiously from her refuge to gauge the extent of the aftershock. Everywhere she trod there were pools of water draining away quickly into small tributaries as if the whole area was once a tidal estuary being drawn back out to sea.

Nothing remained of the once great lake other than the numerous diminutive streams that poured back into its basin and a gigantic mountain of armour plated scales.

Isla climbed up onto the boulder to get a better view. And there in front of her was a huge dragon. So gigantic and imposing was it, that when it stretched out it colossal scaly wings it cast the mountains into darkness. Its long powerful neck held aloft a dark menacing glare, with eyes as black as the deepest caves and teeth as long as sabres. This was a creature of the underworld and spine chilling nightmares, its presence striking fear into all who looked upon it. But Isla did not fear it as it was a creature of her making. Born of the earth as she was and created by her to protect the Grayweald from Lhanna and her armies.

Now was the time to fulfil its destiny.

"Fly!" she shouted as loud as she could. "Fly and save the Grayweald!"

The dragon reared up and let out a deafening roar and burnt the sky red with its fiery breath before beating its enormous wings and taking to the sky. As Isla watched the creature disappear across the horizon she began to ruminate if what she had done was right. She never intended on harming anyone but knew she had to stop the slaughter of the innocent. Ironically fighting a battle with her conscience which no dragon could help her win.

Back at the Grayweald the goblins fought on in desperation for their lives against the relentless force that pushed them further and further back. The land was strewn with the fallen and the earth ran red from the carnage.

The goblins retreated into the mountains and tried in vain to regroup but it was hopeless.

Or so it would have seemed, as just then when it looked as if all hope had failed them Lhanna's army suddenly stopped dead in its tracks, distracted by something in the distant sky. A huge object could be seen flying towards them and it was gradually getting bigger and bigger. The army panicked and began dropping their weapons and running in fear as a gigantic dragon flew in to view right over their heads, roaring and swooping with rage. Lhanna watched aghast as her once mighty army were reduced to nothing more than a horde of scattering mice.

"Stop! Come back here and fight! This creature is no match against me! I am a daughter of the celestial spirit" she yelled furiously, yet still they fled.

So vehemently she grabbed a discarded spear from the ground and rode at full speed towards the creature hurling it at him with great force and accuracy while casting a magical spell. The spear appeared to glow like a flame as it soared across the sky towards the dragon's heart. But this was a beast of earth and sorcery, and the spear simply broke in two. Lhanna could not believe her eyes, she knew her weapon was enchanted and should never have been deflected. Realising the dragon's immense power she was reluctantly forced to retreat with her army back to Lhansburg. The Goblins rejoiced when they saw Lhanna riding off into the distance with her fleeing army and so named the Dragon that saved them that fateful day, Geborga, meaning guardian, protector.

"What an amazing story!" said Laila slumping back in her chair.
"Wait Laila, I have not finished yet" said Yan. "Sure the battle to save the Grayweald was over but you didn't seriously think that Lhanna would simply accept such a defeat. It tortured her mind every day from that day onward, fuelling her hatred and her desire for retribution. She knew that only her sister Isla had the power to conjure up such a

terrifying creature as a dragon and now it was time to get even".

 "But how would she do that?" asked Laila. "Isla has Geborga and he is as powerful as Lhanna, isn't he?".

"Yes but nothing is ever permanent, so it would only be a matter of time" said Yan getting up from his seat and wandering into the kitchen to check on the pottage. Laila sat there pondering his last statement and then looked inquisitively at Jack sitting opposite her who appeared none the wiser. He just shook his head in bewilderment.

Yan returned to the room with two large bowls of steaming pottage and placed them onto the wooden table. "Mind yourself it's hot!" he said sitting down to eat.

"What did you mean when you said it's only a matter of time?" asked Laila.

"Well shortly after Ura valley everything seemed quiet and peaceful again.

Lhanna locked herself away in her magnificent palace. Geborga had disappeared from sight and Isla lived happily in the Grayweald.

Then one quiet summer's day a hunter on horseback appeared in the Grayweald in pursuit of a young stag.

He chased it through the bramble and shrub for
some distance as it darted briskly to and thro to
evade capture until finally he drew forth his bow
and brought the stag to ground. Dismounting from
his horse he was suddenly startled by a womans
voice.

"What brings you into the Grayweald?" she asked.
He turned around to find Isla standing there in a
flowing lace dress of emerald and gold.

"Forgive me my lady, I assumed that this part of the
forest was common land" he said apologetically. He
was the most handsome man she had ever laid eyes
on. In fact one could say he was beautiful. Isla's
eyes opened wide in wonder and she came over
quite faint at the very sight of him. It was a
sensation she had never experienced before in her
life. Her heart began to race and her hands began to
sweat.

"Erm, no it's fine, of course you can hunt" she said
stuttering nervously as if almost intimidated by his
presence. "Forgive my rudeness it's just that I don't
receive many guests in this neck of the woods so I
was a little surprised to see you here that's all".

"Forgive my intrusion my lady" he said bowing
politely. "Do you live in this part of the forest?" he
asked.

"Yes!" replied Isla looking bashful.

"Then I shall make sure I visit here more often in future" he smiled while lifting the young stag onto the back of his steed. "

Please do! You are more than welcome" she said as he mounted his horse.

Leaning down he kissed her hand

"Till the next time my lady" he said, and with that rode off into the woods. Isla watched him like a woman possessed as the figure of the hunter disappeared into the distant trees. Will she ever see him again she wondered.

Well as the months passed the hunter frequently visited Isla in the forest. They grew to know each other well and not surprisingly she fell deeply in love with him. Never revealing her true identity she eventually won over his affections just as nature intended.

Swearing his undying love for her he would often shower Isla with gifts of flowers and animal furs as symbols of his affection, although she never did much care for the furs as she had always protected animals from harm, yet she couldn't bring herself to offend the man she loved so dearly.

One late September he left the Grayweald for a few weeks to hunt the stags that began rutting in the highlands.

"I won't be long my love" he said to her as he prepared to depart early that morning.

"One moment!" said Isla walking over to a small wooden box on her window sill. She opened the box and carefully removed a large bright red ruby from within.

"Take this" she said handing it to him, "Although I can't be with you in person, I can be with you always in spirit".

"This talisman is precious to me and is a symbol of my heart. Carry it with you always and be careful not to lose it".

He studied the shining stone in his hand.

"It is beautiful my love and I am deeply honoured" he said stroking her cheek affectionately

"I shall carry it close to my heart and I'm sure it will bring me luck in the hunt".

They held each other close for a moment before parting company.

"Come back soon" she whispered under her breath as she waved him goodbye.

Two weeks of hard travelling it took the hunter to reach the highlands. Camping out en route in the cold unforgiving September rain before finally sighting the magnificent herds of red deer high in the hills. It was a vision that restored his otherwise fading morale.

He watched as the imposing stags clashed their antlers and tore at the ground in displays of strength, all the time igniting his expectations. Three large stags stood their ground motionless and defiant on the ridge as each measured up the competition.

A deep bark suddenly bellowed a short distance away and immediately the stags retreated hastily off the hill. The hunter watched mesmerized as a huge white stag appeared from out of the mist. It was a giant and stood as big as a shire horse. He rubbed his eyes in disbelief. This was a beast of legend, a mythical creature from every hunters dream. This was the prize of a life time. Leaping on to his horse he rode like the wind up to the ridge in an attempt to flank it but the white hart simply bounded up the steep vertical slopes to the frustration of the hunter who could only watch it vanish as quickly as it came. The next day he picked up the trail of the stag and perused it to the edge of the forest. Tenaciously for miles he chased the beast but to no avail.

Day after day he saw the white hart and day after day it eluded him until one morning whilst tracking in the forest he met a frail old woman out collecting firewood.

"You are wasting your time chasing the white stag" she said. "It can never be caught, as it is said that he is the incarnation of a wise shaman. Many have pursued him for as long as I have been alive and none, no matter how wily have ever so much as got near him" she chuckled.

"Well his fortunes are about to change today my good lady" said the hunter confidently.

"You must know of the bracken pool then" she muttered before trundling off with her bundle of firewood.

"Wait!" shouted the hunter. "What was that you said about a pool?"

"It is the place where the white stag rests every evening of course" she said looking back over her shoulder. Running up he seized her arm.

"Please I beg of you, will you show me the pool where the white hart rests". The old woman looked up at him and shook her head.

"Never!" she snarled. "

But I have spent many days of fruitless pursuit for him my good lady" said the hunter in a desperate tone.

"You and a thousand others before you but that is no concern of mine, I will not betray such a sacred creature, now leave me in peace!" she replied shrugging of his grip.

He reached into his pocket and pulled out three gold coins.

"Take these as a payment for your sacred knowledge" he said. The old woman stopped briefly and looked with interest at the coins.

"That's not enough for such a highly desirable prize" she said.

"It is all I have" replied the hunter.

Then I wish you luck" she laughed.

No wait a moment I have this!" he said holding out the ruby heart reluctantly. Her eyes lit up as she held it in her hands, examining it scrupulously.

"What is its value?" she asked.

"I cannot say what it would fetch but it is of great value to me". "

Why?" the woman asked.

"It is a token of love from my sweetheart" he said solemnly.

"Then it is equivalent in value to the prize you seek" she smiled putting it in her pocket.

"No wait good lady, forgive my imprudence but I cannot give it to you. I'm sorry but it is worth too much to me and I cannot betray my love". The woman stared bitterly at him

"And will I not also be betraying the love of such a sacred creature? For a stone that is only of value to you?"She asked him.

Torn between desire and devotion he paused in thought.

"It is a mythical beast worthy of a king" said the woman softly, pushing him to make a decision.

"The ruby is yours! I accept!" he said hastily.

"A wise decision sir and one you won't regret" she said before pointing towards a grove further down the valley.

"Follow the track to the grove until you come to a large fallen beech tree then head ninety paces west, you will find a pool concealed amongst the bracken. There you shall hide and wait until dusk as that is when the white hart comes to drink at the pool".

The hunter thanked the woman and headed down towards the grove.

Concealing himself amongst the bracken and upwind of the pool he waited with bated breath. Dusk crept into the stillness of the grove and nothing stirred. He listened intensely for the slightest sound but heard nothing at all other than a wood pigeon cooing in the distance.

But just then the white stag appeared out of the mist like an apparition alarming the hunter. Large and intimidating it stood with antlers reaching up like oak boughs. Proud and gracefully it moved with the faintest sound as if it were a shadow in the twilight.

The hunter's heart pounded in his chest as his fumbling hand reached for his quiver.

As focused as a cat in ambush he slowly drew forth an arrow and laid it delicately along the nocking point, never ceasing to take his eyes from the stag. Easing the bow string back until it creaked under the tension he lined up his target and took a deep breath before letting loose his arrow. It flew straight and true, striking the stag in the neck. The creature reared up and shook its head in an attempt to free it. The hunter leapt to his feet with another arrow ready for the kill but the stag just bolted into the thicket with the hunter hot on its heels.

Meanwhile on the other side of the woods the old woman stood examining the beautiful ruby.

Now I am in possession of that which you value so deeply Isla, and it is that which shall prove to be your downfall" she murmured whilst caressing the stone lightly with her fingers

Then the old woman's face gradually began to transmute as the years of fatigue and burden fell from her features. The sag and jowls of age erased under a metamorphic spell until eventually revealing herself in her true form, that of Queen Lhanna

She had deceived the hunter with her sorcery to gain the ruby and had acquired the talisman without force. This meant that she now possessed the charm of Isla's love. Given to her from the man she so adored. Such power over her sister lit up Lhanna's eyes as she grasped the ruby tight in her fist.

Hurling it with great force at a rock she vociferated loudly, hexing the talisman and shattering it into a thousand pieces. Causing the stone to explode and release its energy out into the universe.

At that moment the hunter fell to his knees as if struck by pain. Holding his solar plexus he gasped desperately for breath.

Tolerating his agony he staggered on in eagerness for the stag that now lay mortally wounded a hundred yards ahead of him. Creeping nearer the hunter calmly slipped his dagger from its scabbard. He noticed the creature's laboured breathing as it lay injured amongst the blood soaked bracken of the grove. His heart sank momentarily to see such a gracious creature laying there but knew what he had to do. Plunging his dagger into the heart of the stag he felt its body tremble violently before suddenly transforming into the body of a woman. He leapt backwards in shock and confusion before approaching the woman who lay there cold and still. Lifting her head gently he looked into her eyes and wailed uncontrollably. For they were the eyes of his beloved Isla

"What have I done!" he screamed as he held tight the body of his true love. The pain of grief tore at his heart and soul as he mourned the overwhelming pain of such a loss. At that moment Isla's frail corpse crumbled into dust in his arms and disappeared upon the wind swirling in frantic squalls until there was nothing left.

Realising what he had done the hunter rode immediately at speed to Isla's home in the woods only to find her lying dead upon her bed" said Yan as he tried to suppress his feelings at the conclusion of his tale.

Taking a deep breath he sighed as if he too had felt the hunter's pain while Jack just lowered his head solemnly. Laila wiped the tears from her eyes.

"How sad" she said shaking her head. "So Isla was the stag all along?" she said.

"No!" exclaimed Yan "The stag was merely an animate being; an apparition conjured up by Lhanna to deceive the hunter into giving her the talisman. With the love talisman in her possession she had the power to put a curse on Isla, and by destroying the charm she could destroy her".

"What happened to the Hunter after that?" Laila asked.

"He eventually became a servant of Lhanna's, possessed by her magic. A hollow shell of a man who no longer knew how to love, his mind corrupted by her evil".

In the legend of the story I will only refer to him as the hunter and not by his real name".

"Why is that?" Laila asked looking somewhat baffled.

"Because when he was a hunter he was a good man who won the heart of the beautiful Isla. Now he is a corrupt and despised servant of Lhanna's. Some call him her prince but others know him as Ibora!" replied Yan with distaste.

Chapter Eight

Knap stone Circle

Laila was deeply moved by the story of Isla's demise at the hands of Lhanna, but couldn't quite comprehend why Ibora would become a servant to the woman who had not only deceived him but took the life of his true love, until Yan began to divulge more.

"After Isla was taken from this world Lhanna became the absolute supreme being. A deity worshipped by millions and holding power over almost every living thing, even the heartbroken Ibora.

By putting him under her spell she made him her consort and a shell of his former self. He was now her slave, forced to search the land for gold and other precious object to appease his rapacious Queen, and in return she gifted him with the shamanic powers to do her bidding. By transforming himself into magpie he was able to move around unnoticed, collecting precious objects as well as spying on anyone with dissenting opinions opposed to the new imperialistic dogma. The Witches and Wizards, who revered the natural order of things as Isla once did where now considered subversive elements and were hunted down and turned to stone, and their venerated trees burnt to the ground during a dark time in our history known as the Banishing.

"I heard about the Banishing!" said Laila interrupting

"It was a terrible time of persecution. Many were exiled and sought refuge by living like hermits in the remotest parts of the Grayweald".

"Were they safe there?" asked Laila.

"Well at least they are for the time being. You see after her defeat at Ura valley Lhanna never dare enter the Grayweald again. One can only assume it was through a fear of her presence reawakening Geborga. Even the mere mention of his name would chill her to the core. Only bands of mercenaries raid the Grayweald now, enlisted purely to locate and destroy the venerable world trees.

"So does Geborga live in the Grayweald?" asked Laila.

"I have no idea where he is if I am to be honest. After Ura valley he was never seen again. Some say he still lives beneath Lake Glaslyn and will one day return again, others that he died when Isla departed this world. One thing I do know for sure and that is he is not here anymore. And as long as Lhanna remains unaware of that fact then the Grayweald is safe for now.

Right let's eat before the pottage ends up turning into cold slurry" he said abruptly dipping some buttered bread into his bowl.

There followed a short interval of clattering spoons in bowls and slurping before the cacophony culminated in Yan belching, followed by the exclamation "Delicious!".

"Did you enjoy that Laila?" he asked.

"Yes it was very nice, thank you Yan".

"Would you be so kind as to give me a hand with the washing up? Jack is a little bit too big to help out in the kitchen" said Yan collecting the bowls and cutlery from the table.

"Of course" said Laila following him into the kitchen.

The walls of the kitchen were lined with shelves full of glass jars containing herbs and spices and all manner of wild plants and seeds.

"Here, I'll wash and you can dry" said Yan handing her a cloth.

"Ok!" she smiled. "Do you mind me asking you something?" said Laila whilst drying the cutlery.
 "Sure as long as it's not about Geography" he jested.
"No it's not about that" she replied naively. "Is it true that you're a wizard?"
Yan glanced discreetly over his shoulder into the library at Jack.
"And who told you I was a wizard?" he asked looking at him accusingly. Jack said nothing, he just raised his shoulders as a gesture of his innocence.
"It was a Goblin who told me" Laila replied.
"Well your Goblin was correct, I am a wizard" he said casually rinsing a bowl in the cold water.
"Really? That's amazing! I have never met a real wizard before, but looking at you I would never have thought you were one" she said.
"Oh and what do wizards look like then?" he asked.
"Well you don't have a long beard for a start" she replied to which Yan chuckled loudly.
"You've been reading too many children's books" he said. "Long beards are very dated and not practical. They just get in the way and look scruffy"
"Do you have a magic staff then?" she asked.

"No, only really old wizards tend to have them but more as a walking aid than an instrument of power".

"How about a wand?"

"No I don't need them but apprentices find wands useful as a tool to help them focus their energy".

"Well what do you have?" asked Laila looking a little disillusioned.

"I do have a pointy hat and blue robes incorporating moon symbols"

"Really!" she barked excitedly.

"Yes but they are purely a ceremonial garment, not something I wear every day. They help to put me in the mood for magic, just the same as when you get dressed up to go to a party, it makes you feel different. And in magic it's all about feeling and being focused" he said wandering back into the library and picking a book from the shelf with a pentagram on the cover.

"It's all very well reading about how to do it but you have to know how it works, you have to be receptive to the energy that connects all living things". Laila wasn't too interested in the science lesson, she just wanted to see some magic and thought this was a good opportunity to ask

"So do you know how to change into something else, like an animal?" she asked.

" If you mean can I perform anifornum, of course its simple" he said and before she could blink Yan transformed himself into Jay, flying up high onto Jack's shoulder, then swiftly gliding into the middle of the room before reappearing as himself. Laila and Jack were both totally astounded.

"Wow! How do you do that?" asked Laila jumping up and down euphorically.

"By knowing that one's form is merely the perception of one's mind" he replied, as if it was as easy to undertake as sitting down.

"What do you mean?"

"Well you have to really believe you're a bird to become one" he said. "You have to take on its characteristics; you have to feel your arms getting lighter as your wings appear".

"Do you think you could you teach me how to do that Yan?" asked Laila tugging his hand.

"Yes go on Yan! It would be interesting to see if Laila possesses any magic" said Jack nodding his head and hinting to Yan that this would be a good opportunity to confirm any doubts.

"Oh please Yan!" begged Laila.

"Alright! Alright just stop badgering me!" said Yan placing a log on the fire and stoking the embers with a stick. "You have to realise that you have got to believe in order for this to work".

"I do believe!" said Laila eagerly.

"Ok let's begin; firstly you have to select the creature you intend to be. Most witches use creatures referred to as Familiars as they are easiest to master such as Hares, Cats, Crows, frogs, etcetera"

"I would like to be a crow please Yan so that I can fly like you did" said Laila.

"Ok! Now close your eyes and imagine you're really a crow and not yourself anymore.

Can you feel your nose becoming long and pointed like a beak, and the nimbleness of your body and arms as your wings begin to grow? " he asked.

"Yes I can!" yelled Laila leaping up on to the bench and waving her arms whilst making a loud "Qwark! Qwark!" sound unaware that no transformation had actually taken place at all. Yan and Jack glanced uncomfortably at each other as Laila stood on the bench doing an embarrassingly bad crow impression.

"It's working Yan I can feel it!" said Laila, but Yan just shook his head in bewilderment.

"Oh my word Laila I don't believe it! You have transformed yourself into a crow!" bellowed Jack whilst winking at Yan and trying desperately to suppress his laughter.

"Take to the air my magnificent Corvus and let us see you fly!" he said sarcastically as Laila leapt from the bench towards the ceiling flapping her arms frantically. Only to come crashing back down again onto the study table and somersaulting onto Jack's lap.

Yan and Jack then roared with laughter.

"That was brilliant!" Yan chuckled.

Even Laila saw the funny side and couldn't resist joining in the mirth.

After the amusement of Laila's disastrous attempt at anifornum had subsided Yan got up from his seat and peered out of the library window at the waxing moon overhead.

"I have some business to attend to tonight, so I may be gone for a little while. There's some firewood in the shed and food in the cupboards so please make yourselves at home" he said

"Where are you going?" asked Laila.

"I have to see someone, but I should be back around sunrise at the latest" he smiled before closing the door behind him.

"I think I had better fetch some more firewood before we run out. I won't be a minute" said Jack squeezing out of the door, leaving Laila sitting cosily by the open fire.

As he made his way towards the shed he bumped
into Yan walking across the lawn dressed in his
ceremonial robe and tall pointed hat.

"I had a feeling you had some important spiritual
business to attend to" said Jack admiring his attire.

"Yes my friend I still have a few questions that need
answering regarding the Brisingamen so I will need
to consult the ancestors at the Knap stone circle.
Take care of Laila, I should be back by dawn" he
said patting Jack on the arm.

"Safe journey!" said Jack as he watched the wizard
wandering off into the darkness.

After collecting some wood from the shed Jack
returned to the library to find Laila fast asleep on
the bench by the fire. Gently he laid a blanket over
her and placed a log on the embers.

"Let's hope Yan can help you get home" he
whispered before settling down with a good book
on Ginkgo's.

Yan meanwhile made his up way through the
moonlit woods that surrounded the silver
Mountains. His shadow looming large and distorted
across the stems of the soaring pine trees. Silent and
at one with its surroundings yet unperturbed by the
distant howls of wolves and other creatures of the
night, following the hidden tracks that only the

wiliest foxes were acquainted with, heading to the circle of the ancients.

Eventually he exits the pine forest and ascends a high narrow ridge overlooking the trees before making his way up a little further towards a knap where a huge circle of roughly hewn stones stood pitched upon end.

Like a small gathering come to pay homage to the moon, they appear almost out of place in the untamed isolation of the mountainside and yet oddly belonging to it. Yan proceeds to skirt the periphery of the circle reciting an incantation under his breath before entering the heart of the monument. Once inside he kneels down in the direction of the moon and glances around at the stones encircling him. The light from the moon causes the monoliths to sparkle in the caliginosity, as the silica refracts the moon rays, making them appear as if dusted in a coating of sugar.

Yan removes some incense and a white candle from his pocket and sets them ablaze whilst repeating his incantation. The smoky essence of jasmine fills the circle with a fragrant mist, as subtle murmurs begin to emanate from the stones. Ancient voices awoken from their slumber, returning to speak their wisdom once more.

"Yan Overton you have come here in search of answers" whispered a voice from one of the monoliths. Yan turns to see the carved features of an aged man's face slowly appearing from within the stone before his eyes. His features hardened and furrowed by the toil of longevity.

"A wizard learned in the sacred arts seeks our council?" said another venerable face from an adjacent stone. "Omniscient brothers I seek your guidance. A young girl by the name of Laila has come to me from beyond this world in search of the legendary Brisingamen which she once had in her keeping, but has now has fallen into the possession of Queen Lhanna" said Yan.

"The Brisingamen does not reside in this world" declared the tallest of the monoliths.

"Freja is the keeper of the Brisingamen" said another recumbent stone.

"But is it not true that she lost the necklace?" asked Yan seemingly confused.

"No it is not true!" they replied in unison

"But I don't understand? I heard that Lhanna's servant Ibora recently passed through one of the last remaining spirit doors on a quest for the necklace and returned with the mythical jewel".

"It is true that he travelled to an alternative place in time and returned with a jewel but it was not the

Brisingamen. The necklace that Lhanna now
procures has no power or value whatsoever" said
the stones. Yan shook his head in bewilderment
"But surely Ibora would not have journeyed into
this other realm unless he was absolutely certain of
it being the sacred necklace"
"He was deceived" the stones replied
"By whom?" Yan asked, but there came no reply.
"What about the girl? Why is she here? What part
does she have to play in this?" he asked.
"We have no knowledge of the girl; she is not of
this world. But if destiny has lead her to you in the
search to recover the stolen necklace, regardless of
how insignificant the necklace may appear you
must see that she fulfils that destiny and returns
from whence she came with the necklace back in
her possession as soon as possible, as her presence
in our world will affect the course of future events.
You must act quickly to maintain balance, in not
just this realm but that of the young girls. Retrieve
the necklace by whatever means you can and
deliver her to the last ancient hawthorns at Puoa
Landum. But beware Yan you must not enter the
city of Lhansburg in your quest for the necklace or
the same fate that met us will befall you. Lhanna is
well known for her aversion to wizards and she will
sense your presence in the web that binds all

transcendent souls. The girl must take this journey alone or with a mortal being you can trust, in order to enter Lhansburg undetected. Yan stood up and held his arms high.

"Blessings to you my omniscient brothers and hail to the moon!" he hollered before distinguishing his candle and heading back down into the pine forest

As the morning sun began to rise the welcoming sight of Dial house homed into view amongst the trees. Yan had travelled quite some distance through the night with plenty to deliberate on his journey back, and by the time he had reached home he was weary yet absolute about his objectives. Jack stood waiting in the middle of the lawn with a hot mug of tea in his hand.

"Here you go Yan, the pines told me you were on your way so I thought I would make you a brew" he said handing him the warm beverage.

"Ah lovely" said Yan taking a sip and sitting down on a garden bench.

"How is Laila?" he asked.

"She's still asleep, all the excitement from yesterday has worn her out" he smiled.

"I know how she feels, I have had some a pretty staggering revelations to deal with myself" said Yan leaning back in his seat.

"It appears that Laila's necklace is not the Brisingamen as I had initially assumed" he said with an air of disappointment in his voice. Jack grimaced with intrigue.

"Not the Brisingamen? Then what is it?"

"Just an ordinary child's necklace by all accounts, apparently of no significance, let alone power: Ibora was deceived into believing it was the Brisingamen, for what purpose and by whom I do not know. The sad fact is that Laila by no fault of her own, or so it seems has unfortunately been caught up in all of this"

"Poor Laila! So she was telling the truth all the time".

"Yes I know, and there was I doubting her integrity" said Yan hanging his head in shame

"So what happens now?" asked Jack.

"We get her necklace back and escort her to the ancient hawthorn in Puo Landum" Yan replied.

"That is totally impossible" said Jack with resounding certitude.

"Laila's necklace is now in the possession of the most powerful sorceress on earth and she has locked it away in her impenetrable palace at Lhansburg. To attempt such an outlandish enterprise would be tantamount to suicide. And even if by some miracle you did manage to retrieve the necklace you would then have to travel with a 'Sapien' to Puo Landum which is in the heart of Goblin country, it is not a realistic proposition. If the necklace is of no importance then why even run the risk of going to Lhansburg at all? Let me take Laila from here straight to Puo Landum At least in the company of a Green Man she will pass unnoticed through the Goblin lands".

"I cannot dispute that your discourse is logical Jack and I would normally agree with you, but I believe that everything happens for a reason which would suggest that Laila's necklace was not accidently mistaken for the Brisingamen as we would be lead to presume, but is of some deeper relevance. And if destiny is somehow predetermined then she is also here for a reason".

"And what reason would that be?" asked Jack.

"I wish I knew my old friend, all we can determine for certain is that she came into this world in search of a stolen necklace and so I must do my best to see she that she gets it back"

"But that would mean travelling to Lhansburg!" said Jack in dismay.

"Exactly!" Yan groaned. "I never said it was going to be easy"

"You can say that again! How on earth do you propose on getting her into the citadel without

Lhanna knowing? She is as ubiquitous as a Green Man" Said Jack getting in a fluster.

"Don't you think I've already thought about that Jack? I spent the whole evening mulling over that exact question, and as luck would have it I have come up with a solution.

It is obvious that neither I nor you will be able to accompany Laila into Lhansburg as our presence there would instantly give her away, so later today I will have a word with my apprentice Kieran. I will ask him to escort her to the city where they can liaise with my old friend Lon Atilla. Lon will get the necklace for Laila and they will rendezvous with you in Lhansburg woods. From there you can take her to the ancient hawthorn in Puo Landum".

"Who is Lon Atilla?" asked Jack.

"He is an old friend I have known for many years who lives in Lhansburg. He is a Changeling, half Sprite and half Human although to the onlooker he does appear predominantly more human in form. But being that he is also genetically a Sprite means that he possesses the ability to move faster than the blink of an eye if he so chooses. Anyway, he used to work as a spit boy in the citadel kitchens and knows the palace like the back of his hand. He would often boast about an occasion where he had audaciously frequented Lhannas chambers using his great celerity and stealth to steal gold coins and other objects" Yan chuckled.

"But surely it is impossible to enter Lhanna's chambers? She has guards everywhere and she would easily feel the presence of a Sprite in the citadel"

"Yes Jack but as I said, he is not a Sprite he is a Changeling which means that his biological human aspect helps cloak him from her extrasensory perception. In a city filled with other humans he is psychically invisible and far too fast for any of her guards to see".

"Can we trust him?" asked Jack.

"I have heard it said that Lon is a bit of an opportunist but I trust him wholeheartedly. And anyhow he is our only hope of getting the necklace back so we don't have much choice" said Yan putting his finger to his lips as he watched Laila appearing from the house with hair like tangled wool.

"Good Morning Laila! Did you sleep well?" asked Jack.

"Yes I had a really deep sleep" she said rubbing her puffy eyes.

"Well I will go and make some breakfast" said Yan giving up his seat to Laila.

"What are we doing today Jack?" asked Laila.

"Yan has arranged for you to travel to Lhansburg to collect your necklace" said Jack.

"Really! That's amazing! I thought Lhanna had it? How did he get it back?" asked Laila.

"Well he hasn't quite procured it as yet but Yan assures me that an acquaintance of his who lives in the city should be able to obtain it for you. All you have to do is make your way there, and his friend will do the rest". "Does that mean that you won't be coming with me Jack?"

 "I'm afraid it does Laila, I am a Green Man and could never enter the city. I will travel with you up until the borders of Lhansburg wood and then I must return to the forest" he said.

Yan then came teetering up the lawn with his wicker tray loaded with food and crockery.

"Here we are! A nice bit of scram to get you started for the day" he said putting the tray on to the garden bench. "Jack says that we are going to the city, and your friend there is going to get my necklace back for me" said Laila gleefully before biting into a bread roll. Yan looked at Jack with an expression of unease and let out a short cough to clear his throat.

"I won't be going Laila" he said to which she returned a perplexing glare.

"You see us Wizards are not really welcomed in Lhansburg so my apprentice Kieran will accompany you there. He knows the way to the city and will take good care of you. I'm expecting him this afternoon actually so I had better get you ready to depart as soon as he arrives".

"I'm ready" said Laila sitting up right.

"You can't go to Lhansburg dressed like that" said Yan running his eye over her rather quaint attire. "Your clothes are alien here and you would draw a lot of unwanted attention. I have some linen in the loft. I will put something together more suitable for you to wear" he said and scurried off into the house.

"Will I be going home?" asked Laila?"

"That's the plan" said Jack "Once you have collected the necklace you will meet up with me in the forest of Lhansburg and from there I will take you to an ancient hawthorn located in a secret location on the far side of the Grayweald. then it is home to Warren pond for you young lady" he smiled.

"That's fantastic! I'm, so excited" exclaimed Laila leaping onto his leg.

"Come now Laila, eat up! You have a long journey ahead of you and you will need the energy" said Jack lifting her back onto the bench.

That afternoon Laila tried on her new clothes which basically consisted of a crudely stitched oversized blue linen tunic that hung below the knees and fastened around the waist with a brown leather belt. "It's not very pretty!" She said staring vacantly at her reflection in the mirror.

"It's perfect" remarked Yan.

"Oh yes indeed! You look just like a Lhansburgian peasant girl" he said admiring his handy work.

"You have to remember Laila you are not at the Warren pond now. This is how people dress in Lhansburg so if you want to blend in then you have to dress accordingly".

Just then there was a knock on the door and a young boy around the age of fifteen entered the room. He was tall slender and handsome with shoulder length wavy blonde hair.

"Good afternoon Yan" he said whilst acknowledging Laila with a polite smile.

"Hello Kieran I would like you to meet my good friend Laila" said Yan.

"I want you to accompany her to the city of Lhansburg for me".

"Lhansburg!" replied Kieran in bewilderment. "But I thought I was helping you with the composting today sir?". "There has been a change of plan my boy; we have a far more pressing engagement.

Come in to the library I will tell you what I require of you over a cup of tea" said Yan pushing past him in the doorway.

Jack was sitting in the library when Yan, Kieran and Laila walked in, much to Kieran's surprise.

"Oh my word!" he exclaimed on seeing the huge wooden giant sitting in the corner.

"Jack this is my apprentice Kieran, Kieran this is Jack the Green Man" said Yan casually hanging the kettle on the hook by the fire, and paying no regard to the shock on Kieran's face. Jack nodded courteously whilst Kieran smiled back nervously. He then sat down slowly with his eyes fixed in wonderment upon the Green Man.

"Ok here is the plan" said Yan standing with his back to the fire.

"Jack will accompany you and Laila to Lhansburg wood, and from there you will take the main road into the city. Once inside the city you will make your way to the Strugglers Inn near the citadel walls where you will need to locate someone by the name of Lon Attilia. He is a short weasel faced man with a large diagonal scar above his left eye, you can't miss him. He is also a creature of routine and can always be found drinking in the Strugglers so be sure to ask the innkeeper of his possible whereabouts if you have trouble finding him, but avoid any other interaction whilst you are there unless it is absolutely necessary. Once you have made contact with him tell him you are friends of Yan Overton and ask him if he knows the name of my cottage before you hand him this envelope" said Yan passing Kieran a small sealed brown envelope with the word 'Lon' written on it.

"Now you must not lose this is that clear?" said Yan sternly.

"Yes sir!" replied Kieran putting the envelope into his breast jacket pocket.

"Guard it with your life and don't hand it to Lon until he mentions Dial house, is that understood?. He will then give you your instructions from there. You will be travelling incognito with the pseudonym of David and Elizabeth Slight. If anyone asks you; you are brother and sister looking for work in the market"

"May I ask what this is about sir?" asked Kieran curiously.

"It is better you only know what you need to know" said Yan pouring out the tea.

"You will probably need to stay in Lhansburg over night so here's some money for a room. The Strugglers inn has lodgings so I suggest you stay there until you hear back from Lon. Once he has undertaken my request you must make your way immediately towards Lhansburg wood where Jack will be waiting.

Avoid too much unnecessary interaction with anyone, just get in and out as soon as you can" said Yan emphasising the point by thumping his fist on the table.

"I understand sir" said Kieran apprehensively.

"Right! There's not a moment to lose, I have put together some essential supplies for you both in this haversack" said Yan passing Kieran a large grey canvas sack with a rope strap. "Jack will be going with you as far as Lhansburg wood as I said and from there you're on your own" Kieran's eyes were filled with anticipation of what was to come which Yan quickly sensed and so gave him a fatherly embrace.

"I trust you will do me proud my boy" he said patting him on the back.

"Can I ask you something sir?" said Kieran with a curious expression.

"If it's regarding my absence on this trip then I'm afraid that is a conversation for another day" said Yan turning away.

"No actually it was about that cup of tea you said you was about to make me" he replied cheekily.

"Go on, be off with you!" smirked Yan whilst pretending to kick him up the backside for his impertinence.

They all huddled out of the door chuckling towards the gate before saying their farewells.

"I will see you in a couple of days then" said Yan confidently shaking Kieran's hand.

"I won't let you down sir" said the determined young man proudly before parting company. Yan then walked over to Jack.

Looking up at the lofty Green Man he could do nothing more than smile.

"You are truly a gift of nature Jack and I am as always, honoured to be in your presence" he said. To which Jack shook his hand and bowed his head respectfully.

And finally the old wizard approached Laila who stood a short distance from the others.

"Goodbye Laila, I hope you return home safely with your necklace to Warren pond. The boys will take good care of you" he said shaking her formally by the hand but Laila couldn't contain herself and just threw her arms around him tightly, as she felt a closeness to the avuncular old wizard.

"Thank you Yan for everything I'm going to miss you" she said sorrowfully.

"And I will miss you too" he said looking somewhat awkward in receiving such an affectionate hug.

"Come on now Laila put Yan down" said Jack with a chortle.

"Yes you had best make tracks while the sun is up" said Yan. "And when you get back to Warren pond you can tell your friends that not all wizards have beards and staffs!"

"I will! And thanks again" she said running off to catch up with Kieran and Jack who had wandered off a few hundred yards ahead.

Yan stood by the gate and watched as the three of them departed for Lhansburg. In his stomach he felt anxious but knew he had done all he possibly could. All he could do now was wait and hope.

Everyone was quite contemplative on the march to Lhansburg wood. For mile upon mile they quietly perambulated the thickets and coarse bracken without uttering a word. Two juveniles pursuing their lofty ligneous guardian through the unspoilt deciduous woodlands like cubs to a bear.

Jack in silent communion with the trees and Laila musing of home. And poor Kieran reserved yet totally discombobulated about the whole adventure.

"So how is it that you know Yan Miss?"He asked as they negotiated their way through some vicious brambles. "I think you had better refer to her as Elizabeth. It may appear a little formal if you're going to try and pass your selves off as brother and sister in Lhansburg" said Jack.

"Yes you're right Sir, forgive me" said the young man graciously.

"And you don't need to call me Sir either" demanded Jack firmly. "You can stop staring at me as well" he said glaring down at the ogling youth.

"I am so sorry Jack" he said nervously. "I know it's not polite but I have never met, let alone seen a Green Man in my whole life".

"I never would have guessed" mocked Jack to which Laila burst into laughter.

"Jack doesn't mean to be rude he is really nice when you get to know him" she smiled as Jack marched on ahead.

"I met Yan through Jack since you ask" said Laila.

"So do you know what all this is about? The journey to Lhansburg I mean" asked Kieran.

"It's better you only know what you need to know" bellowed the ever attentive Jack, in reciting Yan's behest.

There then followed a brief spell of awkward silence before Laila began to speak again.

"So what do you do then Kieran?" she asked.

"I'm Yan's apprentice" he replied.

"Wow! So you're going to be a wizard one day then?".

"Well yes! but I have got a long way to go yet. Yan says I have to identify the names and uses of every plant, shrub and tree and after I have done that I must spend a year in the wilderness in total isolation before I am ready to begin learning the sacred knowledge and incantations of wizardry".

"That sounds really tough! Well you are in good company here because Jack knows all the names of the trees and plants and he can talk to them too can't you Jack?" said Laila.

"Yes" he mumbled nonchalantly before stopping dead in his tracks as if alarmed by something ahead. "Shush! He said. "The trees tell me there is a horse and wagon some distance away on the main road heading towards Lhansburg. There is only one male occupant and he is appears to be carrying fruit and vegetables on board. Perfect! We can head it off east of here if we hurry".

"Hang on Jack why are we chasing after a wagon?"

"Because there is a strong possibility that it is heading to Lhansburg!"

"But I thought you were taking us to Lhansburg?" said Laila looking bewildered.

"I am Laila but I can only take you so far before I start running into people working and living near the city. And anyhow you stand a much better chance getting in on the back of a traders wagon than you would by trying to walk in through the gates".

"But what if he doesn't give us a ride?" asked Laila.

"Don't worry he will" said Kieran confidently. "I may be only an apprentice wizard but one of the first things Yan taught me was the art suggestion".

"There you are Laila!" said Jack pointing at Kieran in approval. "You have a fledgling wizard with you. Now come on lets be quick, we have to seize this opportunity!" he said grabbing her by the hand and dragging her off briskly through the forest.

The way to the main road was just less than twelve miles so Jack ended up having to carry Laila and Kieran on his back for most of the way so as to make up time. It was early evening when they finally arrived by the roadside and Laila was feeling a little apprehensive.

"I'm scared Jack" she said looking down the long wide dusty road that lead off into the horizon.

"You have nothing to fear Laila. The trees will be watching over you all the way as will I" he said putting her mind to rest.

"You are the best friend I have ever had" she said embracing his towering leg affectionately.

"Thank you Laila" replied Jack bashfully. "Now quickly you two, the wagon approaches so I have to go but I will see you in a day or two in Lhansburg woods. Goodbye and good luck!" he said before disappearing silently without a trace.

Laila and Kieran looked at each other apprehensively as they stood alone by the remote roadside. They each felt the disquiet of uncertainty. And then in the distance a horse and wagon trundled into view.

"Leave the talking to me Laila" said Kieran hailing the wagon down as it drew near.

"Whoa!" said the driver bringing his horse to a stop.

"I'm sorry to trouble you Sir but would you be by any chance be heading to the city of Lhansburg?" asked Kieran holding onto the horses bridle.

"Yes I am, why?" asked the driver suspiciously. He was a short rotund man with silver grey cropped hair and rosy red cheeks. His clothes were drab and worn as if he had been working out in the fields.

"My sister and I are travelling to the city in search of work, would you have any room for us on your wagon?" asked Kieran courteously.

The man looked over his shoulder to the back of his fully laden wagon and let out a sigh

"No! I'm sorry but my wagon is full" he said.

"Now if you don't mind I have to be on my way".

"It is a lonely journey to Lhansburg and you will be very pleased of the company" said Kieran looking the man straight in the eye.

"It is a lonely journey to the city so climb aboard! I could do with some company" echoed the man in a sudden volt-face which bewildered Laila.

"Come on Elizabeth!" said Kieran climbing up onto the back of the wagon and holding out his hand.

"How did you do that?" she whispered under her breath as he pulled her on board.

"Just a little trick" he said with a wry wink.

"Are we all comfortable?" asked the man.

"Yes thanks!" replied Laila.

"Move on!" He commanded the horse and of they went.

"The names Horatio by the way" Said the stout man politely.

"I'm David and this is my sister Elizabeth" said Kieran from the back of the wagon.

"How far have you come David?" Horatio asked.

"Not far" replied Kieran laconically.

"And you're looking for work you say?"

"Yes that's right".

"Well I might be able to help you there" said Horatio.

"I have a stall in the market where I sell my vegetables and it can get a little busy sometimes, so if you want a couple of days work I could do with a hand".

"Great! Thanks" said Kieran looking at Laila with an apathetic expression.

"Where will you be staying in the city, do you have any family there?"

"We have an uncle there who will be putting us up. I must say the countryside around here is beautiful" said Kieran swiftly detracting from the probing chit chat. "Yes it is! The soil is very good" remarked Horatio as he looked out in reverence upon the lush verdure.

Hazel and field maples divided pastures into neat rectangular plots, washing the breathtaking scenery into a pastiche of emerald hues. Miles of overgrown hedgerows meandered ceaselessly along the roadside with only a handful of rustic small holdings appearing intermittently en route. Cattle and sheep grazed upon the tranquil hills where rivers ambled beneath a cobalt sky. This was truly a paradise to behold and one that captivated the soul.

"We should reach the city by nightfall I reckon"
said Horatio as the evening drew in.

"Is it far?" Laila asked.

"No not at all, look you can see the citadel tower
from here" he said pointing to a tall grey column
rising up high above the far off distant trees.

"My goodness!" said Laila with astonishment.

"You haven't seen anything yet" Horatio chuckled
as they cantered on to Lhansburg.

Chapter Nine

Lhansburg

The overwhelming magnitude of Lhansburg was quite an intimidating sight to greet the observer as it loomed ominously into view against the barren untamed mountains that surrounded it. The sky was as black as jet but for the plenitude of stars and the effulgent light that emanated from the city. The roads all around were a hive of activity filled with the sound of a thousand voices shouting and laughing, talking and trading in a jangled whirlpool of commotion.

Beggars and thieves grappled amongst the pandemonium whilst bards sang their melodious tales beneath the profusion of flaming torches that illuminated the merchant's marquees.

Laila watched enthralled by the spectacle as she had at Grasmont. The humdrum of Lhansburg life was as fascinating to her as anything she had witnessed so far and thus her excitement and anticipation began to grow.

The temperature was cold that evening as the little wagon approached the bustling city gates with their huge granite towers.

Armed sentries controlling rite of passage into the city stopped Horatio as he drew nearer.

"Halt!" ordered one of them approaching the vehicle. He walked slowly around the wagon examining it carefully whilst scrutinizing Laila suspiciously.

"Do you have a traders permit?" he asked Horatio.

"Yes officer!" he replied handing him a piece of neatly folded paper. "The children are hired help" he said restlessly as the sentry perused over his permit for what seemed like an eternity.

"Ok Mr Smythe you may proceed" he said with a stony eyed glare as they trundled off into the metropolis. Laila looked up as they passed beneath the magnificent stone arch that lead into the city. Gigantic white marble effigies of a beautiful slender woman in pleated robes were everywhere to be seen looking down imposingly upon the occupants of Lhansburg. Her delicate flawless features intricately carved with the intention of striking awe into the onlooker.

"Who is that woman?" Laila asked.

"I presume you are joking!" laughed Horatio.
"That is Queen Lhanna of course" he said in a
matter of fact way, whilst Laila stared on in wonder.
"So where does your uncle live?" asked Horatio as
they clattered down the narrow cobblestone streets.
"He said he would meet us at the Strugglers Inn"
replied Kieran.
"I know the place well. If you give me a hand
unloading my stock I will take you there" said
Horatio to which Kieran reluctantly agreed.
They pulled into a side street full of traders
offloading bread, meat and fish from carts and
wagons. The stench from the seafood and livestock
was overwhelming amongst the scent of burning
tallow.
"Hello Horatio! Should be a good day tomorrow"
hollered a man carrying a basket of apples.
"What time do you call this!" quipped another.
It was a friendly lively atmosphere and Horatio was
obviously quite a popular figure amongst the stall
holders.
"It's always like this before market day" said
Horatio dismounting. "Now could you pass me
down those vegetable baskets please David" he said
unlocking the padlock to a dilapidated timber shed.
Inside it looked like a small barn with bales of hay
and thick timber beams.

"We will stack the baskets over there" he said pointing to a corner of the store. "This is where I bunk down when I'm in Lhansburg" he said.

"Why don't you rent a room?" Kieran asked.

"Because there wouldn't be anything left in here by the morning to sell" Horatio laughed.

After unloading the wagon they rode onto the Strugglers Inn.

It was a small red brick tavern close to the citadel walls with an elegantly painted wooden sign outside of a man being taken to the gallows by a lynch mob.

"I'll come in with you" said Horatio climbing down from the wagon.

"There's no need, we will be fine I'm sure" said Kieran brashly.

"That's as maybe David but I also happen to be quite parched and they serve good ale in here" he said tethering his horse.

The atmosphere inside the inn was boisterous, and filled to the brim with the raucous laughter and loud conversations from the diverse cross section of society that occupied the tables. From gentlemen to yeoman and the unsavoury looking vagabonds who shuffled about in the dimly lit corners. Laila couldn't help but feel a little uneasy amongst the din and the curious looks they received as they approached the bar.

"Yes, what would you like?" asked the landlady raising her voice to be heard above the drone.

"Two pints of your finest ale please and a mug of punch for the young lady" Horatio replied.

"I don't drink" said Kieran tapping Horatio gently on the shoulder.

"Well it's about time you did" he chuckled "And anyway it's impolite to refuse a drink.

We will grab that table over in the corner" he said carrying the drinks awkwardly between his fingers across the crowded floor.

"Please excuse me a moment Horatio, I will be with you in shortly" said Kieran before turning to speak privately with the landlady.

"Forgive me Madam but do you know if a Lon Attilia is in tonight?"

"No, Why who wants to know?" she asked with a suspicious look.

"I'm just a friend. I was supposed to meet him here".

"Sorry I can't help you" she said.

"Oh ok! But if you do see him would you be so kind as to tell him I'm looking for him?" asked Kieran to which she nodded listlessly.

"Do you have any rooms available?" he asked hesitantly.

"There are two rooms free at the moment but they won't be free for long as it's market day tomorrow".

"Great! I wish to take one" he said pulling out the money that Yan had given him.

"That's a ha'penny a night and that don't include food" she said handing Kieran a brass skeleton key with the number three scratched into it.

After paying her, he and Laila joined Horatio at the table.

"Where have you been? I've almost finished my ale" he said lifting a half filled ceramic mug. "Now come on drink up!" he insisted.

"I have never drunk ale before" said Kieran looking apprehensively at the frothy bronze beverage.

"Go on! Get it down you!" said Horatio. "What's the matter with you? It ain't poison" he laughed.

Kieran lifted the mug to his lips and began to slowly sip the ale. Each mouthful he swallowed was followed by a wrenching expression of distaste, yet still he managing to finish his pint.

"Right it's your round!" said Horatio slamming his empty mug down hard onto the table.

"You mean you want more?"Asked Kieran surprised.

"Well it is customary to buy a drink after you have been bought one.
And don't leave me drinking on my own either, get yourself one" Horatio called as Kieran wobbled off to the bar.

As the evening progressed Kieran began to feel a little worse for wear. Not possessing a strong head for ale it wasn't long before he ended up slumped face down across the table
"Is he ill?" Laila asked with concern.
"No, nothing a good night's sleep won't put right" said Horatio helping the inebriated Kieran to his feet and dragging him upstairs to his room. Laila rummaged through his pocket to retrieve the room key whilst Horatio assisted the young wizard to his bunk.
"I'll pass by in the morning to see how he is. Good night Elizabeth" he said closing the door gently behind him and making his way back down stairs to the bar.
On his way down the stairwell he noticed a small brown envelope on one of the steps. Picking it up he examined it with interest.
"It must have fallen out of the lad's pocket". I'll give it to him tomorrow" he mumbled before putting it safely into his pocket.

 Meanwhile Laila sat on a stool in the cold
emptiness of the room. The dim light from the street
outside filtered through the gap in the window
shutter. She looked at the unconscious Kieran
draped across the mattress and leant back against
the wall and began to think of home again before
falling soundly off to sleep.

Early the following morning Laila was awoken
suddenly by the sound of restless horses and raised
voices coming from outside in the street. This was
immediately followed by the thunder of boots
racing up the stairs towards her room and the door
being smashed clean off its hinges.
In charged several heavily built soldiers in black
hoods shouting aggressively and tearing the room
apart.
"Get the girl!" ordered one of the men.
Before Laila could think she was seized roughly by
the arms and dragged backwards down the stairs
kicking and screaming. Kieran leapt from his
slumber in the commotion and tried desperately to
help Laila but his attempt was futile as three of the
soldiers then set about beating him unconscious and
hauling him out onto the landing.
"Leave the boy!" ordered the captain. "We came
here for the girl!" he said. So callously they

abandoned Kieran at the top of the stairwell face
down in a pool of blood and departed as quickly as
they came.

Laila meanwhile was hurled into a wooden cage on
the back of a horse drawn carriage and driven at
speed through the cobbled streets of the city into the
heart of the citadel. Peering through the bars of her
pen like some pitiful circus animal hauled out for
the entertainment of prying onlookers who lined the
streets she could only imagine what her fate had in
store.

The horses finally came to rest in a wide square
bailey with high curtain walls filled with soldiers in
red and black tunics. Although they encircled the
cage in which she was detained they stood
motionless to attention with their backs to her. Only
her captures in their black hoods faced Laila if
somewhat apprehensively.

"Don't look into the witch's eyes" advised the
captain as two hooded henchmen holding manacles
stepped forward.

"I'm not a witch! There must be some mistake!"
Laila yelled in terror as she found herself being
manhandled roughly into leg irons and then dragged
unceremoniously across the courtyard into a huge
empty room with no windows and a flat glass roof.

Inside stood a tall elegant man dressed in a black and blue silk tunic, with an ermine collared cape draped neatly over his broad shoulders. He was very well turned out and his resplendent fineries and his persona was dignified yet intimidating as he walked slowly back and forth with his hands behind his back. He never spoke a word. Only the heels of his boots on the stone floor could be heard in the distressing hush of the room as he scrutinized Laila in the arms of his henchmen. And then he suddenly paused as if reaching the destination in his thoughts before turning towards his captive with a contemptuous glare.

"Well Elizabeth what brings you to Lhansburg?" he asked. His tone was soft and gravely with an air of malevolence.

"I have come to look for work in the market" she replied nervously.

"Oh really?" he said sceptically before clapping his hands together loudly making Laila jump with fright. A man then entered the room flanked by two guards.

"Is this the girl?" he asked the man.

"Yes sir!" the gentleman replied dolefully. Laila looked up to see Horatio standing there with a sombre expression on his face.

"Thank you Mr Smythe you have been very cooperative and judicious in bringing this to our attention. You will of course be rewarded for your assistance" said the inquisitor pulling out a small brown envelope from his pocket with the word 'Lon' written across it.

Laila could not believe her eyes. Horatio had betrayed them and sealed her fate for a meagre profit.

"You are free to leave now Mr Smythe" said the inquisitor.

As Horatio was lead from the room he glanced remorsefully over at Laila in the arms of the soldiers before leaving. His eyes etched with the penitence of his treachery.

"I put it to you young lady that you are not only a liar but not a very good one at that" said the inquisitor raising his voice as Horatio left the room. "And further more your name is not Elizabeth at all but Laila. And your intentions were not to work in the market but to steal the Brisingamen from Queen Lhanna. Am I correct?" he asked aggressively to which Laila made no reply.

"There's no point in trying to deny it anyway, your pilfering intent has clearly been disclosed of in this letter, but I also happen to have my own reasons for knowing your story to be nothing more than a total fabrication.

I knew your face seemed familiar to me yet I couldn't quite recollect where I had seen you before until now. Would the name Warren pond be of any significance to you?" he asked with an attentive gaze.

Laila could not disguise her shock. How could he possibly know about the pond she wondered?

"We met their once briefly, but you may not recognise me in this reality" he said.

"So maybe this will jog your memory!" he shouted. And with that he lifted his arms up high above his head and transformed himself into a Magpie. Circling the room and screeching menacingly around her head before returning back to his original form in the centre of the room.

 "Prowler!" gasped Laila.

"The name is Prince Ibora!" he yelled

"And if you think your feeble thaumaturgy is going to reunite you with the Brisingamen you are grossly mistaken. You may possess the power to pass through a spirit door but you will find it a far more arduous undertaking to pass through a prison door" he smirked. "I can make this easy for you or very difficult indeed, that will depend entirely on you.

All you have to do is cooperate. Now tell me the location of the hawthorn tree" he said.

"What hawthorn?" Asked Laila confused.

"You know exactly what hawthorn I'm speaking of. The spirit door of course! The ancient hawthorn you passed through into this world and the one you intend on returning through. Now don't play games with me, I am not a very patient man" he growled.

"I don't know what you are talking about?" replied Laila nervously.

"All I remember is falling asleep under a tree up at Theydon woods, honestly".

"That is not the tree to which I refer and you know it!" he said grabbing Laila by the throat.

"Now I will ask you one more time, where is the tree?" he said staring straight into her eyes.

"I swear I don't know" she gasped fearfully "It was gone when I returned to it! All that was left was a rotten stump!". He then loosened his grip and stood proudly upright with his back turned to her.

"You hereby stand accused of treason and sorcery against the supreme ruler and will stand trial in five days. In the meantime you can stew in the pangs of your iniquity. Take her to the tower!" He ordered, and with that Laila was hauled off without mercy up a narrow set of winding stairs and thrown into a dark damp prison cell.

273

Later that day in another part of Lhansburg, Kieran was being nursed by the staff at the Strugglers Inn.

"Now drink this" the landlord said as he passed Kieran a warm beverage.

"You've taken quite a beating!" said his wife as she mopped his blooded brow.

"Why those soldiers would take it out on such a young lad is beyond me".

"Where's Laila?" asked Kieran perturbed.

"If you're talking about the girl, the soldiers took her away" said the landlord.

"I have to go and save her!" he said attempting to get up.

"You're not fit to go anywhere at the moment" said the landlady restraining him.

"Sound advice indeed" said a voice at the door. Kieran looked up to see Yan standing in the doorway.

"Yan!" he exclaimed with surprise.

"I am the boy's uncle" explained the old wizard introducing himself to the landlord and his wife.

"I am indebted to you for taking care of my nephew" he said politely.

"We just wish we could have helped him sooner sir" said the landlady. "It's outrageous the way they left him there on the stairs".

"You have done more than enough" replied Yan handing them a gold coin and ushering them courteously to the door.

"Well we best leave you alone then, and if there is anything you need we will be down stairs sir" said the landlord and his wife humbly retreating to the bar.

"Thank you, you have been most helpful" said Yan closing the door behind them.

"They have taken Laila Sir!" groaned Kieran.

"I know" replied Yan calmly. "Allow me to introduce Lon Attilia" he said as out from behind him stepped a short gaunt figure in a hooded cape with cropped hair and pointed ears.

"Lon informed me of Laila's fate just before noon, so I flew here as fast as I could by the power of anifornum. News travels fast in this city and it wasn't long before he had heard about the exploits of a certain Horatio Smythe".

"What has Horatio got to do with this?" Kieran asked.

"It was he who informed the authorities of our objective" said Lon.

Kieran grabbed for his jacket and began to rummage nervously through the pockets.

"It's gone! The letter for Lon, it has been stolen" he cried.

"Yes I know and now Laila is in grave danger" said Yan sitting down on the bed with a look of desperation on his face. "I knew I shouldn't have divulged so much to Lon in my letter" he said remorsefully.

"So what are we going to do?" Kieran asked.

"It is my intention with the help of Lon to rescue Laila from the citadel at nightfall" said Yan.

"I'm coming with you!" said Kieran languidly clambering to his feet.

"No!" Yan insisted. "It is only a matter of time before Lhanna senses my presence here and I will not put you in any further danger".

"But this is all my fault, I have failed you Sir and I want to make amends" he said fervidly. Yan looked at him with an avuncular smile.

"My dear boy you have not failed me. Laila's misfortune is not of your doing. You simply carried out what was asked of you and for that I am deeply grateful. These events are the result of me not having the foresight to see that my plan could have gone wrong. I should have sent Laila back to Warren pond with Jack when I had the chance instead risking her life in the pursuit of that wretched necklace. It's probably better in Lhanna's hands anyway as it has not brought Laila much luck" he said.

Just then there was a knock at the door and a voice beyond it hollered, "Carriage for Master David!"

"I have arranged transport for you back to Dial house" said Yan. "You will serve me better if you are there taking care of my plants". Reluctantly the despondent Kieran made his way downstairs to the waiting carriage and said his thanks and farewells to the publicans.

"I will see you tomorrow, adieu!" shouted Yan as he watched his lugubrious apprentice glance back at him from the carriage as it trundled off down the cobbled streets of Lhansburg.

"We best lay low until nightfall" said Lon looking around nervously. "I know a place on the far side of the city where we can hold up until then" he said leading Yan off through the maze of back alley"s where only the waifs and strays dare frequent.

As they made their way across town Lon appeared troubled by something.

"What is it that you cogitate but do not share?" asked Yan sensing his agitation.

"I'm confused as to why your apprentice Kieran was not also apprehended by the citadel forces? It just doesn't make sense?" he said.

"I'm confident there is a reason for it, but to focus your energy on such a negative concern at this time would be unproductive" said Yan.

The streets were narrow and quite claustrophobic with the volume of people and the tall buildings that hemmed them in, and the fetor of raw sewage was overpowering. Even amongst the daily hustle and bustle of Lhansburg normality, Yan felt something was amiss.

"I believe I have just discovered the answer to your enigma Lon" he whispered.

"We are being followed! Don't look now, but there is a man in a brown hooded cape following us. He has shadowed us since leaving the Strugglers inn".

"Leave him to me" said Lon vanishing as quick as a flash, and reappearing behind the pursuer with a knife against his throat.

"What business do you want with us?" he asked.

"I have none my friend, I am merely on my way to see the cordwainer" he gulped, as Lon's blade pushed hard against his neck.

"Well you're going the wrong way my friend, so I suggest you turn your feet around and point them in the opposite direction while you still can" he snarled, before the man swiftly had it away on his heels.

"It appears they may have already felt your presence here" said Lon on his return.

"Then we have no time to lose, we must make our way to the citadel now" said Yan.

"But it is not yet dusk! To even consider breaking into the citadel tower in broad daylight is simply ridiculous".

"We have no choice Lon; the scout that was tailing us will be returning now to inform the Queens guard of our location, and soon these streets will be running alive".

"We can hide! I know a place where they will never find us" said Lon.

"No Lon, they know we are here, and it will only be a matter of time before we are found. We must act now and use this situation to our advantage. As you said yourself, to consider breaking into the citadel in broad daylight is simply ridiculous. So let's hope they also share your belief" he smiled before striding off.

They proceeded expeditiously across town to the heart of Lhansburg. Pausing cautiously in doorways and cutting through the back alley's of the city to avoid detection whilst occasionally having to dive for cover amongst piles of domestic refuse as armed units raced by in their perquisition.

It was a hair raising journey but eventually they arrived within eye shot of the citadel walls where hordes of sentries stood posted on the allures.

"There's a stairwell on the right just inside the gatehouse" whispered Lon from their concealed position. "It takes you to a gallery that leads to the tower. That I'm sure is where Laila will be held".

"There's quite a lot of open ground between here and the gatehouse" said Yan watching the ever vigilant sentries pacing to and fro.

"It's not a problem for me but I can't vouch for you old man" quipped Lon.

"Never underestimate the forces of nature" smiled Yan.

He closed his eyes and clenched tight his fists before reciting an incantation under his breath. Gradually a fine mist began to descend upon the city, rapidly increasing in density.

Before long the citadel was completely enveloped in a thick billowing fog where only the calls of disconcerted sentries could be heard in the nubilous gloom.

"Now is our chance, meet me on the stairwell" said Yan disappearing into the brume.

Like a shadow under cover of night, Yan managed to pass by the guards on the gatehouse unnoticed, meeting promptly with Lon at the top of the stairwell.

"What took you?" laughed Lon as Yan ascended the stairs.

"Insolent Sprite!" he mumbled. "Now guide me to the tower" he said impatiently as they raced along the gallery.

At the end of the gallery was a large wooden door from where the inarticulate murmur of voices emanated.

"The tower guard are stationed behind this door" said Lon in a low voice.

"How many do you think?" Yan asked.

Lon held up four fingers.

Drawing forth his sword slowly from its scabbard he turned the handle and pushed open the door. Instantly the soldiers charged the intruder with howls of rage as the wizard stood standing in the doorway with his sword held aloft.

"Lay down your weapons and no harm will come to you!" he roared but to no avail.

And so with the grace of a cat and the speed of a sprite he swiftly dispensed of the tower guard. Appearing almost motionless in his agility, as all around his adversaries collapsed to the ground. Lon watched astounded in the doorway. "I have never seen anyone wield a sword like that!" he gasped.

"I have lived longer than most to perfect it regrettably" said Yan. "Now where do we go from here?".

"This way!" said Lon dashing off down a long narrow passage leading towards a spiral staircase.

"There are two floors we have to pass through before we reach the top of the tower where the prisoners are held. And they are both heavily manned" said Lon.

"I have to save Laila" replied Yan resolutely making his way up the stairs. Lon used his swiftness to survey the defences in advance of Yan.

"There are six soldiers on the first floor and two on the second" he said appearing out of thin air in front of the wizard.

"Leave this to me" said Yan approaching the top of the stairs.

"Who goes there!" shouted one of the guards wielding a spear as Yan loomed into view from out the doorway. But before he even had a chance to speak, Lon had cut deep the soldiers throat, spilling his blood everywhere and causing his comrades to swiftly take up arms and attack Yan.

There then ensued a brief exchange where within a moment, six men lay dead upon the floor. Yan looked around, abhorred by his actions.

"Why must it end in cold blooded murder?" he said shaking his head.

"Such is the price of a warrior's valour" said Lon seemingly indifferent to the butchery, as he wiped the cruor from his face.

Yan was perturbed by the almost macabre gratification in the Changeling's demeanour.

"Then valour is senseless virtue" he said in disdain.

"But it was a case of kill or be killed" said the Changeling confused.

"Maybe so Lon, but with the malefaction done, I can find neither solace nor deliverance in those words" he replied as he made his way to the stairs.

"Yan!" called Lon after him. "If we are to free Laila from here, then killing is what we must do" he said.

"I know my friend" replied Yan remorsefully "That is what troubles me".

Making their way up the spiralling steps to the top of the tower Yan insisted that Lon abstain from attacking the guards.

"If I can avoid bloodshed I will" he said.

"Then why not use magic?" asked Lon.

"Because Lhanna would instantly be alerted to the source of the magic and none of us will get out of here alive" he said ascending the final flight.

Entering the tower they they managed to catch the jailers completely off guard. With a sword and a dagger at their throats the jailers proved very cooperative.

"We have come for the girl Laila" said Yan stony eyed.

"And be quick about it!" said Lon shoving the jailers against the wall.

Without resistance the jailers opened the heavy iron door to the cell.

There in a darkened corner, huddled over like a pile of rags was Laila. At once Yan rushed to her side.

"Laila can you hear me? It's Yan, I have come to take you away from here" he said softly. Laila looked up through abandoned eyes.

"Yan is that really you?" she asked in a susurrus tone.

"Yes Laila, now drink this" he said holding a hipflask to her lips.

"What are you giving her?" Lon asked.

"It's a potion to help revive her" said Yan.

"Lhanna's reputation for contaminating her prisoner's water with hemlock is well founded" he said.

Rapidly the potion began to take effect and before long Laila was back on her feet.

"How do you feel?" Yan asked.

"Much better thank you" Laila replied adjusting herself. "How is Kieran, is he alright?" she asked. "He is fine don't worry, I sent him safely back to Dial house this very afternoon" said Yan removing her leg irons.

Just then the sound of a bell could be heard ringing loud across the citadel.

"It's the alarm. We had better get out of here quick!" said Lon, locking the jailers in the cell behind them.

They quickly raced down the stairs as fast as their legs could carry them until they arrived back in the long gallery where a large group of armed soldiers stood at the other end blocking their exit. Yan drew his sword and stared long and hard at his opposition.

"Lon and I will clear a path for you to escape" said Yan turning to Laila.

"But we'll never get past those soldiers" said Laila trembling fearfully.

"Yes we will! Remember anifornum Laila, you must believe in me when I tell you that you can be as fast as the march hare if you so wish. They will never catch you. Be fleeting and head for the forest" he said, before he and Lon ran head on into the waiting guard.

The piercing clash of steel resonated through the gallery as the old wizard and his friend fought fiercely to clear a passage for Laila but with reinforcements arriving in their droves they were soon overwhelmed.

"Run Laila! As quick as the hare, be gone!" called Yan from beyond the fray just as two burly guards rushed her from behind. Nimbly she managed to give them the slip before darting off down the gallery towards the exit as fast as she could. Suddenly and inexplicably everything around her seemed to rapidly increase in size. The gallery expanded into a gigantic hall and its soldiers into towering giants. She felt herself falling forward onto all fours as she raced at lightning speed towards the exit, eluding capture by dashing briskly between the legs of the guards.

Out through the citadel gates and along the city streets she raced without stopping until finally reaching the sanctuary of Lhansburg woods.

Chapter Ten

On to Puo Landum

Back in the citadel gallery Yan and Lon fought wearily on against the odds in a bedlam of butchery, desperately holding back the advancing tide of might that bore down upon them.

Like the irascible swarming mites of a desolated nest the soldiers soon overran the citadel until any hope of an escape seemed inconceivable.

But then as quickly as it had begun it mysteriously ended. The once inexorable army suddenly and inexplicably ceased their advance leaving Yan and Lon standing there, gasping for breath amongst the bloody massacre.

"This does not bode well my friend" said Yan panting from exhaustion.

"Get out of here now Lon while you can, and make sure Laila is safe" he said gripping the hilt of his sword tight.

"But Yan!" cried Lon, only to be cut short.

"An evil presence too powerful for us to defeat comes this way Lon, now leave!" he insisted. And within a flash the Changeling disappeared from sight leaving Yan standing alone and defiant like a rock in a torrent.

A brief standoff then followed as he stood his ground within the silent ring of steel. Nobody moved or said anything as if they had been frozen in time. And then from the back of the gallery there came a ripple of movement that created a domino affect all the way to the front. Every soldier present in the building fell subserviently to his knees as the figure of a tall slender woman entered the gallery. Dressed in ivory silk robes she parted the obsequious hordes while making her way directly towards Yan.

"It will take more than a sudden mist to conceal a wizard from me" she said furiously in her stride. Yan could feel her power radiating through every fibre of his soul and throughout the entire citadel. Knowing he was no match for her he instinctively looked around for a way out. Glancing up he noticed an arcade of arched windows near the ceiling of the gallery, so as quick as a flash transformed himself into a jay and flew rapidly up towards the light and freedom. In an instant she swiftly drew a dagger from the scabbard of a nearby soldier and vehemently threw it at the bird, hitting it square in the flank and bringing it tumbling back down to earth in a hail of feathers. Bending down she picked up the lifeless creature from the cold stone floor and pulled the dagger from its side.

"See how easy it is to kill these fearful priests" she scoffed. "Now where is the girl?" she asked turning to one of her officers.

"She escaped, your majesty" he replied gingerly.

"And how does a child evade the elite guard?" she asked.

"She changed herself into a hare and we just couldn't catch her" said the officer with a look of shame on his face.

"But I will dispatch a unit immediately for Lhansburg wood your majesty" he said in a staunch attempt to redeem himself.

"No! It takes a hound not an army to catch a hare" exclaimed the Queen abruptly.

"Set loose the black dog!

"Yes your majesty! Right away" said the officer making his way hastily down to the citadel dungeons.

In the dark waterlogged tunnels that ran beneath the citadel were the dungeons, where Lhanna kept a bizarre collection of zoological curiosities from

Lubber fiends to Grindylow's. It was a cold dank place lit only by the intermittent torches that flickered in the gloom.

On arrival at the dungeon gates the officer was confronted by two armed sentries who stood quickly to attention on his approach.

"The Queen has ordered that Black Shuck be released to hunt down an escaped witch. Go immediately to the castle kitchens" he commanded them. "And return here with a hare's carcass".

The sentries promptly hurried off and before long reappeared with a butchered hare in hand.

"Now open the gates" demanded the officer.

Slowly pushing open the heavy iron gates to the dungeons the officer and his subordinates descended into the murk of the catacombs. Strange squeals and growls echoed from beyond the vaults as they proceeded through the caged menagerie to the black dog's enclosure where all that could be seen were two large red glowing eyes. "Hold up the hare and let the hound catch the scent" ordered the officer as they drew nearer. Cautiously the sentry approached the bars of the cage.

A deep agitated grumble like thunder bellowed from the shadows.

"Now take the carcass to Lhansburg wood and cast it into the nearest pond you come to. I will give you

ten minutes before I release Shuck" said the officer.
The sentry froze for a moment in absolute horror
before swiftly taking to his heels.

But no sooner had he left the officer ordered that the
black dog be set loose. Slowly and fastidiously the
key to the lock was turned until the clunk of the
locking bolt resounded in the hush

"Stand clear!" yelled the officer diving for cover in
a recess as the gates of the cage burst open with an
almighty crash.

 Out charged a huge black dog as big as a calf with
razor sharp teeth and claws, its eyes burning
brightly as it panted with rage. It sniffed the air and
looked around briefly and then tore off in a
whirlwind of dust much to the relief of the officer
and his adjunct trembling with fear in the recess.
Out of the citadel gates and through the streets the
black dog hurtled, smashing through market stalls
and sending people and horses fleeing for their lives
before disappearing into Lhansburg wood, leaving
behind him a trail of devastation.

By this time Laila had stopped running and
gradually returned to her natural form. Tired and
enervated from all the excitement she rested a while
to contemplate over the extraordinary happenings
beneath the shade of a beech tree. It was so quiet
and peaceful in the woods, just the soft twitter of

bird song to sooth the spirit. But the tranquillity was only transient as her attention was suddenly drawn to the strange sound of brushwood snapping in the distance. Rapidly the sound began to grow in volume forcing Laila back on to her feet again. Agitated she looked about for somewhere to hide but with no time to think she instinctively ran in the opposite direction to the noise and deeper into the woods. But no matter how fast or far she ran the sound seemed to track her every movement and at great speed. Before long she could feel the tremor of heavy feet pounding against the ground and the terrifying pant, of whatever it was racing in pursuit of its prey. Turning around Laila could see a large black dog around two hundred yards away amongst the trees rushing straight towards her. She tried to outrun it but it was no use. The dog was far too agile and had leapt on her from behind within a flash, pinning her face down on to the ground. She could feel the piercing pain from its sabre like claws in her back but no matter how much she struggled she just could not move. Glancing up from the corner of her eye Laila could only watch as the terrifying beast licked its teeth and opened its wide powerful jaws to take a bite at her when all of a sudden there came an almighty thump and the next thing she saw was her assailant hurling through the air like a stone.

"Leave her be!" roared a voice in rage from out of the trees, which startled Laila. She looked up to see Jack standing tall amongst the branches. He looked huge and powerful with a stern expression on his face. Never had she seen him look as intimidating as he stood there in confrontation of the ferocious black dog that now walked menacingly through the undergrowth towards him. Hastily she took cover behind a fallen tree as the two mighty adversaries faced off.

"I mean you no wrong Black Shuck, but I will not allow you to harm this girl" said Jack loud and resolutely. But the snarling wrathful canine was apathetic to reason, and with eyes of burning rage sprang up at Jack rabidly. Anticipating the lunge the Green Man quickly sidestepped the dog, catching it in mid air by the throat in a crushing grip before holding it up high at arm's length.

"I am the guardian of the forest; go back to the fens in the east where you belong" he bellowed as the creature growled and wriggled violently to free itself.

"You are no longer a slave to that tyrant Queen, now be gone" he said. And with that he carefully and very cautiously lowered the black dog back down before loosening his hold and resuming a defensive stance. The dog however did not seize the opportunity to retaliate as would have been expected but appeared unbalanced and shaky for a while as it stood there convulsing at Jack's feet, as if it had been stunned in the struggle. And then the most peculiar thing happened. The dog shook himself down and then walked up to Jack and licked his hand before trotting off placidly into the forest as if nothing at all had happened. Jack watched dumbfounded for a moment until it disappeared out of site.

"Well I never?" he gasped.

You can come out now Laila" he said looking down at her two tiny eyes peering over the fallen tree Leaping up from behind her refuge she sprinted towards him in total elation.

"Oh Jack you saved my life!" she cried as she hugged his leg tightly.

"We have to stop meeting like this, it's becoming a routine" he smiled.

"Where is young Kieran?" he asked.

"It's a long story" replied Laila wearily.

"What about your necklace, did you get your necklace back?"

"No" she said shaking her head in disappointment.

"I had to escape the city in a hurry and I was lucky to get out alive, what with all those soldiers chasing me. "And where did that evil dog come from?" she asked.

"The trees told me about Black Shuck leaving Lhansburg and entering the forest in pursuit of a hare. I knew straight away that it had to be a witch hunt". Laila walked a short distance away from him with her head hung low. "What's the matter Laila?" he asked.

"It was me Jack, I was that hare" she said as if ashamed.

"I know you were. You performed anifornum" he said walking over to comfort her. Laila looked at him bewildered, as if surprised that he knew.

"I don't know how it happened Jack, honest I don't!" she said.

"It's ok Laila. To possess such magic is a wonderful gift".

"Does that mean that I am a witch then?" she asked.

"No, but to be a witch is not a bad thing at all" he chuckled.

And then his face suddenly dropped and he quickly stood upright and gazed around

"Someone comes this way" he said impulsively picking Laila up and putting her up high into the crown of an oak tree.

"Now be still, you'll be safe there" he said stepping back amongst the trees and vanishing into his surroundings.

A short time later a sprightly character appeared in the clearing shouting at the top of his voice.

"Laila! Laila!" he hollered as he scouted about through the tall bracken.

Instantly Laila recognised the voice as Lon Atillia's.

"Lon!" she called. "I'm up here". Lon looked up into the branches of the huge oak tree with surprise.

"How on earth did you get up there?" he asked.

"Jack put me here" she said.

"Who's Jack?" came Lon's reply just as a huge leafy figure materialised out of the trees.

"I am Jack!" he bellowed much to Lon's astonishment.

"It's alright Lon, Jack is my friend" she laughed on seeing the expression of terror in the Changeling's eyes. "Where is Yan?" she enquired.

Lon lowered his gaze solemnly.

"The last time I saw him he was about to be confronted by Queen Lhanna in the citadel" he said with a sigh.

"What was Yan doing in Lhansburg? Will someone tell me what's going on here?" demanded Jack.

"Not now Jack, just get me down from here quickly! We must go back to Lhansburg and save him" Laila cried.

"I'm afraid there is nothing we can do to help him now" said Lon despondently.

"He's right Laila" agreed Jack lifting her gently down from the tree.

"Against Lhanna we can only but fear the worst" he said mournfully before she burst into tears in his arms.

"He might not be dead" she sobbed. "He is a wizard; he might have used magic to escape".

"No power on earth could save him against Lhanna. She is a supreme being and a ruthless one at that" said Lon.

"He lost his life trying to save mine" she sniffed with tears rolling down her face.

"I know Laila, but you have to realise that Yan would not have entered Lhansburg blindly. He knew the dangers and the possible sacrifices he would have to endure to free you. He was a good and brave man" he said softly whilst suppressing his own grief behind a reserved disposition.

"Even after eight hundred years, letting go is never easy" he mumbled to himself.

They sat a while in reflection, dealing with the sorrow in their own individual way as dark clouds gradually formed overhead. Light rain began to fall, as if the sky too lamented the loss of the old wizard. "We had best take shelter" said Lon severing the pensive atmosphere, as he stared up at the murky skies.

"We shouldn't sit around too long either as I'm sure it won't be long before Lhansburg scouts head this way". Jack rose to his feet and looked west towards the hazy sun. "It's only stratus, follow me" he said strolling away into the thicket.

"There are some big Yew's growing not far from here under which we can shelter till it passes he said. Despondently Laila tagged slowly behind as they wandered amongst the tall trees forcing Jack to stop occasionally and wait for her to catch up.

"Would you like me to carry you?" he asked concerned.

"No I'm fine thanks" she replied unconvincingly. Jack could sense the feeling of pain and anguish that swelled deep within her heart, after all she had been through it was understandable. He realised too the burden of responsibility now placed upon him to deliver her safely to the ancient hawthorn in Puo Landum.

That afternoon they took shelter beneath the dense crown of a large Yew tree and watched the rain pass over beside the warmth of a fire. Laila drifted soundly off to sleep and all was calm but for Lon's restless pacing that didn't go unnoticed by Jack.

"What is troubling you?" he asked.

"If you must know, I don't think it was wise to have lit a fire in the woods this far from Lhansburg. You're putting Laila in grave danger, and for all you know Lhanna's soldiers could be out there lurking in the woods" he said uneasily looking around.

"Well I can assure you that no one cares more for Laila's welfare than me, which is the reason why I built the fire, to keep her warm" said Jack raising his voice.

"And as for soldiers lurking about in the woods, there are none".

"And how would you know?" asked Lon.

"Because I am a Green Man and the trees are my kin, now sit down!" he insisted.

Lon vanished in an instant and then reappeared perched on the low bough of the Yew with an indignant expression on his face while Jack just shook his head at the sheer gall of the Changeling.

"How would a Green Man know what lurks in the woods" he quipped silently to himself before going on a short saunter to converse with Elms.

There was certainly no love lost between the pair of them, making for a sullen and awkward mood that evening when the moon appeared over the forest. Not a single word was exchanged throughout the entire night until sunrise the next morning when Laila awoke.

"Morning Jack, morning Lon" she said stretching from her dormant slumber.

"Morning Laila, I prepared you some breakfast" said Jack walking over to hand her some roasted roots and salad leaves.

"And I put my coat over you last night Laila to keep you warm" declared Lon from his bough in the tree, as if competing for her favor.

"And I kept the fire going all night" came Jack's swift riposte.

"Thank you both very much, that's really kind of you" she said cheerfully.

"You're welcome!" they replied in unison.

"Whenever you're ready Laila we will head off" said Jack.

"I'm coming with you!" announced Lon springing keenly down from his perch.

"I'm sorry but this is a journey that only Laila and I can undertake. I appreciate all that you have done but I fear your presence on this venture would only prove a hindrance" said Jack.

"Yan asked me to see that Laila was safe and that's what I intend to do" replied Lon staunchly.

"Well as you can see she is very well so you have honoured that request. Now if you don't mind.....".

"Whoa! Hang on!" exclaimed Lon. "That is not what I meant. I'm here to protect her" he said.

"No harm can come to her when she is in the company of a Green Man!" vociferated Jack in an irritable tone. "STOP!" yelled Laila pulling the reins on the incessant bandying.

"Has anyone thought about asking me what I might want? You're both arguing about me as if I wasn't here" she said. Lon and Jack fell silently abashed.

"I say that Lon comes with us" she said conclusively.

"Alright Laila, if that is what you wish" agreed Jack annoyed.

"It is Jack, and I would also like you two to try and get along!"

"I will do my best" he mumbled.

"Good! Well I'm ready to go then" she said walking over to him.

Looking up she smiled and held his hand.

"As long as I am with you Jack I am happy" she said heartening the Green Man and putting a big proud grin on his face.

"Ok! Let's head north to Puo Landum!" he said, picking her up in his arms and carrying her off into the forest with the spritely Lon alongside.

"How do you know we are heading north?" she asked. "Because the moss grows thickest on the north side of the trees of course" he said in a matter of fact way.

On their journey Jack communed with the trees all around him, enlightening Laila and Lon on his conversations with them and all the wonderful occurrences that were taking place at that time within the Grayweald.

"There are a pair of sparrow hawks nesting in a tree up ahead of us, and also in a hollow oak not far from there is where a large colony of Noctule bats resides" he said getting carried away in his arboreal monologues.

So engrossed was he in his garrulous discourse that it diverted his attention momentarily from a large fallen ash limb lying hidden amongst the ferns in a tract of open ground through which they were passing. Without looking where he was stepping the huge Green Man inadvertently stumbled clumsily over the branch, falling forward like felled timber pole and propelling Laila straight into a clump of vicious stinging nettles.

"Oh my!" he exclaimed dropping her into the unforgiving trichomes.

Just then within the blink of an eye Lon leapt into the air and caught Laila in his arms, saving her from the uncomfortable landing.

"Thank you Lon!" said Laila a little shaken.

"Are you ok?" he asked putting her down safely.

"Yes fine" she replied.

"I bet you're glad I came along now Jack?" quipped Lon smiling cheekily as the lumbering green giant picked himself up from his fall. He looked at Lon for a second as if insulted by the remark and then began to chuckle loudly, much to the Changelings delight.

"Yes I am glad" he smiled. "As Yan would always say; everything happens for a reason. And thanks to you being here Laila remains unharmed" he said walking over and patting Lon approvingly upon the back.

From what appeared as just a minor incident changed the entire atmosphere, and propitiated the animosity between the two of them . Gradually a mutual respect began to blossom from that point onwards. Even the long hike through Lhansburg forest became filled with nothing but conversation and laughter, which made the expedition to Puo Landum more of an adventure for Laila. A far cry from the arduous journeys she had previously endured.

Around nightfall they reached the river Ura with its steep earthen banks. It was wide and deep and roared like thunder in the wind as it snaked through the mountainous wilderness.

"The river divides the borders between the sovereignty of Lhansburg and the Goblin lands of the Grayweald" said Jack looking out across the sweeping expanse of water.

"We have to cross to the other side to get to Puo Landum" he said.

"Puo Landum" gasped Lon. "Why are we heading to Puo Landum?"

"We have important business there" replied Jack.

"But how are we going to get across?" asked Lon.

"I'm not a very strong swimmer" he exclaimed, gawking into the dark implacable river.

"There is a crossing point a bit further down. Follow me" said Jack leading them a short distance along the bank to a sheltered outcrop.

"There it is!" he whispered pointing to a wide timber bridge spanning the river. "Once on the other side we are in Goblin country and they don't take kindly to intruders so stick close to me" he said.

Just then Laila noticed four tiny figures moving
around on the bridge

"Look, Goblins on the bridge!" she cried.

"Shush Laila! They are the bridge wardens; we
don't want to alert them of our presence" whispered
Jack. "Damn!" he exclaimed. I totally forgot about
the wardens".

"What are they doing there?" asked Laila.

"They are there as observers, to give advance
warning of any intruders entering into Goblin
territory".

"So how will we get past them?" she asked.

"I'm not sure? Let me think about it" he replied
scratching his leafy head.

Lon then began sniggering loudly to himself.

"What are you laughing at Lon?" Laila asked.

"Why! Isn't it obvious?" he smirked before
disappearing and reappearing behind her.

"I'm a Changeling and I can get across that bridge
easily without being seen" he smiled.

"But how does that help Laila and I?" asked Jack.

"Simple! I will create a diversion for you both to
cross. All I have to do is lure the wardens off the
bridge which shouldn't be too difficult if they are as
unfriendly as you say they are" he chuckled
confidently.

"Please don't hurt any of them Lon" begged Laila.

"Don't worry, no harm will come to them" he said reassuringly.

"Do you really believe you can lure them off the bridge long enough for me and Laila to be able to get across?" asked Jack intrigued by the audaciousness of the Changeling's disposition.

"Leave it to me" said Lon.

"But you'll have to be quick though Jack. As soon as you see the wardens leave the bridge you'll have to run for it!" he said.

"No problem! I will carry Laila and make it over the bridge in a couple of quick strides" said Jack.

"Ok let's do it then" said Lon, keen to get going.

Jack guided Lon down to the edge of the forest and as close to the bridge as he dare.

Three hundred feet lay between their concealed position in the thicket and the bridge approach.

"The trees are telling me that there is a fifth Goblin on the other side cooking fish on an open fire close to the bank" whispered Jack. "

Aww! I'm so hungry" groaned Laila.

"Where are we going to meet up once we get to the other side?" asked Lon.

"Don't worry about that, we will find you. Just cover as much ground between you and the bridge as possible. And good luck" Said Jack.

"See you there" smiled Lon and vanished into thin air.

With his amazing celerity he had crossed the bridge undetected by the wardens, only to reappear from out of nowhere beside the Goblins fire on the other side of the river.

Standing nonchalantly beside the fire he decided to sample some of the salmon, much to the astonishment of the Goblin cook, who just froze with shock.

"It needs a bit more salt" he said with a calm and casual smile before running off into the darkness. The Goblin cook could not believe his eyes, and it took a moment for him to comprehend what had just happened. And then at the top of his voice he hollered to his companions on the bridge.

"Intruder! Intruder!" he yelled just as the four Goblins came running up with swords drawn.

"What is it?" asked one of them.

"A Sapien just materialized out of thin air and ate some of the salmon" said the cook in a fluster.

"Hey have you been at the mead again?" asked another Goblin.

"No! I swear it! It went that way" said the cook pointing into the darkness.

"Come on let's get it!" said one of the goblins drawing a burning torch from the fire and scampering off into the undergrowth.

"You stay here and keep an eye on the bridge! And you had better not be eating our share of that salmon" said another before joining his colleagues in the search, leaving the cook alone and confused. With the coast now clear Jack swiftly leapt out from the thicket and ran fleet-footed across the bridge with Laila clinging tightly onto his back.

On reaching the other side of the bridge he ran straight into the Goblin cook who was standing beside the fire. Jack stopped fast in his tracks and for a minute the two of them just eyed each other up. Never had the Goblin cook ever seen anything like a Green man in his life before, and just gaped in absolute amazement.

"Get the fish" whispered Laila in Jack's ear.

"I'm just going to relieve you of this salmon if you don't mind?" said Jack politely bending down and picking the fish from the embers before dashing off into the night.

Not a moment later the four Goblins arrived back at the fire.

"No sign of a Sapien out there anywhere!" said one of them puffing breathlessly from his search. "Are you sure you didn't imagine it?" he asked.

"Hey! Hang on, Where's the fish gone?" exclaimed another.

"You won't believe me if I told you" said the cook a little dazed.

"Try me" he said folding his arms irascibly.

"Well a giant walking tree with a Sapien growing out of its back stole it" said the cook with a nervous smirk. "Oh really?" he growled angrily looking around at the unified dubiety of his companions. "Get him lads!" he yelled, before they all set upon the poor Goblin cook.

Meanwhile somewhere in the darkness of the woods, hidden amidst the tall ferns and bramble, Lon waited nervously for Jack and Laila to appear. "Where are they? What's taking them so long?" he muttered restlessly to himself as he lay low amongst the bracken fronds.

Just then from out of the faint hush of the woods he heard the unsettling sound of footsteps heading slowly towards him. Each furtive step munched down through the crisp vegetation as it approached his refuge. Unsure whether the prowler was friend or foe Lon remained motionless. Holding his breath as the footsteps drew near. All was still for a moment in the blackness except for the sudden strange puerile chuckles of suppressed laughter.

Hesitantly Lon glanced up to see Laila and Jack smiling down at him.

"Found you!" laughed Laila.

"I must confess it was a very good hiding place" remarked Jack.

"Well it couldn't have been that good. How on earth could you have found me amongst the ferns? It would be hard during the day but at night, impossible!" said Lon.

"I told you that us Green men converse with trees did I not?" smiled Jack.

"We have a fish for supper!" said Laila excitedly holding up a large cooked salmon wrapped in a burdock leaf.

"Sounds good to me" said Lon climbing out from his hiding place.

"But first we had better put some distance between us and the Goblins" said Jack. "The trees tell me that there is a glade nearby that is sheltered from the wind, so let us make our way there before we rest for the evening" he said leading them off once again through the tenebrous woodlands and the sanctuary of the trees.

Laila and Lon where in good spirits that night. Laughing and joking about the Goblin cook whilst enjoying the salmon around and blazing open fire. Relaxed in the knowledge, that whilst in the

company of the ubiquitous Green man no harm
could come to them in the Grayweald.

"It must be great to be able to move as fast as you"
said Laila looking across the fire at Lon sitting cross
legged on a fallen branch.

"It is useful I guess but I have always been quick so
I don't know any different" he said modestly.

"How did you become so fast?" she asked
enthralled.

"I am a Changeling" he replied.

"What is a Changeling?".

"They are sometimes referred to as the possessed.
Human Sprite hybrids" interjected Jack.

"That's correct" said Lon looking somewhat
abashed.

"An incubus assaulted my mother in the woods" he
said. "Consequently I was born, but I was rejected
at birth by my stepfather, and outcast by the people
of my village as a demon child. My mother had
heard rumours of a wizard living in the mountains
called Yan. So she took me to him in an attempt to
exorcise the spirit, but there was nothing he could
do other than offer me sanctuary.
And so I lived with Yan until the age of ten before
seeking my fortune in Lhansburg" he said.

An awkward silence instantly fell upon the camp.
Laila could not think of anything to say in reply to

his divulgement and just sat button lipped, unsure whether to sympathize or admire the Changelings inherent abilities. Observing her discomfort Jack quickly piped up.

"You had better get some rest now Laila. We still have a way to go tomorrow and I want you to be up early" he said.

"Ok Jack" she said curling up beside the fire.

"Goodnight Laila" said Lon putting his cloak over her.

"Goodnight Lon" she smiled.

Chapter Eleven

The Treacherous Tide

The Green man was up and out bright and early with the dawn chorus as usual, foraging amongst the undergrowth when Laila awoke from her slumber. Lon meanwhile lay snoring in the foetal position on the opposite side of the fire upon a bed of dry bracken.

"You're up early!" remarked the ever resourceful Jack appearing from out of the greenery, arms laden with food and firewood.

"I know" said Laila drowsily rubbing her eyes.

"I had this really strange dream last night Jack, about a dragon. It was lying in cave underground surrounded by water and it was calling to me as if it wanted me to help it, but I couldn't do anything. It's not that I didn't want to, it was just that it was far too huge and scary".

"I wouldn't concern yourself with it Laila, it's only a dream. It might be just your subconscious mind expressing the feeling of being trapped in this world

and yearning to be back home" he said with a
cheery smile.

"Yeah I guess?" she said resting her head back
down again.

"The important thing is, we are on our way to the
ancient hawthorn, so your dreams of home will
soon be a reality" said Jack as he fed some more
wood onto the fire.

"What was that you were saying about an ancient
hawthorn?" asked Lon waking suddenly from his
sloom.

"It is our reason for heading to Puo Landum" said
Jack.

"What, to find a hawthorn?" he said. "But all the
hawthorns were destroyed during the Banishing!".

"Your assertion is based upon rumour my friend.
Yes it is true that nearly all of the ancient hawthorns
were destroyed but one still remains, the last of its
kind known as the Omega tree, hidden beyond the
axes of destructive ignorance".

"You mean to say that a world tree still exists in
Puo Landum?" asked Lon surprised.

"That is correct" said Jack.

"My word! That's amazing!" He gasped. "But
how do you expect to get anywhere near it? I mean,
Puo Landum is in the heart of Goblin country and

everyone knows that the Goblins are a ferocious, barbaric race".

"On the contrary Lon, the Goblins are a very civilized race".

"But you said yourself that they didn't take kindly to strangers".

"Yes, but unfortunately they have been persecuted for so long now that they forced to be defensive, but that is not to say they are in anyway uncultured. After all it was they who recognised the sanctity of ancient trees".

"That's as may be, but how confident are you that we will be unharmed if caught entering Puo Landum" Lon asked.

"I'm afraid I cannot answer that, but I have heard it said that their elder is an extremely wise and learned individual".

"Well let's hope he is as merciful as he is wise" Lon quipped.

After breakfast they cleared away any signs of their presence in the woods and continued their journey north following a tributary of the river Ura downstream. The terrain was steep and the weather fine so Laila and Lon decided to pause briefly for a swim in the inviting yet cold waters of a picturesque glen where ferns, mosses and broadleaf sapling's issued from every crack and fissure of the towering vertical outcrops, fragmenting the sunlight into an illumination of crepuscular rays below.

Whilst splashing contentedly in the tranquillity of the pellucid mountain river, Laila couldn't help but sense an air of unease in the Green mans demeanour, as if something was amiss.

"Is everything ok Jack?" she asked, stepping out of the water and making her way carefully up the slippery lichen covered boulders to where he sat reflectively gazing into the canopy above.

"We had best make our stay here brief" he said softly.

"Why what's wrong?" asked Laila perplexed.

"The trees tell me that fifty horsemen from Lhansburg have just crossed the Ura Bridge".

"So what does that mean?" she inquired.

"For a detachment of horsemen to risk crossing into Goblin lands can mean only one thing. They are coming for you Laila" he said with a look of foreboding in his eyes.

Laila stumbled back aghast.

"I don't understand, why would they be after me? I don't have the necklace anymore" she cried.

"I know not their reasons but I do know they are heading in this direction"

"Then we must leave now!" she said in a tremulous voice.

"Indeed we must" replied Jack standing up and beckoning Lon from the river. Speedily the Changeling arrived, curious to his summoning.

"We must leave now and proceed with haste to Puo Landum" said Jack.

"Why?" Lon asked.

"Because it has just come to my ear that a detachment of around fifty soldiers on horseback are on our trail". "But how did you not notice them earlier? Surely the trees could have told you some time ago that they were looking for us" said Lon agitated.

"It was not until they crossed the Ura Bridge that I considered them to be a threat. I believed they would never cross the border but my convictions were erroneous. So we must now act fast and put as much distance between us and them as possible. Their hounds have obviously picked up your scents, so from here onwards I will carry you both along the course of the river as far as possible" said Jack picking Laila up in his arms.

"Now climb upon my back Lon, we have a long journey ahead of us and we cannot delay any longer" he said bending down on one knee.

Wading through the treacherous turbulent river Jack made his way downstream in urgency. With the rolling white waters billowing and crashing into his mighty oak limbs unyielding in their ferocity, the journey became gruelling and hazardous. Leaping from waterfalls and immersed to the waist in the bitter cold water the Green man drove on tenaciously until eventually the river opened out into a vast wetland.

"This is as far as we can go along this course" said Jack looking out over the boundless landscape of gorse and heather.

"So where is Puo Landum?" asked Laila.

"About forty five miles in that direction" he said sitting down on the ground and pointing out into the distance.

"So what are we waiting for?" she said eager to move on.

"I cannot travel out over open ground. I will be like a fish out of water" he replied.

"Without the trees to guide or inform me of any peril that may lurk out there we could be easily ambushed and I am not prepared to put you in anymore danger Laila" he said.

"So what are you suggesting we do then?" piped Lon.

"We keep to the perimeter of the marsh under the safe cover of the trees". Lon scanned the forest margin stretching away as far as the eye could see. "But if we keep to the edge of the woods it's only going to treble our journey" he said.

"Well that is our only option" replied Jack.

"No it isn't!" he exclaimed.

"We could easily make it across the marsh in a few hours".

"No Lon!" retorted Jack. "To walk across the marsh is to walk blindly into the unknown".

"But to follow it around is going to take us days and we will lose the advantage on our pursuers, don't you agree Laila?" said Lon turning to her for support in his argument.

"Yes I'm afraid I do" she replied regretfully.

"Please Jack, let us cut across the marsh. I want to go home and I just don't think I can take much more of this running" she sighed.

Jack pondered for a moment as he looked out upon the wide barren marsh.

"Quickly then!" he said abruptly "There's no time to lose".

Grabbing Laila around the waist Jack bounded apprehensively out onto the open marsh as fast as his lofty legs could carry him. His lengthy strides propelling him forward with such immense velocity that it wasn't long before poor Lon struggled to keep up with the pace.

"Wait for me!" he called as he fell exhausted to his knees. "I need to rest a moment".

"We have no time for resting" said Jack. "I will carry you the rest of the way".

"No!" insisted Lon. "All I need is a couple of minutes just to catch my breath" he said panting heavily. Jack looked around nervously.

"Hurry now Lon, we must go" he said reaching down to assist the Changeling

"Look!" yelled Laila suddenly.

"What's that?" she asked, pointing at a cloud of dust far away on the horizon heading towards them at speed.

"It's them, they have discovered us!" said Jack. "Now we must fly" he roared.

So impetuously he grabbed the resting Lon by the scruff of the neck and dashed off hastily, with the Changeling swinging to and fro in his hand like a poachers sack as he carried him over the boggy plain. After a couple of miles Jack's pace began to decrease as the fatigue finally began to set in.

"They are gaining on us!" screamed Laila looking back over his shoulder at the horsemen galloping behind at full stretch, the ground rumbling and shaking under their hooves like drumfire.

And then unexpectedly Jack stopped dead in his tracks, as if he had given up any hope of trying to escape and turned to face his pursuers. Slowly and carefully he lowered Laila and Lon down.

"We Green men were not designed for running" he said inflating his chest and tensing up his mighty limbs. "Protect Laila at all costs" he said turning to Lon who could only stand and stare at the impending assault.

Bending down Jack calmly picked up a large boulder from the marsh and inspected it carefully whilst the horsemen raced ever nearer to him. And then like a shot from a cannon, he launched the stone straight at them with such immense force that four horses and six men were instantly killed as they crashed over one another like skittles but yet still the rest thundered onward. The hounds were first to arrive on the scene and rushed eagerly into the encounter, snarling and howling as they bayed for blood. Lon quickly and without hesitation drew forth his blade and with his amazing speed and dexterity dispatched those that tried to get anywhere near Laila whilst Jack simply crushed the rest under foot. They were soon followed by the cavalry who charged in and rapidly overwhelmed them.

Jack fought ferociously on against the onslaught, slaying men and horses in a desperate attempt to protect Laila but with such large numbers he eventually began to lose ground as the circling hordes lassoed ropes over his arms and legs until finally managing to restrain him.

"Lon quickly! Cut me free from these bindings!" bellowed Jack as he floundered in vain to break loose from the tangled web of ropes that pinned him down like a feeble fly, but Lon did nothing.

Two horsemen hastily dismounted and seized Laila by the arms.

"Let go of me!" she screamed as she tried to shake them off and yet still Lon did nothing.

"Help me!"She begged him as they forcibly dragged her away but the Changeling just glared indifferently at her.

"Well done Lon!" said a mounted officer riding over to him. "You have served the Queen well and will be rewarded handsomely for your collaboration in catching the fugitive".

"My duty is to serve" replied Lon bowing his head subordinately. Jack was dumbfounded. The only person in the world he felt he could have confidently relied on in safeguarding Laila's welfare was the last person he expected to betray her.

"You traitor!" He yelled, pulling violently on his restraints. "I knew I should never have trusted a Changeling" he said.

"You will soon regret your insults Jack" replied Lon abruptly. "Firewood is in short supply out here on the marsh so I suggest you keep your mouth shut" he retorted to a raucous chorus of laughter from the assembled soldiers.

"Right listen up men! We only need to stay in Goblin territory for as long as is totally necessary" said the commanding officer. "So I will need a dozen men to escort me and the girl back to Lhansburg. The rest of you can finish binding up the Tree man for transportation. He will make an interesting addition to the Queens menagerie" he remarked smugly.

With hands and feet bound tightly together Laila was thrown across the back of a horse and whisked off unceremoniously across the marshes. Looking back she could see the pitiful sight of the Green man lying entangled in ropes upon the heather whilst soldiers beat him with rocks.

"Jack!" she screamed as the torture of their separation gouged her heart.

En route to Lhansburg she wept incessantly much to the annoyance of the commanding officer.

"Lon, will you quieten that wretched child down until we at least cross Ura Bridge, otherwise she will wake every damn Goblin in the Grayweald" he said.

"Certainly" replied Lon falling back on his steed to ride parallel to the grief-stricken Laila.

"Save your tears Laila they won't be of much help to Jack now" he said mordantly.

"How could you do this to us?" she sniffed. "We trusted you; we thought you were a friend of Yan's".

"Oh believe me I am a friend of Yan's. It's all thanks to him that I am to become a very wealthy man" he smirked.

"Don't you feel anything? Don't you feel bad for what you have done?" asked Laila.

"No! not at all. It's a dog eat dog world out there and I don't want to be eaten".

"But I don't understand why you fought with Yan to free me, only to take me straight back there again?" asked Laila confused.

"It was all just a clever deception" he laughed.

"What you fail to realise Laila is that the great Queen is all powerful and can have anything she so desires. And the only thing she desires more than anything is the location of the last remaining world tree, and thanks to you and Jack, she will soon know".

"But what does she want with the tree?" inquired Laila.

"You ask a lot of questions Laila but I guess you might as well know. It has been portended in the pool of omens that a terrible dragon will return one day soon into our world through the branches of an ancient hawthorn and change the world of men".

"Geborga!" whispered Laila silently under her breath.

"So by order of the Queen all world trees must be immediately destroyed" continued Lon.

"And what about me, what is going to happen to me?" asked Laila.

"I have no idea, that is up to the Queen to decide. But I suggest you do as your told and keep quiet from now on if you know what's good for you" he said before riding off to rejoin the leading group of riders.

They rode on for quite some distance at speed through the forest before the commander finally ordered his riders to stand down at a bend in the track. Laila was relieved, be it only for a short while as she found the entire journey lying face down across the back of a horse very uncomfortable indeed.

"The Ura Bridge is approximately a mile from here, I want two men to ride ahead on a reconnaissance" said the commanding officer pointing to two riders. Immediately they galloped off down the track while the remainder began to form a defensive shield of horses around Laila.

"It seems you have been quite a busy girl" remarked the commanding officer strolling over to Laila.

"I don't know what you mean?" said Laila irritably.

"Attempting to steal the Queens necklace, breaking out of Lhansburg and travelling through Goblin country with a giant walking tree, I'd say that's being pretty damn busy" scoffed the commander. Laila decided not to rise to his jibes, choosing instead to rudely ignore him by closing her eyes dismissively much to the embarrassment of the commander.

"Well you'll be a lot busier from now on explaining yourself to Queen Lhanna when we get back to Lhansburg he snarled turning away abruptly to the sound of a few suppressed chuckles amongst the ranks.

An interval of anxious silence amongst the unit then followed as the horsemen waited in anticipation of their reconnaissance rider's return. No one said a word; just the glancing tension in their eyes spoke volumes.

And then sounds of galloping hooves were heard drawing nearer as out from the trees appeared the two returning horsemen breathless from their ride. "The crossing is clear, no Goblins in the area to report of Sir!" said one of the riders to the commanding officer. "But we did sight a large bull Ogre feeding in the river close to the crossing sir" said the other rider. "How close?" asked the commander.

"Only a few yards down from the bridge pilings sir" he replied.

"Damn!" exclaimed the commander infuriated. "That's the last thing we need, twenty ton of bull Ogre on our hands. Is there another passing point along this stretch of the Ura?" he asked his Lieutenant.

"I'm afraid not sir, there are no other bridges suitable to withstand horses for some considerable distance" came the reply. "Then we shall proceed with caution to the bridge" he said resentfully.

Slowly and reticently the soldiers moved out towards the Ura Bridge in single file with weapons drawn. Only the jangle of reins and exerted puffs from restless horses revealed their presence in the

Grayweald, a presence unperturbed by the monstrous creature that loomed in the raging depths ahead of them.

Halting the procession three hundred yards from the bridge approach, the commander paused briefly to assess the situation.

"We shall proceed surreptitiously across the bridge in pairs so as not to provoke the beast" he said organising the unit into teams of two.

Apprehensively the first two horsemen rode out to the bridge, stopping just short of the approach before warily stepping onto the wide timber boards that spanned the boiling river. Their hearts racing as each clunking step seemed as if it was knocking loudly for the Ogres attention.

Nervously they tried to calm their jittery horses as the Ogre surfaced, spouting huge clouds of fine mist from his nostrils as he came up for air, shaking the pilings in his wake as he plunged back down again, oblivious to them being there .Resolute and ever vigilant they gradually inched their way across the bridge until eventually arriving safely on the other side to the relief of their commanding officer.

"The girl shall be next to cross" said the commander selecting one of his men to escort Laila across the bridge. "Keep a tight rein on her" he said with a steely glare before dispatching the rider.

Nearing the bridge Laila could hear the Ogre thrashing around in the water and sensed an air of trepidation in her escort's demeanour.

"Don't make any sudden noises" he said in a low shaky voice as his horse stepped gingerly onto the bridge. Laila glanced down through the timber rails at the swirling black water churned up by the Ogre and remembered a similar sight the day she met Fenndeor by the lake.

And then suddenly out of nowhere like an exploding geyser the Ogre burst up from the depth in a crescendo of slurry causing the horses to rear up in alarm, and buck Laila off onto the boards of the bridge with an almighty thump.

The sudden commotion from the horses caught the Ogres attention, so inquisitively he waded over to investigate. Towering over the bridge he looked down at Laila laying helpless on the deck and sniffed her hair before to make a deep gruff "Choo, choo!" sound. Laila recalled the sound as being that of a greeting noise made by Ogres and quickly realised that the huge Ogre was none other than Fenndeor himself. But before she could call out to him the horseman leant over frantically and grabbed her violently by the scruff of the neck, throwing her across his horse and galloping off with her back to his commanding officer. The Ogre in his fury let out a ferocious growl and briskly pursued the rider with long determined strides.

"What are you doing man!" yelled the terror stricken commander as he watched his rider racing towards him with a gigantic enraged Ogre trailing close behind.

"Drop the girl! Drop the girl!" he exclaimed as Lon and the rest of his unit briskly scattered off in all directions, fleeing in fear of their lives and for the river crossing to Lhansburg.

But it was too late for Laila's captive as the Ogre had quickly caught him up. Pulling him violently from his horse he tore his limbs clean from his body before tossing his discarded remains into the branches of a tree much to Laila's horror. And then capriciously he turned and lifted her up gently from the back of the horse in his blood soaked hands and placed her down gently on the ground.

"We have to help Jack, Fenndeor! They have got Jack" she said calling up to the humongous Ogre With a sweeping glance Fenndeor surveyed the trees for his friend but there was no sign of the Green man. Addled by his absence he looked down at Laila distraught.

"He is on the marsh!" she said vehemently jumping up and down.

Carefully he picked Laila up in his mighty hand and made his way off with her in the direction of the marsh, crashing through the trees like a charging elephant.

They hadn't travelled much more than a mile when the sound of the second unit could be heard a short distance ahead of them. "Stop Fenndeor! Put me down" said Laila, pausing for a moment amongst the trees and listening intently to determine the direction of the troops.

"It's them! The soldiers, the ones who have got Jack" she said softly. Fenndeor let forth a deep rumbling growl. "It's ok Fenndeor, we will save Jack but we have to surprise them in case they try to harm him. You wait here a moment and keep out of the way and I will go and see where they are. And please don't hurt them" she said lovingly patting his arm.

Traipsing a few yards through thick bracken she left the immense Ogre hidden amongst the trees and stepped out of the brush on to a bridle track. She recognised it as being the track she had previously passed through when she was being taken hostage. The far off clamour from the approaching horsemen began to intensify in the peaceful remoteness of the forest. So Laila decided to boldly wait for them to appear in the middle of the track.

Before long the cavalry finally emerged from out of
the woods some distance from her, dragging the
sorrowful Jack along on ropes behind them.

"Let my friend go!" she shouted angrily at the top
of her voice.

"Look!" exclaimed one of the horsemen on
sighting her.

"It's the girl! How on earth did she escape?"

"After her!" shouted the second Lieutenant as his
horse reared up violently. Without hesitation six
riders immediately tore off down the track towards
her brandishing their swords. Laila decided that this
would be a good opportunity to make a quick exit
so sprinted as fast as she could back into the
undergrowth with the horsemen close on her heels.
Stopping a short way in, she stood beside a tree to
catch her breath just as the riders appeared from out
of the bushes.

 "You stupid child" they said as they dismounted.
"You may have escaped us once but you won't get
away this time".

"Oh really? Well that's where you're wrong!" she
said tersely. The soldiers looked at each other and
began to roar with laughter.

"And what are you going to do little girl" said one
of the soldiers derisively.

"Not I!" smiled Laila. "Him!" she said pointing casually up towards the canopy. The soldiers looked slowly upwards only to be greeted by the terrifying face of an immense swamp Ogre peering down at them through the branches of a tree. Two of the soldiers instantly fainted whilst the others just fell trembling to their knees.

While this was happening the rest of their unit awaited patiently for their return on the bridle track. "What's taking them so long? I wouldn't have thought a small girl would be that difficult to catch" said the second Lieutenant looking out into the discerning calmness of the forest confused. He had almost given up on waiting any longer for them and was just about to send out a small search party when four dismembered soldiers suddenly fell out of the sky right in front of him with an almighty crash causing the distressed horses to lurch backwards. "Arm yourselves, we are under attack!" yelled the second Lieutenant as every man simultaneously pulled out their swords and stood their ground in the middle of the track. Uneasily they looked around and waited.

A momentary lull followed before the steady pounding of gigantic footsteps moving through the trees broke the calm. The very ground they stood upon shuddered under their feet as each step came ever closer.

"Stand your ground!" ordered the second Lieutenant raising his sword, as a huge Ogre stepped out from behind the trees onto the bridle track in front of them. Impressive and imposing it stood there motionless, bearing down on them in the middle of the track unyieldingly, shortly accompanied by the diminutive figure of a small girl.

"I'm sorry about that. I asked him not to hurt your men but he just wouldn't listen to me!" she shouted apologetically but the soldiers could not speak. All they could do was look on aghast at the astonishing sight of Laila standing as bold as brass in front of such a gigantic, formidable creature as a swamp Ogre.

"Anyway!" hollered Laila interrupting their gapes. "Me and my friend Fenndeor here would like you to release the Green man if you don't mind". There was a short silence before the second lieutenant spoke.

"And if we agree to release the Green man how can you assure us that your Ogre will not attack my men?" He asked.

"I promise" Laila replied.

"I'm sorry but your assertion is not enough. The Ogre has already ignored you once already to the detriment of six of my best horsemen" said the second Lieutenant."We do not wish to engage in any confrontation with you or your Ogre. All I ask is that you let us pass safely and we will surrender the Green man to you".

"You have my word" said Laila turning to Fenndeor. "Please let them pass Fenndeor, don't hurt them" she said pleading to him .

Acknowledging her request the giant Ogre moved back slowly to one side of the track allowing the cavalry to pass safely by him.

Cautiously in single file the soldiers moved out, riding past Fenndeor at a deliberate pace.

Nervously looking up at him staring back at them as they went on their way, until the final horseman had passed, galloping off in haste toward the Ura Bridge.

Laila ran speedily over to Jack who lay bound up in ropes on the track.

"Jack, are you alright?" she asked stroking his leafy locks affectionately.

"All the better for seeing you Laila" he smiled.

"Quickly Fenndeor, break the ropes" said Laila calling over the lumbering beast who snapped the ropes like bindweed.

"Thank you Fenndeor" said the Green man climbing back to his feet and looking none the worse for his ordeal.

"I have so many questions Laila, I don't know were to begin?" said Jack

"How did you find Fenndeor?" he asked.

"He was in the river next to the bridge we crossed, and he rescued me from the soldiers".

"You are indeed a loyal friend" said Jack patting the Ogre gently, causing the creature to bellow with delight. "And what of that traitor Lon? What happened to him?" he asked.

"He escaped with the rest of the soldiers, but before he left he told me that he had been working for Queen Lhanna all along" said Laila. Jack shook his head in disbelief.

"I knew I should not have trusted that insidious Changeling" he said with distain.

"No, it was all my fault" said Laila. "It was me who allowed him to come with us on this trip" she said lowering her head in shame.

"You have a good heart Laila and should not blame yourself for putting faith in people" said Jack holding her hand. "What has been done has now passed. I'm just confused as to what he expected to achieve by deceiving us all this time?".

"He told me that all he wanted to know was where the last hawthorn tree was growing because it is rumoured that a dragon would one day return from it or something?" said Laila.

Jacks eyes widened.

"Oh my word, so that would explain why Lhanna had all the hawthorns indiscriminately felled! It's all falling into place" he said in astonishment.

"Geborga the dragon was the only thing left in the world powerful enough to stand between her and the conquest of the Grayweald. If Geborga is prevented from returning into this world through the Omega tree then she will surely invade the Grayweald and destroy the forests to fuel her expanding demand for land and power".

"What are you saying?" asked Laila.

"It is obviously Lhanna's intention to fell the last hawthorn Laila" he said.

"We must leave immediately with the greatest of urgency to Puo Landum. Lon would have informed the Queen by now of its whereabouts, so there's no time to lose".

"What about Fenndeor?" Laila asked.

"He cannot come with us. He does not belong here, he belongs in the rivers and lakes" he said turning to the giant Ogre.

"Go now Fenndeor my friend and return to the
river, you have done well and I am indebted to you.
I promise to come and find you again soon" he
smiled. The huge Ogre made a loud 'Choo!' sound
before wandering off placidly into the undergrowth
and out of sight.
"Come now Laila we must go" said Jack picking
her up and putting her on his shoulder. "The Omega
tree beckons and time is short".

Chapter Twelve

The Omega Tree

Once more Laila found herself on a never ending journey through thick forest in the company of her friend the Green man.

"How far is it to Puo Landum?" she asked.

Jack began to chuckle quietly to himself. "You are always asking me about the distance of things; it's as if knowing is somehow going to make the journey shorter".

I'm sorry Jack I'm just tired I guess".

"No need to be sorry Laila, you have every right to know. It's about thirty miles across the actual marsh but we will stick close to the margins this time as it's safer. We'll camp over tonight so you can get some rest and we should arrive in Puo Landum in about a day or two" he said.

After a long hard days ramble Jack eventually set up camp for the night close to the marsh undercover of some towering hornbeams.

A cool breeze blew in from the east across the peaceful wetland as the evening sun set low in the sky. The view across the boundless landscape was outstanding, so Laila sat down to admire the scenery and contemplate for a while in the peaceful bliss.

"Are you ok?" asked Jack strolling over.

"Yes I'm fine, I always like to sit and think about things when I'm in a beautiful place, it makes me feel happy inside" she said.

"I know exactly what you mean as I often do the same thing myself" he replied sitting down beside her. "Sometimes I have the strangest thoughts Jack, like flying to other worlds and meeting fairies and stuff but nothing quite as strange or as real as all the things that have happened to me here. I still keep thinking that maybe this is all just a dream and I am going to wake up any minute".

"Soon this will all be nothing more than a dream when you get back to your world Laila" he smiled. Laila looked up at the Green man lugubriously and sighed.

"I know this sounds silly but I kind of don't want to leave. Not without you anyhow" she said lowering her head. "You are the best friend I have ever had and I will miss you terribly when I get back".

"Hey come now Laila, don't speak like that.
Sadness is detrimental and so we must not dwell too
long on it. Anyhow, you never know what the future
holds so don't waste your time on such silly
pessimistic thoughts. Who knows, I may come and
visit you by Warren pond someday" he said softly.
"And what if you don't and I never see you again?"
asked Laila despondently.
"And what if we had never met?" He answered.
But Laila gave no response to his retort. Instead she
just looked out pensively across the wild marsh with
the tears rolling slowly down her cheeks. Jack felt
awkward and slightly uneasy in the quiet
melancholia and struggled to think of anything to
say that would be of any comfort to her so instead
decided to alter the mood.
"Hey I thought these places were supposed to make
you feel happy inside?" He quipped forcing Laila to
break into a grin.
"You always make me smile" she chuckled.
"Well that's nice to know, now come on over and
sit beside the fire before the temperature drops as it
can get pretty inclement around the marshes at
night" he said walking back towards the
hornbeams.

"Ok I will be over in a minute" she said, deciding to sit a while longer to watch the far off clouds changing shape over the marsh.

The fire was a blaze when she had returned to camp and Jack was busy roasting Burdock roots in the ashes

"Not long and your food will be ready" he said delicately prodding the embers with a long green twig. "How are you feeling?" he asked.

"I'm good thank you. I was just watching the clouds over the marsh changing shape and making pictures in the sky" she said.

"Yan told me that Witches and Wizards do a similar thing to foresee future events" said Jack.

"Apparently you are supposed to focus on something you wish to know the answer to, and the clouds will respond by forming a picture".

"I don't think I would really want to know what happens in the future in case it's not nice" said Laila grimacing.

"It's only a window into possibilities. It is not carved in stone, only what could happen if things remain unaltered" said Jack.

"But if Yan knew how to do that then why didn't he see that by going to Lhansburg to rescue me he would be killed?" she asked.

"Maybe he knew that all along and was prepared to make that sacrifice. You have to understand Laila that to Wizards there is no such thing as mortality. It is just another passing season in their spiritual development. They live by the laws of nature and believe that all living things from the tiniest blade of grass to the mightiest tree exist as pure energy and therefore can never truly die as they are an integral part of the matrix that makes up the universe". Laila looked at him with a puzzled frown.

"Are you saying that Yan is not dead then?" she asked.

"Yes I am!" he smiled "He is the wind in the trees and the light of the moon" he said looking up into the night sky.

"But will I ever see him again?".

"I'm sure you will" he smiled handing her some cooked roots wrapped in dock leaves. "Now eat up and mind your fingers as they are hot.

"Wow these are delicious" said Laila enjoying the burdock roots. "What are they?" she enquired. But Jack for some unknown reason ignored her, it was as if he couldn't even hear her at all.

"What's the matter?" she asked perplexed as he sat there looking rigid and focused.

"Hush!" he whispered listening intensely to the breeze in the leaves. "The trees are speaking" he said.

"What are they saying?" she asked.

"They tell me that a great number of soldiers from the south and the west assembled yesterday afternoon and are now converging upon Lhansburg".

"Are they going to attack the city?" gasped Laila.

"No this is not an incursion Laila; it is a call to arms. It appears that Lhanna is summoning her troops to Lhansburg".

"Why would she do that?" Laila asked bemused.

"It presume that she now knows the exact location of the Omega tree and is gathering her forces with the intention of invading the Grayweald and felling the last of the spirit doors". Laila instantly leap to her feet in horror.

"If she chops down the hawthorn at Puo Landum then how will I ever get back to my home, I may never see my Mum and Dad ever again!" she cried.

"You have nothing to fear Laila, I will make sure you get back to Warren pond safely, you have my word" said Jack rising to his feet resolutely.

"But how can you stop her, she is too powerful?"

"Yes it is true that she is far too formidable an adversary for me to stop and I have no intention of trying. But we have the advantage of being only a day or so from Puo Landum. We should arrive there by overmorrow if we keep a steady pace, long before her forces even depart for the Grayweald. By which time you would have returned to your world" he asserted.

"I really hope you're right" she said running over to him and embracing his thick fissured leg.

"I'm sure of it! Now try and rest as I want to be on the trail before the storm cock sings" he said affectionately stroking her head.

So Laila laid down on her thick bed of soft dry ferns beside the fire and gazed up at the moon before drifting off to sleep.

It was dark when Jack awoke her from her sleep the next morning. The only sound was the distant haunting shrieks of the rough and tumble foxes at play.

"Wake up Laila" whispered Jack. "It's time to go" he said handing her a drink of elder flower in a birch bark container. "Drink up" he smiled. "We are off to Puo Landum".

The cold misty wood was dank and grey with an earthy scent of humus hanging in the air. Jack had extinguished and removed all traces of the previous

evening's fire before he had awoken Laila. She
began to shiver in the cold snap of dawn.

"I will carry you some of the way, it will be
quicker" said Jack bending down to pick her up.

"It's ok" she replied stepping back tired and
fractious from the early start. "I need to warm up
and stretch my legs".

"Whatever you say" he said graciously. "But we
need to push on today as I also heard last night on
the wind that two dozen men at arms with rache's or
hunting hounds crossed the Ura bridge at dusk.
. I can only assume they were sent with the
intention of tracking you down"

"Oh no not again!" gasped Laila, scanning the
surroundings. "How far away are they?"

"Don't worry" said Jack calmly. "They are no
match for me, and anyway they are at least a day's
travel from here. If we follow the river course and
avoid making too many stops en route we should
make it to the Omega tree in good time and with
more to spare" he said with a confident smirk.

"Now come along we have an appointment with
Warren pond.

It was a magical morning to watch the sun rise
amongst the great oaks of the Grayweald, whilst the
chilly mists of night slowly dissipated into the air.

The dawn chorus played like a piped symphony, rattling through the branches of the trees as every bird came together in a crescendo of song, with the accompanying low drones of buff tailed bumblebees hovering amongst the foxgloves springing forth from the secluded clearings.

As she strolled amongst the tranquil beauty of the Grayweald Laila had a sense of foreboding that the verdant paradise that she had grown to know and love would be nothing more than a memory when she had returned to her home. Not just for her, but for Jack and all the creatures of the Grayweald.

"If Lhanna does enter the Grayweald when I am gone what will you do?" she asked.

"I will do as I have always done. I will retreat into the isolation of the forest" said Jack. "Although how long that will last I cannot say".

"Surely the Goblins will be able to stop her from destroying the forests" she exclaimed.

"I fear the Goblins will offer little resistance if she invades. After all it was only Geborga who turned the tide in their favour during the battle of Ura valley, and without their dragon as an ally they are virtually defenceless against her".

"But Lon said that the dragon would return one day soon through the branches of a hawthorn tree maybe that soon is now!"

Jack stopped and knelt down in front of her and held her gently by the hand.

"My dear Laila, how much I would give for that to be true, but it would be futile to put ones faith in such a remote prospect at this time. People have been predicting Geborga's return for as many years as I care to remember and still he has failed to appear. What Lon told you we must treat as pure speculation. Now I don't want you to trouble yourself anymore with such barren thoughts, all you should be thinking about now is returning home to Warren pond" he smiled.

"But Jack, how can I go home knowing that you and the creatures of the Grayweald could die?" she said anxiously.

"Sometimes we have to learn to accept the things we cannot change no matter how harrowing they may seem; it is the way of things. Even as we stand here now in the apparent tranquillity of the woods there is death and suffering taking place all around us. Day and night and in the tiniest copse, life struggles to exist".

"But I can't help caring" said Laila.

"I know you can't Laila and it is quality that is admirable but I need you to be stronger now more than ever".

"Why?" she asked.

"Because our struggle is not yet over" he replied walking off through the bracken.

Meanwhile from every corner of the earth the battle vehement hordes descended upon the city of Lhansburg. Equipped and accoutred in a display of theatrical pageantry that would stir all patriots to arms. The streets heaving with flag waving crowds clamouring "Hail to the Queen!" as they joyfully welcomed the blade wielding servants of power who gathered in the city square in their thousands. Lining up in orderly quadrate columns the Queens legions eventually covered the forum like a sweeping chequered cloth as they waited ceremoniously and patiently for their sovereign to address them amongst the raucous cheering populace of Lhansburg.

Their rambunctious din quelled only by the fanfare of trumpets that heralded the Queens approach. Immediately an obeisant hush fell upon the lips of the gathered multitude with just the sound of the flapping standards daring to break the formality of the silence as the divine Lhanna with her long golden flowing hair and red velvet robes arrived ostentatiously on a magnificent horse drawn chariot flanked by horse guards in resplendent gold tunics..

Terminating in the centre of the square she looked out over an ocean of idolatry faces.

Raising her hand in acknowledgment they erupted like a crashing wave in adoration.

"Hail Lhanna! Hail Lhanna!" they roared emphatically with hands held aloft in a reverent salute to their ruler whilst she stood reserved and regal in absorption of their adulation.

Once more she raised her hand to silence the rapturous hoi polloi, and promptly the dissonance faded.

"Champions of the empire, noble compatriots of Lhansburg, we come together at a time of great change in our world, a time when all that we have endeavoured so long to uphold and protect now lay imperilled.

For as I speak to you this day, hostile forces are amassing close to our borders in an abhorrent act of aggression and violation of our peaceful existence.

A peaceful existence we have sacrificed too many lives to preserve, and if this were not so then how quick we would be to dishonour the memory of our brothers, sons and fathers those whose blood still stains the earth at Ura valley.

Yet in this grievous moment it is in our unity that we must place our faith, for it is our unity that gives us strength, and liberates us from the adversity of oppression.

As soldiers alone you stand; side by side an army you become, and those who dare to defy our resolve rue the day they heard our name!" she asserted, to a deafening wave of "Hail Lhanna!"

"Now take up arms courageous sons of Lhansburg for Queen and empire, and condemn to death those who in foolish disregard invoke the storm of our wrath, for today we fight for honour, for liberty and for peace!" she yelled as once again her words incited a rousing cheer of "Hail Lhanna!" that seemed to last forever.

Slowly back through the furore her chariot wound its way under the indefatigable screams of devotion from the assembled multitude. Above the jubilation she remained composed and dignified like a sculptured effigy for all to worship.

"This is a momentous day!" she declared to her Marshal as he escorted her chariot back to the palace. "For too long I have waited to avenge our defeat at Ura valley and today at last we will receive our restitution.

Gather the nobles for briefing in the imperial chambers" she said alighting from her chariot in the palace courtyard.

"Tonight Marshal we prepare for war".

Later that day emissaries to the seven kings and
nobles from the imperial forces assembled in the
annex to the imperial chambers where they were
gracefully received by the private secretary.
"The Queen awaits, please follow me" he says
cordially before ushering them into a long hall with
a rectangular wooden table at its centre.
He then invites them to be seated before
respectfully retiring to the annex, leaving them
sitting in silent repose.
Moments later trumpet blasts reverberate through
the hall as the officials rise to their feet.
Two sentries push open the large oak doors to the
chamber and Lhanna enters the room accompanied
by Prince Ibora.
The nobles in their obeisance go down on one knee
and bow their heads as she takes her seat at the head
of the table.
 She then orders the officials to rise and be seated.
"I will keep this brief gentleman as time is of the
essence.
The location of a world tree has recently been
discovered in the region of Puo Landum and I have
no doubt whatsoever that this is the very hawthorn
we had been searching for, for some considerable
time, so on receipt of this intelligence I had an

expeditionary force dispatched immediately to Puo Landum.

I am confident that within a few days as a result of their mission, all portals to and from this world will be sealed, finally purging us of my sisters evil dragon and leaving the Grayweald totally exposed. I therefore command all forces advance forthwith to Ura Bridge and be on standby for an invasion at sunrise in three days" she said abruptly concluding her briefing.

"I beseech your majesty please pardon my insolence" piped one of the nobles. "But if the expeditionary force is successful and the Grayweald is left defenceless, why does your most gracious majesty require us proceed this day with such promptitude? To muster our armies to march upon the Grayweald at such short notice would be an ambitious and arduous undertaking".

"Arduous!" exclaimed Lahnna tersely. "Arduous is the interminable torment I have endured every day since our defeat at the talons of Isla's repugnant creation, and now we have the winds in our favour I will not falter" she said rising from her seat. "Now go gentlemen and seize this moment. See that our reprisal is made swift and severe for tomorrow will be our greatest triumph, our final conquest, and our coup de grace to the Goblin nation!"

The following day and far off in the forests of the Grayweald, Laila trotted wearily along in Jack's wake for a time and a distance, until he finally he came to pause for a moment to give attention to the wind in the boughs.

"Puo Landum is close by. The trees tell me the forest is filled with Goblins" he said under his breath.

"Five of them are heading this way. Quickly now Laila, let me embosk you in the crown of this tree for a moment until they pass" he said placing Laila high up into the branches of a sycamore before concealing himself artfully amongst a network of branches.

Not a moment later from her coverture, Laila observed a group of Goblins passing merrily right beneath her feet in single file along a well worn track, oblivious to her presence, their arms laden with brushwood.

As quickly as they arrived they had disappeared much to Jack's relief.

"I was concerned that they might have spotted you up in the tree as you are hardly indistinct" he said appearing like an apparition from the backdrop of leafage.

"We have to be extra careful now as we are in the very heart of Goblin country and there are Goblins around every corner".

"So how will we get to the Omega Tree without being seen?" asked Laila looking around nervously. Jack looked at her with a disparaged expression "Through stealth, arborescent ubiquity and other clandestine means of course. As long as there are oaks in the woods you will pass unseen in the veil of the Green man" said Jack proudly.

"Now stay close to me, the Omega tree is only about a mile east of here" he said before slinking off again into the undergrowth.

The distant bedlam of Goblin activity resonated throughout the forest as Jack and Laila made their way tentatively towards the ancient hawthorn, with the sound gradually encompassing them as they drew nearer their objective.

And then appearing through the gaps in the trees like a vision, they came across a glade suffused with sunlight. It was extensive and elliptical, encircled by a ring of large roughly hewn monoliths and at its heart stood a stupendous ancient hawthorn.

"The Omega tree!" said Jack, falling to his knees in awe. Even Laila couldn't help but be overwhelmed at the site of such a magnificent tree. It was as wide as it was high and the crown was as radiant as a bouquet with the prismatic multitude of clooties hanging from every twig.

"It is the most beautiful tree I have ever seen" said Laila mesmerised.

"Yes it is indeed! But we must remain hidden as there are Goblins present in the glade" said Jack peering behind a tree.

After a short spell of observing the glade from a safe distance Laila was quickly able to discern that the hawthorn was by no means in an isolated area, simply by the plethora of Goblins that were frequenting the site. Every so often she would see a small party of them milling around the buttress of the great hawthorn before departing again.

"How will we ever get close to the tree without being noticed? There are so many Goblins about" she whispered quietly under her breath.

"We will have to be patient and wait until nightfall when they are sleeping and then we will have the site to ourselves" replied Jack confidently.

And so they waited and waited and watched the evening sky grow dark without any signs of a cessation in the activity around the sacred hawthorn tree.

To make matters worse Goblins even began arriving in the darkness with burning torches to visit the glade much to Laila's despair.

"I'm cold Jack" she said shivering in the gloom.

"Right, that's it! I have had about as much as I can take" he said vehemently storming out from behind the trees in a burst of rage.

"Come along Laila" he exclaimed. "I'm taking you home" and with that he marched off through the bracken as bold as brass and out into the centre of the glade in full view of several stupefied Goblins.

"I am a Green man! guardian of the forest. I come to pay homage to the sacred hawthorn" he bellowed assertively expecting to scare the Goblins away. But they just stood there aghast at the sheer sight of him. Fixed with terror and unable to move or say a word.

Subsequently an uncomfortable lull ensued until the sudden appearance of Laila from out of the shadows.

"What are you doing Jack?" she asked.

"A Sapien! A Sapien!" yelled the Goblins on seeing the figure of a young girl stepping out of the blackness, and ran off screaming into the night.

"I was attempting to clear the glade of the Goblins but it appears your ubiety here is a far more intimidating prospect than mine" he chuckled.

"Why did you walk out right in front of them like that?" asked Laila perplexed. "I thought you didn't want us to be seen?"

"I didn't Laila! But we have come too far to be hindered from our quest by a few tiny Goblins".

"But they know we are here now and might come back!" she cried.

"That is very probable so let us not waste time. The Omega tree is ready to receive you so go now Laila, escape this place before they return on mass".

"What do I do?" she asked with an anxious look.

"Go to sleep beneath the crown of the hawthorn just like you did in Theydon wood" replied Jack.

"I can't just fall asleep like that. I need to feel relaxed or tired and at the moment I'm neither.

"Why don't you just try lying down at the base of the tree and closing your eyes and focus your thoughts on something? Maybe that might work" said Jack.

Apprehensively Laila approached the tree and curled up in a ball at the base of the bole and closed her eyes tightly. As she lay there concentrating as hard as she could she began to think about her Mother and Father and imagined them standing there beside Mr Tree and calling her over.

"Where have you been Laila? We have missed you so much precious child" they cried passionately with arms out stretched. She could almost feel the cool zephyr caressing her skin as it wafted across the Warren pond to greet her home. And then suddenly and inexplicably, just as it had done before at Theydon woods, she began to feel a slight tingling sensation in her toes that started to gradually spiral up through her body.

"Hurry now Laila the Goblins are coming!" exclaimed Jack from beyond the ether, breaking Laila's concentration and startling her abruptly from out of her entrancement.

Instinctively she leapt to her feet, her heart pounding in her chest from the sudden shock.

"What is it Jack?" she exclaimed.

"Damn! I knew it would only be a matter of time before the Goblins returned on mass. The trees tell me they are heading this way so we had better leave now while we have the chance" he said grabbing her hand.

"No Jack!" said Laila releasing her hand from his grip and stepping backwards.

"I want to go home; I'm tired of all this running. Don't you see? This is my only chance to get back to where I belong".

"But the Goblins will be here soon, we don't have much time" he said looking around.

"I don't need much time; I know what to do Jack, I know how to pass through the spirit door! I was almost there just now, back at Warren pond with my Mum and Dad. Just give me a moment longer with the tree that's all I'll need" she begged.

"I wish I could Laila but I fear time has forsaken us" he replied solemnly.

"What do you mean?" she asked perplexed. Jack despondently turned his gaze to the perimeter of the glade where the flicker of glowing torches could be observed appearing from out of the darkness in all directions. Staggering backwards towards the tree Laila cowered in terror as the approaching flames encircled them.

"I forbid any harm to betide you!" bellowed Jack standing tall and puffing out his chest menacingly.

Within moments the glade was besieged with hundreds of enraged Goblins brandishing spears and daggers.

"Stay back or I will crush you! Roared the Green man as the cadaverous throng began to surround him, cautiously keeping their distance whilst hissing loud and acrimoniously at the timber giant bearing down over them. Resolutely they launched their spears in fury at the intruder, whooping hysterically as each projectile pierced the ligneous interlopers flesh.

"Your feeble weapons are powerless against me!" yelled Jack, tearing the spears from his chest and trampling on any Goblin that dare stray too close to Laila.

Undeterred the tenacious mob intensified the bombardment leaving Jack charging around the glade like a wild ox protecting its calf from a pack of wolves. After each defensive surge the Goblins would make bold attempts at seizing Laila from the bulwark of the Green man. Rushing in at every opportunity to drag her away into the undergrowth, whilst trying desperately to restrain her as she kicked and screamed frantically to free herself. But Jack was quick to see them off, flailing his arms tempestuously at the tiny marauders and slamming them into the trees like ripe fruit.

But eventually despite his best efforts and persistent determination to safeguard her from the Goblins a handful of the armed antagonists managed to evade his blows and overwhelm Laila.

"Come any closer Green man I swear I will kill the Sapien!" hollered a Goblins amidst the mayhem. Jack turned around to see one of them holding a spear up at Laila's throat.

"If you harm her I will destroy you!" He vociferated whilst stepping forward aggressively.

"No Jack!" shrieked Laila. "Do as they ask!" she begged, halting him in his tracks.

"Yes, do as you are told!" the Goblin sneered, pushing the spear sharply into Laila's neck.

"Let her go! What use is the girl to you?" asked Jack, his fists clenched tight with suppressed fury.

"The Dalock's will decide that at Puo Landum" replied the Goblin hauling Laila off into the night at knife point with his cohorts alongside.

"And don't try anything foolish if you want your Sapien unscathed" he yelled as Jack followed on behind at a compromising distance.

Fringed by a large crowd of tiny Goblins he trailed Laila into the heart of Puo Landum.

Like a gigantic trophy from the spoils of some imperialistic expedition he paraded through the Goblin town to the astonishment and amusement of a thousand inquisitive eyes.

Eventually the spectacle came to a halt outside a huge marquee at the edge of the municipality.

Most of settlement was made up of tents and marquees as the Goblins of Puo Lanadum had originally derived from nomadic tribes. Their woven tents were large and elaborate and by no means primitive, but the largest of them all was a big top called the grand marquee where the elders gathered and where Jack and Laila found themselves that evening.

A brief hiatus then followed with Jack immotile amongst the throng, as the gathered mass cheered and hissed triumphantly beneath the giant's legs. Their excited din increasing in its intensity until reaching an ear splitting crescendo before unexpectedly desisting, as out from the marquee stepped a lone Goblin dressed in a black hooded robe. He calmly approached Jack while the assembled rabble quickly and respectfully withdrew to a suitable distance. Lowering his hood he looked up at the Green man and smiled.

"Welcome guardian of the forest, my name is Glundaloch; I am chief Daloch of the elders of Puo Landum. We mean you no harm and are honoured by your presence here" he said bowing his head benevolently.

"I hardly consider attacking somebody with spears a courteous reception" Jack sneered.

"Purely an impulsive defensive reaction, you understand. It is not every day that my people come across a Green man in these woods".

"That's as maybe but I am not here to indulge your people's curiosity" he scoffed.

"Then may I be so bold as to inquire the purpose of this visitation?" asked the Goblin politely

"My purpose is no concern of yours" Jack replied sharply.

Acknowledging his reticence to cooperate and not wishing to antagonize the Green man any further the Goblin nodded cordially.

His attention was then drawn towards Laila cowering at spear point.

"I appreciate that you have good reason for being here Green man but what of the Sapien child?"

"She is with me!" replied Jack defensively.

"As I see, but she is a Sapien and I am sure that I need not remind you that this is Goblin country and her presence at our most consecrated of sites is bound to create an extremely volatile situation".

"It need only become volatile if you allow it!" said Jack angrily clenching his fists.

"Wait, Please! May I speak!" barked Laila quickly trying to diffuse the tension.

"Stay where you are scum!" screeched her Goblin captures, pressing their spears hard against her chest.

"Put down your spears and release the Sapien!" ordered Glundaloch to an impassioned wave of disapproving hisses from the grotesque assemblage. Raising his hand the sibilating quickly dissipated.

"Give ear to the Sapian child" he demanded as Laila anxiously approached.

"I know this may sound ridiculous but I really don't belong here" she said.

"Obviously!" replied Glundaloch looking somewhat bewildered by the outlandish comment. "This is sacred Goblin territory and you are a Sapien trespasser".

"No, what I meant to say was, I don't belong here in this world. I am from another world and Jack, the Green man was only trying to help me get home through the hawthorns spirit door" she said.

"Is this true?" he said looking up at Jack.

"Yes!" snapped the Green man.

"Are you a Witch?" he asked her warily.

"No" replied Laila. "I'm just a normal girl. I came to this world by accident".

Glundaloch frowned thoughtfully and scratched his head.

"But that doesn't make sense? How does one unwittingly pass through a spirit door into other worlds?" he asked

"I don't really know myself? I just fell asleep under a hawthorn tree one day and ended up here" said Laila modestly.

"Very few beings are gifted with the ability to transcend the physical universe, even unintentionally" he said. "I can therefore only assume that it was fate that brought you here to Puo Landum".

Laila looked around at Jack bemused.

"And it is her fate to return from whence she came" asserted Jack.

"Of course, I totally agree!" the Goblin concurred. "I have no desire in preventing your Sapien companion from fulfilling her purpose, it would be callous of me to suggest otherwise. But equally it would be impertinent not to at least offer you both the hospitality of our city whilst you are here" he said graciously.

"And why would you want to do that?" asked Jack suspiciously.

"Merely a gesture of goodwill and understanding, seldom are we graced by the presence of such omniscient beings" he smiled.

Jack sighed peevishly

"We have no time for socialising, we have a far more pressing engagement" he said abruptly.

"Why are you so animus Green man?"Asked Glundaoch.

"All I offer you is the hand of friendship?" he said.

"Because I don't trust you devious little creatures, that's why!" growled Jack loudly

Instantly the gathered mass burst into a deafening clamour, jeering and waving their burning torches in a riotous contempt whilst Glundaloch held aloft his hands in an attempt to repress their rage.

"To refuse the hospitality of a Daloch in our culture is considered to be the highest form of disrespect".

"Oh really!" snapped Jack contentiously.

"One moment please!" interjected Laila. "It is very kind of you to ask us to be your guests and we would love to stay here in your city a while" she said enthusiastically.

Abashed by Laila's sudden outburst Jack hastily pulled her to one side.

"What are you doing Laila?" he whispered. "I thought you wanted to go back home to Warren pond?"

"I do more than anything in the world but I don't think I will ever get the chance to if you keep upsetting the Goblins Jack". She said.

"But they are shifty untrustworthy little critters" he replied.

"Then we will have to be shifty too then, or else you are going to have to fight the whole of Puo Landum to get me out of here. I know how you feel about them Jack but can't you at least try to be friendly for my sake?" she pleaded.

Understanding her reasoned exposition he reluctantly nodded his head.

"I will do it for you if that is what you wish" he said turning back towards Glundaloch.

"Forgive my impudence Glundaloch" he said politely. "My rash behaviour was purely an impulsive defensive reaction you understand".

Glundaloch chuckled loudly at Jack's pert remark.

"Then let us put our differences behind us and move forward. Now please won't you join me" he said walking off into the marquee.

Laila looked up at Jack with an air of uncertainty. But all he could do was shrug his shoulders nonchalantly and direct her toward the marquee.

"After you" he said courteously.

Chapter Thirteen

De Fumo In Flammam

As Laila stepped through the awning entrance into the marquee she was immediately taken aback by the scale of the interior.

The pleated draped roof was raised up high by large and intricately carved pine poles allowing even the mighty Jack ample headroom to move about. A timber floor covered the base of the construction and was overlaid with colourful woven matting. Burning torches on slender twisted iron stands were intermittently placed and illuminated the room with a warming glow.

Long prostrate tree trunks set out in a sweeping semi circle commanded the centre of the marquee giving the impression of a bandstand or alter.

"Please make yourselves comfortable" said Glundaloch settling himself down on one of the trunks.

Tentatively Laila and Jack sat down whilst looking around admiringly at the beautiful tapestries that hung from every cornice.

"This is the grand marquee where I and my fellow elders assemble to discuss important matters. Each of the elders here in Puo Landum are savant in his or her own particular field be it art, agriculture or philosophy. And through our shared wisdom we endeavour to contribute for the greater good of our people" he said. But his words were wasted as both Jack and Laila where far too absorbed in the wonderfully woven arrases that covered the walls of the marquee. Their attention only distracted momentarily by the sudden appearance of two Goblins standing by the awning entrance.

"Please come in sisters!" said Glundaloch beckoning them over.

"Allow me to introduce you to our esteemed guests. This is Jack, a Green man and guardian of the woods and this is?" He paused for a moment and gazed disconcertedly at Laila.

"My name is Laila, pleased to meet you" she said politely acknowledging the Goblins with a discreet wave.

"Ah yes that's right! Laila" he smiled looking slightly embarrassed. And may I introduce you to Sardaloch, our elder of spiritual matters and

Juldaloch our elder of the arts". The two Goblins bowed courteously.

"We came here brother on hearing the discovery of a Sapian child at the hallowed tree" said Sardaloch.

"You heard correctly, but she is no ordinary Sapien my learned sister but an astral being, a traveller from another world. She was merely here in Puo Landum using the hallowed tree as a portal to return to her world with the help of Jack the Green man, when some of our people misinterpreted her intentions as hostile".

"An easy mistake to make" said Juldaloch looking over at Laila.

"So what brings you to our world Laila" she asked.

"It was an accident!" Laila replied. "I was resting under a hawthorn tree when I fell asleep. I was trying to get my necklace back from a crazy magpie who I now know was actually a shaman called Ibora. Anyway he mistook my necklace for a necklace called the Brisingamen and...." But before Laila could finish Sardaloch cut her short.

"The Brisingamen you say? How very strange?" she uttered before stroking her pointed chin in deliberation.

"It is commonly known throughout the land, as I'm certain my learned elders will testify that the shaman Ibora is a kleptocrat, assigned to collects sacred artefacts and valuable objects to appease his queen, but what begs the question is why the Brisingamen?, what use would Lhanna have for it?" she pondered.

"Disclose your concerns sister, what are you saying?" asked Glundaloch.

"The Brisingamen belongs to the Goddess Freja and was originally created as an amulet. The purpose of which was to protect its wearer from harm, but whom or what on earth could possibly harm a supreme being as powerful as Lhanna?" she asked.

"A dragon!" asserted the Green man resolutely rising to his feet.

Just then a sprightly Goblin races into the marquee unexpectedly waving his arms and screaming "Fire! Fire!"At the top of his voice, much to everyone's surprise.

"What fire?" asked Judaloch.

"The hallowed tree!" he said in his fluster. "It's on fire!".

Immediately Jack, Laila and the elders rushed with haste from the grand marquee towards the Omega tree.

In the distance a fierce blaze could be observed lighting up the forest. Thick clouds of smoke belched into the night sky whilst Goblins rushed around, arms laden with pails and jugs of water or anything they could get their hands on to help douse the flames. As Jack and Laila drew nearer, the heat became so intense and they were forced to stand back at a distance and watch helplessly as the Goblins laboured in vain to quell the conflagration.

"How on earth could this have happened?" muttered Glundaloch as he gazed solemnly at the last of the sacred hawthorns engulfed in flames.

"This is the work of Lhanna!" growled Jack. "The definitive act before the final conclusion" he said mournfully averting his glare from the searing abomination only to find a solemn faced child standing alone amongst a veil of smoke with tears in her eyes. His heart sank as he approached, cognizant of her misery and at a loss for words to console her grief, he just knelt down and picked her up gently and held her in his arms.

"I want to go home Jack" she sobbed.

"You will go home Laila, back to Warren pond where you belong, trust me I will find a way" he said softly. " You have my word".

.

That evening the Goblins of Puo Landum watched despondently as the once sacred tree became nothing more than a charred empty spine amongst a heap of smouldering black embers. Their sense of woe was as thick as the smog that filled the woods at dawn.

"What say you Green man?" said Glundaloch wistfully as he made his way over to Jack and Laila. "Bestow upon us your great wisdom. Tell us what our venerable trees disclose, is this egregious event an omen"? he asked.

"It is indeed a portent of what is to come sadly" said Jack. "The destruction of the Omega tree will prove to be the catalyst for the desolation of the Grayweald".

"Can this presage be altered?" asked Sardaloch.

"Without Geborga I am afraid not" he replied.

"The lore of the dragon's return, that has preserved the Grayweald for so long burnt within the branches of the hawthorn, as did our hope. All we can do now is prepare ourselves for the coming of Lhanna and the impending tempest of war"

"No! This cannot be, the future is yet to be written, we must seek to find another way" said Glundaloch.

"I shall gather the tribal elders for urgent talks" he said scurrying back to Puo Landum. But no sooner had he gone a noisy fracas suddenly erupted in the woods.

"What could that be?" remarked Sardaloch inquisitively.

"It appears they have discovered the arsonists" replied Jack as he watched an angry mob of Goblins surge forth from the undergrowth with two badly beaten soldiers in tow. Their listless faces covered in blood.

"Burn the Sapiens!" Their captors chanted as they continuously kicked and whipped the perpetrators through the smoke filled glade, before hauling them up in front of Juldaloch.

"What is this?" She asked.

"We found these Sapiens hiding out in the woods. There were several more but we killed them" said one of the Goblins wiping the blood from his blade with an air of satisfaction.

She gazed curiously at the piteous creatures kneeling helplessly before her. Their empty faces void of penitence and feeling

"What are you doing hiding out in Goblin territory?" She asked.

"My business is my own Goblin!" replied one of the men obstinately, to an angry jeer from the intrusive crowd that began to congregate around them.

"These are the culprits responsible for the burning of the Omega tree" exclaimed Jack stepping into the fray. "Is this so?" Juldaloch asked, but defiantly they hung their heads in silence.

"Never fear I can easily crush the truth out of these minions" said Jack grabbing one of the men by the throat and holding him up high in the air with his huge wooden hand.

"No! Please, I beseech you do not harm them. I have not doubt that what you say is true but to punish them will not alter what has been done. Take them to the grand marquee, we can question them further there" She pleaded.

So without hesitation Jack picked up the saboteurs by their legs and dragged them back through the forest like lifeless poultry to the grand marquee where Glundaloch stood in consultation with a number of elders.

Tramping boldly through the awning, Jack hurled the saboteurs across the floor at Glundaloch's feet.

"What have we here?" he asked, stepping back suspiciously from the strange bodies strewn upon the deck.

"These are two of the perpetrators who torched the world tree" said Jack.

"And how do you know this?" asked Glundaloch perplexed.

"The trees see all!" he replied abruptly.

The elders bowed respectfully to the Green man before scampering over to inspect the prostrate figures on the ground.

"They are Lhansburg soldiers" said one of them confidently. "Men at arms to be precise". Glundaloch stepped nearer and shook his head dolefully.

"How absurd it is that the source of my affliction lies benumbed at my feet and yet it is I that feels impaired. If only her pawns realised the implications of their actions?" he grumbled despondently as he paced the floor.

"And now through inane and callous disregard for all that is sacred they have effectively ended centuries of peace in the Grayweald".

The room fell silent and sullen for a time as everyone stood in quiet deliberation.

Eventually the wounded soldiers regained consciousness and sluggishly clambered to their feet. Looking about dazed and confused they squinted in bewilderment at the Goblins surrounding them in the dull lustre of the marquee

"If you are going to kill us then do it now, and be done with it" barked one of the men staring acrimoniously at Glundaloch before spitting on the floor disrespectfully, promptly igniting a brief altercation.

"And what would I hope to achieve from that? Other than perpetuate the inequitable contempt your people already hold for us" said Glundaloch.

"A contempt well founded" snapped the soldier.
"Founded upon what may I ask? An intimate
knowledge or the imbued prejudices spoon fed to
you and your people by Lhanna" he said.
"How dare you speak ill of the Queen! My people
hold our sovereign in the highest regard, and I for
one would not hesitate to give my life in her
honour" replied the soldier proudly.
"How ignoble of you to condemn your children to a
life of destitution and your wife to viduity" said one
of the elders.
"That is the sacrifice of every warrior!".
"Warrior? You speak as if killing were a dignified
profession" Glundaloch quipped.
"Say what you will, but your derision of our
integrity will soon turn around and bite you" the
soldier riposted. "For as I speak the Queens armies
are poised to invade your lands and there is nothing
you or your people can do to stop it. Checkmate!"
he smirked malevolently.
The venerable arbiter was immediately silenced by
the revelation, the immensity of his plight suddenly
dawning upon him. Lowering his head he humbly
walked to one side of the marquee before gazing up
reflectively at the tapestries. Their depictive scenes
glorifying the victory and bloodshed at Ura Valley.

"Emancipate the Sapiens and see that they receive safe passage to the borders" he said to everyone's astonishment.

 "What are you saying?" protested the elders. "These barbarians are responsible for the destruction of the hallowed tree!"

"I am aware of that!" said Glundaloch.

"But to execute them for their ignorance makes us no better than them, let them go!" he insisted. With reluctance the soldier's bindings were cut and they were led from the marquee to acrimonious boos from the awaiting crowds outside.

"What now Glundaloch?" asked one of the elders. "If what the Sapien says is true, we are tinder to a flame".

"It is true I can vouch for that!" interrupted Jack. "The trees forewarned me three days ago about the massing of troops near the Ura River". The elders looked at each other, aghast by Jack's sudden proclamation.

"Did the trees not also forewarn you about the arsonists and the impending threat to the hallowed tree?" asked Juldaloch perplexed.

"Yes, the trees informed me of their presence in the Grayweald, but not their intent. I injudiciously presume their objective was Laila and not the world tree" he said ashamed.

"But what begs the question is how they came to know the whereabouts of the tree in the first place?" asked one of the elders.

"Its location has remained a secret for centuries until now".

"I fear it is I who is responsible for revealing the location of the Omega tree" muttered Jack to a collective gasp of disbelief from the gathered assemblage.

"He is an impostor, he is cursed!" cried one of the elders. "He led the Lhansburg soldiers straight to the hallowed tree" said another pointing his finger accusingly at Jack and provoking a raucous surge of indignation for the Green man.

"Stop! No you are wrong!" yelled Laila impassioned amongst the rumpus.

Climbing up on to one of the prostrate trunks she waved her arms furiously at the elders to grab their attention. "Jack is a Green man and a friend of the trees" she said speaking passionately in his defence. "He would never have told anyone where the hawthorn was. He was betrayed by a Changeling and so was I, so don't blame him for what has happened to the tree" she said.

"We are not! If what your friend the Green man says about your being pursued into the Grayweald by Lhanna's men is true, then you are as much to blame as he is!" Came a reply, followed by a unanimous rumble of, "Here, here!" from the congregation.

"No one is to blame for anything!" asserted Glundaloch stepping onto the podium. "We may all point fingers and argue amongst ourselves but what will we hope to accomplish other than division and hostility? There are far more pressing concerns at this time, such as the imminent incursion of our homelands by imperialistic troops.

I have given the ominous matter some deliberation and would like to forward a suggestion to the council" he said to a hushed marquee.

"I propose we evacuate Puo Landum immediately and head north into the safety of the mountain caves". Instantly the whole place erupted.

"How can you suggest such a thing" exclaimed one of the elders enraged. "To run without a fight is an outlandish proposition".

"It is our brains not our bravery that will preserve us" replied Glundaloch sharply.

"And against such odds in the absence of Geborga, I'm afraid our trouncing is a fait accompli" he said.

"But to live in exile, that is such a desolate existence" said a morose elder.

"I fully understand your concern. It is a desperate situation my brother, but what will you have us do?.

Die in a futile gesture of resistance or live to see another day. The Green man has already foreseen our subjugation, so why heed the warning and await the storm?" he said. But his argument did nothing to quell the ruckus, until Juldaloch made her way through the contentious tumult and pleaded for calm.

"Brothers and Sisters, give ear I beseech thee! The Arbiter is chivalrous and judicious in his exhortations and I cannot help but advocate his reasoning, but may I also be so bold as to propose an alternative suggestion for your consideration. If we united the Grayweald tribes, it may be possible to delay the incursion of imperial forces into our lands".

"And what use is a brief hiatus ?" an elder inquired.

"It would allow us time to evacuate the women and children to the mountain caves of Gamolham" she replied. "It is vital that we safeguard the future of our kind"

"But how can we assure their safe passage through the Grayweald? Imperial forces may ambush them before they even reach safety of the caves" said a voice from the crowd.

"I will see they are lead safely to the mountains" said Jack stepping forward. "Nothing passes unseen by the trees".

"Thank you Jack, we are indebted to you" said Juldaloch humbly.

"What about the unification of the tribes?" asked Sardaloch. "There are deep divisions and rivalries between some of them, how on earth do you intend on getting them all to agree to your proposal?"

"Leave that to me!" said Glundaloch. "It is in their best interests that they put aside their differences".

That afternoon envoys from Puo Landum were dispatched to the various tribal regions heralding Lhanna's imminent invasion of the Grayweald, and requesting urgent attendance of all tribal elders to talks at the grand marquee.

The following day senior representatives began to arrive at the grand marquee. Hundreds of elders from the numerous Grayweald tribes, congregating together for the first time since the battle of Ura Valley, in an atmosphere of apprehension and animosity. Laila and Jack were invited to attended and watched quietly from the wings as the Goblin dignitaries coalesced.

Glundaloch climbed upon his tree stump podium and cleared his throat before requesting the attention of his peers.

"Elders of the Gray weald, Brothers and Sisters, as representative of Puo Landum I would like to

welcome you all to our grand marquee, I wish your
visitation here were for more favourable reasons but
as you are no doubt already aware, Lhanna's forces
are poised to invade our lands and it imperative that
we come together and take some form of action to
safeguard our progeny"..

"Why don't we try and negotiate some kind of
treaty with Lhanna and avert any bloodshed?"
hollered a tribal elder to a rumble of disapproval.

"It would futile to attempt to negotiate with her, she
is a megalomaniac and totally incapable of
compromise." asserted Glundaloch.

"I have heard from a reliable source that
Lhansburg troops only discovered the hallowed tree
whilst in pursuit of the Sapien child" said one of the
elders glancing over suspiciously at Laila.

"Perhaps the Sapien is all that Lhanna desires, in
which case we should take advantage of what we
have and use her to bargain with" he said.

"That will never happen while I live and breathe"
growled Jack. "Laila is my responsibility and stays
with me".

"The Sapien child was never Lhanna's objective
anyway" interjected Glundaloch. "The saboteurs
already knew the location of the hallowed tree.
They were sent into our lands with the sole purpose

of desolating it in an attempt to cripple us before an assault".

There was a moment of loud mumbling as the elders discussed the situation.

"What do you propose we do then?" asked one of the delegates. "Even if we united our forces, we are no match for Lhanna and we only barely survived the bloodbath of Ura valley because of Isla's dragon".

"I am aware of that my friend, but we have a duty to protect the women and children of our tribes. When her armies march into our villages they will spare no one, which will leave us with no other option but to unite our forces and meet them head on. This will allow enough time for a systematic evacuation of all villages in the Grayweald and the immediate withdrawal of our kinfolk to the safety of Gamolham Mountain".

A loud jeer resonated throughout the marquee.

"But Gamolham Mountain is a harsh desolate place, not suitable for children at all" remarked an elder.

"It was the birth place of our ancestors. For centuries they occupied the labyrinth of caves that run through the mountains" said Sardaloch.

"Yes that's correct!" agreed Glundaloch. "And it is the only safe place we have. With the entire Grayweald now encompassed by the empire we have no safe havens left open to us other than Gamolham".

"Even if we did agree to unite, an undertaking of this magnitude would take an eternity to organise. The evacuation of villages alone would be a mammoth undertaking" remarked a voice from the assemblage.

"You don't have any time! They are already here!" exclaimed Jack rudely interrupting the conference. "The trees along the banks of the Ura River have already witnessed Lhanna's forces crossing the bridge south of the Gray weald this very afternoon. You have no choice but to unite now and harry them en route or sit and watch the genocide begin".

It was clear to the elders that Jack's passionate and abrupt address was not a proposition but a mandate for action, and so with that they each drew forth their daggers and threw them into a pile in the centre of the room as a symbol of their tribe's allegiance to a coalition of resistance.

"Where shall we rally our forces?" asked a learned elder. Glundaloch turned around and looked up at Jack. "What do the trees behold?" he asked.

"They speak of a large army currently heading North West through the Lime wood towards Wickham fell" said Jack.

"That will lead them through our lands" exclaimed one of the Goblins. "We can hinder their progress as they pass through the gorge, that should delay their advance to the fells" he said.

"Then Wickham fell is where we shall make our stand" said Glundaloch stepping down from his podium and walking off through the crowd.

"Now make haste brethren as time is precious, and see that those bound for Gamolham rendezvous with the Green man here at Puo Landum before the new moon" asserted Juldaloch.

Laila looked up at Jack. "Am I coming to Gamolham Mountain too?" She asked softly.

"Of course you are Laila I would never leave you alone again" said Jack. "After we have accompanied the Goblins to the mountains we will return to the place of our first meeting. I have a strong feeling that the portal back to your world may have been right under our noses, I just never had the sense to look for it".

"I do hope you're right" said Laila holding his hand.

"Don't you worry Laila I will get you back home to Warren pond if it is the last thing I do" he said.

Meanwhile Puo Landum was plunged into turmoil as its inhabitants panicked to evacuate the village.

Some piled all their worldly possessions on to carts and began to make their way to Gamolham without escort whilst other refused to leave their homes. Claiming it was better to die with a sword in your hand than with an arrow in your back. Large groups of Goblins stood around the grand marquee, engaging in heated discussions as their elders tried desperately to rally support for the battle and enlist volunteers.

Jack and Laila watched reflectively from beyond the awning at the mayhem outside.

"From order in to disorder in one small step" remarked Jack at the scene of outside.

"Have you seen Glundaloch?" asked a Goblin elder approaching them. "We need him to speak to the villagers and restore calm" he said.

"I'm sorry but we have not seen him since the meeting" Laila replied.

"Well if you do tell him he's needed urgently" he said continuing his search.

"Come Laila, let us go for a walk" said Jack wandering off into the thicket.

"Where are we going?" she asked inquisitively.

"To visit a pensive soul" he quipped.

Laila was none the wiser and just followed instinctively. Eventually they came out into an area of dense scrub a few hundred metres from the marquee, where heather and gorse grew in scattered clumps beneath ragged stunted trees.

It was a wild and barren place all but for a solitary figure sitting hunched beneath an elderberry bush.

"It's Glundaloch!" gasped Laila recognising the individual.

"Yes that's right the trees told me I would find him here" said Jack casually.

"But if you knew he was here, why didn't you tell the Goblin who was looking for him earlier where he could be found?" she asked.

"I can only assume that he came here because he did not want to be found" said Jack before strolling over to him.

"It would appear your high station is giving you vertigo" Jack jested as he ambled through the gorse.

"Oh it's you Jack!" said Glundaloch looking up at the looming giant. "I knew that if anyone could find me here it would be you" he said solemnly.

"You are quite sought after back there" remarked the Green man.

"I know, I just wanted to be alone with my thoughts a while" he sighed.

His eyes looked dull and lost as he glared down in a despondent mien.

"If you want us to leave I totally understand" said Jack turning away.

"No, please stay I am grateful of your presence" he said. And so reticently they sat down beside him in the quiet solitude of the scrub.

"I can find no peace here anymore amongst the trees Jack or even in the sanctuary of my own mind" he said wearily. "To foresee the inevitable conclusion of my being is a frightening prospect that compels me to question the very purpose of my existence".

"Do not squander your time my friend with such futile introspection, it will only enervate you at a time when your people, more than ever will look to you for strength" said Jack.

Glundaloch put his head in his hands and gave a deep doleful sigh.

"It pains me to the core that I must blacken their illusions, but I'm afraid they will find no courage here" he mourned. "The truth is I'm scared Jack, I don't want to die this way" he said listlessly getting to his feet and walking a short distance from the tree before pausing to reflect.

"The very idea of ceasing to be is a reality that seems almost inconceivable" he said distraught.

"Why is it that we must endeavour to survive adrift an ocean of despair and suffering in the absolute knowledge that we are all destined to perish beneath its waves.

Only to exist momentarily as nothing more than a fading memory in the thoughts of those who live on. If all that is must end, then do it now and be done with! And release me from the torment of my ruminations" he cried.

And then slowly he pulled a blade from beneath his belt and held it against his chest.

"No!" screamed Laila leaping onto him like a cat. "Don't do it!" she yelled knocking him to the floor whilst Jack quickly seized the blade from his hand.

"Self abandonment is not the solution to your afflictions or that of your people!" he said throwing the blade with fury into the far off distant trees.

"Neither is it your fate!" he murmured. Turning around enraged he picked up the little Goblin by the neck. "Do you not realise that the consequences of your actions will affect not only you but the lives of many of your people and the course of future events in the Grayweald" he said sternly.

"My passing will alter nothing. We are all damned" said Glundaloch woefully.

"Then if you are so indifferent to the world let me help you end it!" said the Green man crushing the little Goblin tightly in his mighty hand.

"No please stop!" pleaded Glundaloch gasping for air.

"What is wrong?" asked Jack. "I thought you wanted to die? Or is it the nature of your death that troubles you?" he said gradually increasing the pressure on his grip.

"No Jack! Stop! Please put him down" begged Laila anxiously watching the little Goblin squirm helplessly in his hand.

"Don't worry Laila I wasn't really going to kill him" he said placing the limp weakened Glundaloch gently onto the ground. "I was merely reviving his sanity so as to purge him of his fatal disposition".

Laila ran over to the shaken Glundaloch.

"Are you alright?" she asked distraught.

"I'm fine!" he wheezed "Just give me a moment to catch my breath".

He lay prostrate on the floor a while, panting for air and wincing in pain whilst Laila and Jack looked on concerned.

"Forgive me" said Jack perturbed "I never meant you any harm".

"No Jack I understand! You just did what you thought was right which is more than can be said of me" puffed Glundaloch.

"I was a fool to allow my emotions cloud my judgment" he said clambering to his feet. "To detach myself from this sorrowful plight at the detriment of my people is not the actions of a prudent elder" he asserted before looking up at the Green man with a resolute glow in his eyes.

"You have made me realise that my anxious mind is a far greater threat than the sword of any adversary" he said, and expeditiously hobbled off through the scrub cradling his ribs.

"Where are you going?" asked Laila.

"To fulfil my destiny!" he hollered before halting in his haste.

"If I am to live, then let it be to lead my people against coercion and suffering. And if I am to die, then let it be upon the hills of Wickham fell" he said valiantly before heading on his way again.

Chapter Fourteen

The Mountains of Gamolham

Through the great forests and across the plains the imperial armies marched unopposed. Like an encroaching tide upon the shores of the Grayweald they flooded the land with their might. A war machine hell sent to murder. Ploughing the soil beneath their feet and devouring the land as they went.

Heading the march was Lhanna herself astride a huge white shire horse with prince Ibora by her side. She had waited many years for this moment and was not going to miss the opportunity to witness her final triumph.

"I had a feeling that the acquisition of the Grayweald would be a breeze once the last world tree had fallen" said Lhanna. "Without their precious dragon to protect them the race of Goblins are feeble and will offer no resistance to our forces" she smiled.

"Indeed your majesty" replied Ibora humbly. "And with the recent defection from a renegade Goblin tribe to our cause, their intentions to ambush us in the gorge will also prove ineffective, as I have already sent a thousand men at arms ahead of us to clear them out".

"Good work Ibora" said Lhanna. "And what news of the rebellion blockade at Wickham fell?" she asked.

"It appears your majesty that their resistance at Wickham fell is purely a stratagem to hamper our invasion, whilst they conduct a mass exodus of their women and children to the refuge of the Gamolham Mountains, under the protection of a Green man and a young witch girl by the name of Laila who escaped from the citadel". Lhanna's eyes widened with menace.

"So they think they can outsmart me by concealing their despicable prodigy in the mountain caves do they?" she uttered in quiet deliberation before abruptly pulling the reins on her steed.

"Ibora!" she said assertively. "Order the infantry to continue their advance upon Wickham fell. I want all cavalry units to escort me immediately to Gamolham!".

"Right away your majesty!" he said sounding the cavalry horn.

At the eve of the new moon on the far side of the Grayweald, tens of thousands of Goblins began to arrive at Puo Landum. Young and old, frail and fearful, carrying their lives upon their backs. It was a desperate scene to behold and one assured to strike remorse upon the onlooker.

Amongst the din and commotion in solemn witness stood the elders.

"What have they done to deserve this?" said Glundaloch looking at the faces of the frightened children.

"Their innocence is all they are guilty of" replied Sardaloch dolefully.

"Yet it is they who pay the price for war" said Juldaloch. "The victims of warfare it seems are seldom those who instigate it".

"True, but we must also remember that even those engaged in combat are victims too. Slaves to the arrogance of others, blindly sacrificing their existence for what they believe is right" said Glundaloch.

"The only campaign worth fighting is that which opposes it" uttered Sardaloch.

"If that be the case my sister, then you give me at least some consolation in the knowledge that I fight not for victory, but for the preservation of the innocent" said Glundaloch parting company to join his troops who stood waiting expectantly upon a nearby hill., their Bowe's and Pike's grasped firmly in their stubby blue hands, reckless and spirited for the battle ahead, like a bevy of fawns to a wolves lair.

As Glundaloch made his way slowly through the town towards the concourse of fighters he suddenly found his path barred by the prodigious Green man. "You must not leave for Wickham fell!" he said assertively.

"Why, what is the reason for your concern Jack?" asked Glundaloch bewildered.

"I have heard that Lhanna's mounted forces have abandoned their advance to Wickham fell and are now heading north east at speed in order to outflank you" said Jack

Glundaloch shook his head in disbelief. "No Jack, they are not attempting to flank us. If they are heading north east then they are heading towards the Gamolham mountains. It appears we have been betrayed. I had a feeling that this might happen" he said despondently.

"There are some venal tribes existing in the Grayweald".

"So what will you do?" asked Jack.

"It is imperative that our people continue their retreat into the safety of the mountains" he uttered. "So I have no choice but to direct my forces north east, so as to impede their progress".

"There is only one track I am aware of that passes through the Gamolham forest which is suitable for horses" said Jack. "They will have no other option but to take that route"

"Yes I know that track well" said Glundaloch. "It isn't very wide which could be to our advantage".

"What do you mean?" asked Jack perplexed.

"With the cavalry columns riding in tight formations through the forest we should be able to hold them back and allow you more time to get our people to Gamolham. But we must act fast as we won't be able to hold them off forever".

Jack nodded his head in acknowledgment and patted the tiny Goblin on the back.

"Good luck Glundaloch, you are a great and gallant leader!" he said before making his way over to Laila and Sardaloch.

"What's happening?" asked Laila as the towering Jack came lumbering over towards her.

"There has been a change of plan. We cannot wait until the new moon, we must leave today" he said.

"But why?" asked Sardaloch. "There are still more refugees yet to arrive"

"We cannot delay any further. Mounted troops have been dispatched to the Gamolham Mountains, it appears your brethren have betrayed you" said Jack.

Just then horns began to sound loudly throughout Puo Landum as the Goblin forces that had gathered upon the hill began to move out.

"Glundaloch is marching north east to intercept the riders so as to give us more time" said Jack.

"Such an honourable sacrifice" uttered Sardaloch pensively. "We would be remiss to squander this given moment. We commence immediately to Gamolham Mountain" she said before gesturing the command to decamp to a Goblin clasping a lur.

Once more the horns resonated above the tumult whilst the elders addressed the jaded masses who griped in languid discontent.

"We depart for Gamolham forthwith, only essential provisions should be carried" they hollered, mobilizing the nomadic horde.

Pandemonium quickly rippled through the crowd as they hastened to gather their belongings as well as their loved ones.

"Will you lead our people to the mountains?" asked Sardaloch looking up at Jack humbly.

"Of course I will" he smiled. "It would be an honour".

Lifting Laila up onto his back, the huge Green man carefully made his way through the throng towards the trees and the distant mountains with an ocean of Goblins scampering in his wake.

The exodus to Gamolham was arduous. After the third day of their expedition many Goblins fell behind through exhaustion and sickness. As much as Jack tried to assist them, by holding back or carrying the infirm he knew that he had to push on without delay as Lhanna's riders were gaining ground with every moment they lost.

"I don't think we will make it to the mountains in time" he said looking back despondently at the wretched multitude that lagged wearily after him.

"If we don't increase our pace before sunset, all we have achieved would have been in vain" he said.

"But we are only days from the foothills" said Sardaloch "Surely we can make it there in time?"

"I'm afraid the only time we have now is that which Glundaloch's resistance can spare us. The Lhansburg riders have already entered the forest and are only a day's ride from here" said Jack.

Realizing the asperity of their predicament, Sardaloch attempted to rally her enervated flock and spur them on for the final push before dusk by singing a traditional Goblin ballad.

Her lowly voice was sweet and soothing amongst the sombre hush and it wasn't long before the song began to lift their morale. Soon the forest rang out with the sound of resolute voices making their way towards the foothills of Gamolham with an air of espirit de corps.

"What a wonderful sound!" said Laila listening intently to the melodic hum.

"It is indeed a magical sound" remarked Jack. "If there is one thing that Lhanna will never take from the Goblin's, it is their spirit" he smiled.

With a renewed vigour the Goblins finally arrived within sight of Gamolham as the sun began to set. Foraging in the forest for deadwood they congregated around their fires beneath a beautiful starlit sky. There was a reposed atmosphere that evening amongst the camp but the ubiquitous Green man was never at ease. Ever vigilant he stood alone in the shadows looking out over the tenebrous wood.

Laila watched him from beside the fire before walking over.

"Are you alright Jack?" she asked.

"I'm fine Laila" he said maintaining his focus upon the trees. "It is Glundaloch who I fear is not"

"I hear it on the wind that his forces are at present positioning themselves for an ambush alongside the track to Gamolham".

"I don't understand Jack? I thought you knew he was going to do that" said Laila perplexed.

"Yes but he is much closer to the enemy than he thinks. If he engages them before first light he will never hold them back long enough for us to reach the mountains"

"So what will you do?" asked Laila.

"There is nothing I can do at this time except wait, and hope they do not encounter one another before morning" he said looking down at Laila affectionately.

"And the best thing you can do Laila is get some rest. We shall be in the foothills of Gamolham by noon tomorrow and it is very rigorous terrain up there" he said.

Laila did as she was asked and bid Jack goodnight before bedding down with the Goblin children beside the fire.

Even in warm halcyon twilight of Gamolham forest the air was filled with the presentiment of the rising sun, but for some, there would be no sunrise.

For as they slept soundly around their fires that night Lhanna and her mounted troops rode on purposefully towards Gamolham and ever nearer Glundaloch's ambush.

"Wait!" yelled Lhanna unexpectedly, before drawing forth her sword and bringing her mighty cavalry to a grinding halt in the middle of the murky wood. The air was sharp and all was still in the eerie gloom but for the whinnying of their anxious horses.

Meticulously she began to scour the road ahead with her cat like vision, piercing through the darkness like a flame.

"There are Goblins here" she asserted. "Dismount and arm yourselves!".

Calmly her riders climbed down from their steeds, their blades primed and glinting in the moonlight.

"They are concealing themselves in undergrowth either side of the track. Now branch off and flush these vermin out" she ordered.

No sooner had they began their advance into the caliginous silence; when the lull was abruptly shattered by the violent swoosh of arrow fire. Several of Lhanna's horsemen fell to the ground while the rest swiftly took cover behind the trees. Lhanna meanwhile remained firm and resolute in the centre of the road. Casually catching arrows like dandelion snow in mid flight and snapping them like matchwood.

"You think you are secure behind the veil of night, let us see how stout-hearted you are when we can see the whites of your eyes" she said flooding the forest in brilliant light and blinding the hidden Goblins.

Impetuously Ibora and his men rushed into the thicket, hacking and stabbing with tumultuous rage whilst the Goblins hastily retreated back into the underbrush.

Even though Goblins are somewhat smaller in stature to men, they are extremely agile and tenacious and it wasn't long before they mounted a counteroffensive. Leaping from the trees onto the soldiers below in their droves, like a swarm of livid wasps.

Lhanna meanwhile looked on composed and apathetic to the bloodshed that raged on about her, doubtlessly revelling in the carnage of her final conquest.

Unlike the timber colossus, who on the far side of the wood bellowed mournfully towards the waxing moon at her annexation, whilst startling the elders from their slumber.

"What is it that warrants such an outburst at this time?" asked Juldaloch approaching the distraught Green man in the dead of night.

"It has begun" he said

"You mean the fighting?" she asked.

"Yes" he replied. "I hoped this wouldn't happen tonight but it has, so we must leave immediately!"

"But the people are weary and in need of rest" said Sardaloch.

"I promised you safe passage to Gamolham but I cannot fulfil that promise if we do not leave now" said Jack.

"Just give us a couple of hours I beg you. They will make up for lost time if they rest a little longer" said Sardaloch.

"All right if that is your wish; but we move on to the mountains at the sounding of the first bird song" he said.

Sardaloch and Juldaloch both agreed and returned to their slumber leaving Jack standing alone in the darkness, poised and attuned to the whispering aspen whose parlance was only cut short by a solitary blackbird signalling the evanescence of the night and the departure to Gamolham.

The elders sounded their horns in the still twilight. Rousing their flock from their sleep and indicating the start of another day's haul. Torpidly the jaded

multitude shuffled on towards the foothills with
Jack, Laila and the elders leading the way.

En route Sardaloch and the other elders
continuously tried to encourage and energized their
people. Pushing them on and boosting their
motivation until by midday they had arrived at the
foothills of Gamolham much to Jack's surprise.

"We have far exceeded my expectations"
exclaimed Jack, commending the Goblins on their
progress.

"The caves are only a day's travel from here" he
said pointing towards a line of grey peaks looming
on the horizon.

"If you continue at this pace you should reach there
by sunrise tomorrow" he smiled.

"When you say 'You', it's as if you're suggesting
that you will not be coming with us?" said
Juldaloch perplexed.

"That's correct" replied Jack. "My work here is
done; I have lead your people safely to Gamolham
as promised and now I have one more promise to
fulfil" he said looking down at Laila affectionately.
"To return Laila back to her world".

"But we are not safely at Gamolham yet" said
Sardaloch in dismay. "We still have the mountain to
ascend"

"You don't need me on this part of the journey"
said Jack. "Besides, I will be of no use to you in the
mountains. There are no trees up there and without
the trees I am blind".
"What about Lhanna?" asked Juldaloch. "What
news do the trees impart on the resistance?"
"The resistance is holding up well" said Jack. "It
appears that the forest is proving to be a real
impediment to the cavalry and they are now reduced
to chasing shadows on foot through the dense
overgrowth"
Sardaloch reached up and held the Green man
gently by the hand.
"Please don't leave now" she said. "Our people
feel safe with you as our escort. They regard you as
their guardian and champion".
Jack was overwhelmed to be held in such high
esteem by the Goblins, and also a slightly
embarrassed, as it wasn't that long ago when he had
a natural aversion to them. But the thing that
disquieted him more was the prospect of heading
into the mountains. Up there he was vulnerable and
exposed and although Glundaloch's forces where
doing exceptionally well in holding back the
advance of Lhanna's cavalry he knew that it was
only a matter of time before they broke through.

Looking around at the expectant faces he sighed and shook his head disconcertedly.

"I am honoured really I am, but I am afraid the decision is not solely mine" he said turning to Laila and throwing the ball straight at Laila's feet.

Now all eyes were directed at her.

"I think it's only right that you take them all the way to the caves Jack" she said feeling a little pressured.

"Hooray!" the Goblins cheered, punching the air with delight whilst Laila stood casting a stern glare at Jack for placing her in such an awkward situation. He shrugged his shoulders in a feeble gesture of penitence before raising his hands in an attempt to suppress the elation and get the Goblins attention.

"May I say, I find you appreciation moving but I would appreciate it if it were moving in that direction" he quipped whilst pointing up towards Gamolham Mountain, before briskly marching off up the rugged track in earnest with Laila in his arms.

"Why did you leave it up to me choose whether to go to the caves or not?" asked Laila as they ascended the steep path.

"I'm sorry about that Laila but I just couldn't think of a way out of it. I was kind of hoping you would have done it for me" he said.

"Why? Didn't you want to take them to the caves?" she asked.

"No, it's not that I didn't wish to take them. It's just that I believed it would have been unwise for you and I to journey into the mountains. With Lhanna and her troops close by in Gamolham forest we are really chancing our luck. At least in the forests we are safe but up here we are defenceless" he said looking around uneasily.

"Oh dear! I'm sorry Jack I wasn't thinking properly" said Laila.

"It's ok Laila, it's not your fault, I should have been firmer. But never mind eh? Let's not worry about it now. As Yan would say: don't put too much energy into negative thoughts" he said in an attempt to cheer her up . "We should reach the caves by early morning and then our work with the Goblins will be done".

"I do hope so" said Laila.

Chapter Fifteen

The final journey

Thousands upon thousands of Goblins, like tiny ants on the march, ascended the craggy steep hills trailing Jack in search of safety and a new life in the womb of the earth.

Gamolham was an immense mountain range with several peaks, littered with vast lakes rivers and waterfalls.

But it was renowned mostly for its extensive cave systems, formed by ancient underground streams which ran like arteries for hundreds of miles throughout the hills. It had long been a safe haven for Goblins but up on the barren slopes of boulders and scree, it was far from a place of refuge for a Green man.

"I wish your people would quicken their pace" said Jack stopping every hundred yards for them to catch up.

"We are unfortunately not as lofty as you" said Juldaloch catching her breath.

"That's as maybe but it will soon be dark and you people will need to make camp for the night" he said looking uneasily out over the forest below. "We will make base camp before sunset you have my word" she said, walking off boldly ahead of him.

The little Goblins drove on expeditiously that day against the unforgiving terrain and by nightfall were almost in sight of the caves.
Huddling together in huge groups in order to keep warm, they avoided building fires or speaking loudly on the mountain to evade detection from Lhanna's spies. Even so the atmosphere was buoyant and positive with Goblins wandering around in the darkness from group to group socializing whilst others pushed on doggedly through the night to reach the caves.
Laila and Sardaloch sat together upon a rock peacefully watching the proceedings.
"We are indebted to you and the Green man for all you have done for our people" said Sardaloch.
"Don't thank me, it was Jack who did it" said Laila modestly. "He is the one who spoke to the trees"
"No, but it was only because of you that he agreed to help us" she said. "He is very fond of you Laila".

Laila looked over at the lumbering giant playing with the goblin children and smiled.

"Yes I know he is, and I feel the same way about him. The hardest thing about returning home for me is leaving Jack" she sighed.

"You won't be leaving without him" said Sardaloch tenderly. "He will always be with you right there in your heart. To have become the friend of such a wonderful creation of nature is an eternal gift, you are a lucky girl" she beamed.

"Yes I know I am" replied Laila Solemnly climbing down from the rock. "Will you please excuse me Sardaloch, all this walking today has made me a little thirsty" she said, politely parting company from the Goblin elder.

Wandering over to a secluded mountain pool she knelt down beside it and looked pensively at her reflection. She began to think of home again and Mr Tree by the Warren pond. The Goblins journey was nearly over yet hers seemed to go on forever. A tear began to appear in her eye before dropping delicately on to the surface of the water, distorting her image amidst the refracted moonlight.

Slowly the ripples dissipated and the surface was still once more. She glanced down again at her reflection only to find a face she did not recognize looking back at her. Bewildered, Laila looked around to see who was standing behind her but there was no one there. Once again she looked in to the pool and once again she saw the face of a beautiful young woman with long dark hair looking back at her.

"Who are you?" muttered Laila curiously, but the woman gave no response. She just smiled warmly back at Laila. So tentatively Laila reached down to her in the clear cold water but there was nothing there.

Unnerved by the strange apparition in the pool Laila returned hastily to the safety of the Goblins.

As she returned Jack noticed a change in her demeanour.

"Are you alright Laila? He asked.

"Erm? Yes I'm fine" she replied looking somewhat discombobulated by the experience.

"Well if there is anything troubling you just let me know" said Jack.

"Yes, thank you Jack I will" she said sitting down reticently upon a large boulder.

While the Goblins slept soundly under their cloaks upon the mountainside, Laila stayed awake, looking up at the star filled sky. She couldn't sleep at all that night as every time she tried to close her eyes she saw the face of the woman in the pool smiling back at her. "Who or what was she?" she thought. Her face seemed familiar to Laila but she couldn't quite remember where she had seen her before.

Throughout the night she lay there deliberating over the experience and by the time she began doze off the sun began to rise as well as a few keen Goblins.

"Good morning Laila, did you sleep well?" asked Jack walking over to her.

"Not really" she replied lethargically.

"Why not? I thought you would have been quite spent after yesterday's hike" he said

"I just couldn't get comfortable" replied Laila, not wishing to burden Jack with her mental turmoil.

"Well you can catch up with some rest later. We are about three hours from the caves so Juldaloch tells me so let's get going" he said picking her up gently. It was a beautiful morning and the Goblins were abuzz with excitement. Refreshed and with an alacrity of spirit they eagerly made their way up to the top of the mountain. Even the airy Jack found it difficult to keep up with them.

Within a few hours the caves began to appear as they ascended the brow of a steep ridge, their wide openings welcoming the enervated wanderers. The children immediately ran joyfully around, laughing and chasing each other whilst their weary parents

headed straight into the caves with their
impedimenta.

Laila and Jack were agape at the size and beauty of
the lush oasis. It seemed almost surreal in its
surroundings.

Gigantic waterfalls surging from high in the cliffs
feeding deep pools surrounded by Sphagnum moss
and Tormentil. Milkwort and Alpine lady's mantle
sprouted from the precipitous cracks and ledges all
around the cave entrances like formal hanging
baskets, and the ground was blanketed in glistening
semi precious stones.

"I can see why they would want to escape here"
said Jack looking around in wonder. "It would be
perfect if only they had some trees up here".

Just then Sardaloch walked over with a big smile on
her face.

"What do you think?" she asked.

"It is a wonderful" remarked Laila.

"I trust you will stay a while and join us in
wassailing the end of our journey" said Sardaloch.
Jack shook his head remorsefully.

"I realise it is considered discourteous to refuse a
Daloch, but we really must be going. Our journey is
still not over and we cannot delay a moment longer.
I'm sorry" he said apologetically.

"I understand" said Sardaloch bowing her head respectfully. "What you have done for us can never be repaid, you are both truly omniscient people" she said bowing once again.

"Will you be safe here?" Jack asked.

"Yes, these caves are numerous and endless and too small for Sapien beings" she smiled

"Well good luck to you" said Jack holding out his hand to her.

"And good luck to you both" she said behind sad eyes.

As Laila and Jack turned around to make their way back down the mountain track a huge cheer went up from all the Goblin's and they began clapping their hands loud and appreciatively.

Jake and Laila waved back at them gratefully before disappearing back over the ridge.

"I will miss the Goblins" said Laila wistfully.

"So will I" said Jack. "But at least we can find some solace in knowing they are safe now" he grinned.

Briskly he made his way down the arduous craggy paths with Laila struggling to cling on to him.

"Do you have to go so fast?" she said nervously as he leapt down one steep incline after another.

"The quicker we are off this mountain and in the forest the better" he replied.

"Once we reach the forest, how far do we have to go to get to the place where we first met?" said Laila, keen to get down from his back and on her own two feet again.

"There you go again!" Chuckled Jack. "Always wanting to know how far things are"

"I'm sorry" said Laila timidly.

"Don't you worry Laila, you will be home soon I promise" he said.

Jack moved with such celerity down the track that before long they were nearly at the base of the mountain. They could see the tops of the trees and one of the vast mountain lakes shimmering in the distance.

"Not far now Laila, once we reach the woods you can have a rest" said Jack.

"That would be nice" said Laila relieved.

As they neared the foothills, the landscape became strewn with large boulders making the final descent awkward and hazardous, so Jack allowed Laila to make her own way down.

Slowly she clambered from boulder to boulder with Jack assisting her occasionally. There was a slight breeze blowing in from the hills that caused the outlying trees to rustle in the wind.

Jack suddenly stopped dead in his tracks and began scanning the terrain. Laila sensed his distress and grasped anxiously to his leg.

"What is it Jack?" she whispered looking around afraid.

"Listen!" he said softly.

But Laila could discern nothing, only the faint hush of the wind. There was a brief lull and then out of the silence came a harsh and abrupt "Cu Cu!" sound.

Startled by the unexpected noise Laila looked around to see a Magpie staring down at her from the top of a large boulder. Jack swiftly grabbed Laila and dashed off down the rugged precipice, leaping haphazardly from boulder to boulder.

Then out from the rocks poured hundreds of Lhansburg troops brandishing swords and pikes, howling with enmity and clambering after them.

Still Jack powered on smashing into the soldiers like a runaway train and sending them flying down the hill. They hurled rocks and pikes at the Green man in an attempt to slow him down but tenaciously carried on until eventually he lost his footing and came crashing down to the ground.

He lay there still for a time panting with exhaustion whilst Lhanna's forces rushed over and surrounded him.

"Get up Jack!" cried Laila desperately as the soldiers began to gradually converge.

"Quickly Jack, please!" She screamed.

Languidly he clambered to his feet like a wounded beast, looking around at the hundreds of soldiers that now surrounded them.

"I'm sorry Laila" mumbled Jack limping over to rest against a boulder. "I cannot go any further" he said breathlessly.

"How very moving!" mocked a voice from the girded horde.

Laila looked up to behold a tall elegant lady dressed in red velvet robes with a magpie perched subserviently on her wrist. Even in her elegant guise she emanated pure malevolence.

"Lhanna" uttered Laila anxiously under her breath.

"You have eluded me once too often little witch and now you have reached the end of your rope" said Lhanna furiously striding over to Laila.

"Your head will be the price for your malefaction!" she yelled grabbing Laila violently by the hair and drawing forth her sword.

With his last ounce of strength Jack lunged forward hitting Lhanna in the chest with such immense force that it sent her tumbling like a stone into her men at arms.

Calmly she picked herself up off of the dusty shale and glared ominously at Jack.

"You have committed your final futile act Green man!" she hollered, holding a sword high above her head whilst casting an incantation. Nervously her forces stood clear as her sword began to glow white like an incandescent flame. And then with unrelenting malice and the celerity of a sprite she rushed the wounded giant, striking him hard like a bolt of lightning across the neck bringing him slumping to his knees before collapsing to the ground at her feet.

Laila immediately dashed over to him, stumbling and screaming hysterically.

"Jack! Jack!" she wailed stroking his leafy locks affectionately "Speak to me!".

He looked up at her through his sad dying eyes and began to weep.

"I'm sorry Laila" he said.

"Don't be silly" sniffed Laila with tears streaming down her face. "I love you Jack" she said hugging him tightly.

All of a sudden he began to cough violently and creeping stems of ivy began to issue forth from inside his mouth, as if they were growing from inside of him. His eyes then rolled slowly back into his head and all went still.

"No Jack, No! Please don't leave me" she cried trying to shake him to, but Jack did not stir.

"Hooray!" cheered the soldiers triumphantly whilst Lhanna looked on with a conceited grin.

"Right little witch!" she said sternly turning to Laila. "Where are those Goblins hiding?" she asked.

Laila said nothing, she just lay there bawling with her arms clasped firmly around Jack.

"I won't ask you again" said Lhanna raising her voice. "Now get up or I will run you through!"

Laila slowly rose to her feet and looked at Lhanna with revulsion in her grief stricken eyes.

"Well? Speak witch!" exclaimed Lhanna impatiently. "Say something!"

"GEBORGA!!!!!" yelled Laila with all her might and for as long and as loud as she could muster much to Lhanna bewilderment and distaste, her voice resonating across the hills like a landslide.

"How dare you utter that name here" roared Lhanna, throwing down her sword in blood spitting fury.

Suddenly the sky cracked and began to turn black as night, as thick grey clouds billowed across the mountains like surging waves, followed by the loud rumble of distant thunder. Lhanna's soldiers looked up apprehensively at the strange phenomenon overhead and began to cower down as the wind began to blow violently around them throwing up soil and shale from the slopes in a whirlwind of debris.

"Your paltry sorcery is no match for me little witch" yelled Lhanna as a storm began to rage and the mountains began to tremor. "I am a celestial child of the Sun and Moon" she sneered.

"RUN FOR YOUR LIVES!" cried her soldiers, dropping their swords and running as fast as they could back down the mountain.

"Where do you think you are going? Come back here now!" bellowed Lhanna. "This witch is no threat to us!" she screamed.

"DRAGON!!!" they howled, tumbling down the slopes.

Lhanna's eyes widened with terror, when in the distant sky she saw the mammoth imposing shape of Geborga the great dragon rising up from the mountain lake like a volcanic eruption, its gigantic wings eclipsing the sky and casting Gamolham into blackness.

"No! This cannot be?" she muttered disquietly. "The Omega tree was destroyed!".

Even Laila was overwhelmed at the sight of the dragon and could only stand gaping in awe at its sheer enormity.

"Nobody has the power to summon the dragon" growled Lhanna vehemently. "Only its creator!" she said turning around to Laila, only to see the apparition of her sister Isla smiling back at her.

"You!" she screamed leaping impetuously at Laila and holding her up in the air by the neck.

"So Isla you have come to seek your retribution have you?" she said grinding her teeth like a woman possessed, whilst Laila hung helplessly from her hand gasping for air.

"Well, vengeance shall be mine sister!" she said squeezing Laila's throat tightly and almost choking the life from her.

And then when it seemed Laila's inevitable end was in sight, a glowing sword suddenly appeared, ripping through Lhanna's chest, impaling her upon its shaft and spilling her blood upon the Gamolham rocks much to the evil Queens horror.

Dropping Laila to the ground she slowly turned, weakened by the transfixion to find Ibora standing there brandishing her effulgent sword in his hand.

"What have you done to me my Prince?" she muttered in a faint voice, her languid eyes filled with pain and disbelief.

"I have avenged my true love" he hollered, and with that, swung the enchanted blade with all his might, chopping off Lhanna's head in one fell swoop.

Laila screamed in dismay at the spectacle, stumbling back amongst the boulders in fear as Ibora staggered towards her through the tempest, holding out her necklace in his blood soaked hands. "Take it Isla" he pleaded. "Let death be my retribution" he said kneeling before her in penitence. Warily she reached out and took the pendant from his hands.

"Forgive me" he begged as the winds of time finally came to claim his soul, reaping the stolen years from his mortal flesh before her eyes.

She watched him age and wither in utter consternation, shielding her eyes as his skin fell from his bones before eventually turning to dust and dispersing in the gale.

Crouching in fear and trepidation Laila remained steadfast beneath the rocks whilst the wind howled and thrashed the mountain in righteous indignation.

Time passed and gradually the storm began to ease until all that could be heard was a gentle breeze. Laila crawled gingerly out from the safety of the rocks and looked around nervously. A thick mist had descended upon the mountain reducing visibility down to only a few yards, so carefully she made her way down the rugged track towards the woods.

All around where the remnants of the storm, windblown debris and piles of broken shale heaped up against toppled boulders. It was a bleak barren sight except for a tiny figure appearing out of the mist ahead of her. As she drew closer she recognised the shape as that of a small dog fox. "Rocco? Is that you?" she whispered softly as she approached. The fox appeared to wag its tail contently, before trotting off a few yards in front, as if to guide her out of the mist. She followed it curiously for a short while until eventually finding herself back in the woods again where the spring flowers carpeted the ground and the air was cold and frosty. The place felt somehow familiar to her as she wandered aimlessly through the trees, and began to recognise features in the landscape as if she had been there before. And then from beyond the thicket she saw a large twisted oak tree beside a pond. Laila could not believe her eyes, it was the Warren pond, and she was finally home again. Overjoyed at the vision she dashed from out of the woods towards the tree, throwing her arms around it in a huge embrace.

"I'm home Mr Tree, I'm home!" she cried as she clung firmly to the fissured bole.

"Welcome home" said a voice from behind her. Laila turned to find Donna standing there with Rocco beside her.

"You will never believe what has happened to me" said Laila, eager to tell Donna of her adventures.

"Would it involve Geborga, Lhanna and a wizard by the name of Yan overton?" she smiled.

"Yes? But how do you know about that?" asked Laila perturbed.

"You don't think this all happened by chance did you Laila? Not anyone can pass through a spirit door into the otherworld".

"You mean to say you set this whole thing up?" gasped Laila.

"Well I can't take all the credit for it" said Donna. "I had some help from a very special friend" she chuckled.

"That would be me" exclaimed a scruffy old man strolling along the bridle track towards the pond. Laila was overwhelmed when the old man turned out to be none other than Yan.

"Yan!" yelled Laila running over to greet the avuncular wizard "I thought you were dead" she said hugging him lovingly.

"It takes more than a dagger to kill a wizard" he said stroking her head affectionately.

"But I don't understand" she said confused.

"Well, we wizards can only die a triple death so the dagger merely wounded me" he explained.

"No not that" said Laila and began to walk away despondently.

"What's troubling you Laila?" asked Yan.

"I thought this was all just a dream. All those things that happened to me back there in the Grayweald. The dragon, Lhanna, even you" she said.

Yan walked over and held her by the hand.

"No Laila it all happened" he said. "I know it's all a bit strange to comprehend right now but it was your destiny to embark on that journey"

Laila looked at him perplexed.

"So is it true Yan? Was I really Isla in a past life?" she asked.

"Now come on, I'm getting thirsty standing around here, the tea rooms should still be open" he said avoiding the question. "We can talk more over a lovely cup of tea" he smiled.

As they made their way over towards the tea rooms Laila had one more question on her mind.

"What happened to Jack?" she sighed.

"How could I have forgot!" he said rummaging through his pockets.

"Here you are Laila" he said handing her a large green acorn.

She inspected the ovate nut in her hand and frowned disconcertingly at it.

"Is this Jack?" she asked in wonderment. Yan nodded his head and beamed from ear to ear.

"It fell from his locks when he was staying at Dial house. You see his energy is eternal and he now exists in this form. If you want to see him again Laila all you have to do is plant the acorn beside a magical spring and Jack will return exactly how you remembered him" said Yan. "And it just so happens that I know the whereabouts of a magical spring".

Laila looked at Yan then she looked at the acorn.

"No Yan, I will plant it somewhere quiet in the woods" she said. "Jack always said that he wanted to be a tree and watch the world go by so I'm going to make sure his wish comes true" she said.

"Whatever you say Laila" said Yan but mind that magpie don't steal it from you" he said running off towards the tea rooms.

"What magpie?" yelped Laila nervously scanning the trees. And then she heard Yan laughing out loud.

"Hey you come back here!" she said giggling whilst chasing after him along the bridal way.

The Laila Mythology

.

Vincent G Learoyd

10768516R00238

Printed in Great Britain
by Amazon.co.uk, Ltd.,
Marston Gate.